Arroyo Circle

ARROYO CIRCLE

a novel

JoeAnn Hart

GREEN WRITERS PRESS   *Brattleboro, Vermont*

Printed in the United States.

10 9 8 7 6 5 4 3 2 1

Green Writers Press is a Vermont-based publisher whose mission is to spread
a message of hope and renewal through the words and images we publish.
Throughout we will adhere to our commitment to preserving and protecting
the natural resources of the earth. To that end, a percentage of our proceeds
will be donated to environmental and social-activist groups. Green Writers
Press gratefully acknowledges support from individual donors, friends, and
readers to help support the environment and our publishing initiative.

GReen
wriTers
press

Giving Voice to Writers & Artists Who Will Make the World a Better Place
Green Writers Press | Brattleboro, Vermont
www.greenwriterspress.com

ISBN: 979-8-9891784-4-5

COVER PHOTO: ISTOCK.COM/CLICKER

Charlotte's Web quotes reprinted by permission of White Literary LLC.
Copyright © 1952 by E.B. White.

MIX
Paper | Supporting
responsible forestry
FSC® C103525
FSC
www.fsc.org

PRINTED AT KASE PRINTERS, ON FSC-CERTIFIED PAPER AND PRINTED WITH SOY-BASED INK, DEDICATED TO SOUND ENVIRONMENTAL
PRACTICES AND MAKING ONGOING EFFORTS TO REDUCE OUR CARBON FOOTPRINT. WITH PAPER AS A CORE PART OF OUR BUSINESS,
KASE IS COMMITTED TO IMPLEMENTING POLICIES THAT FACILITATE CONSERVATION AND SUSTAINABLE PRACTICES. KASE SOURCES
PRINTING PAPERS FROM RESPONSIBLE MILLS AND DISTRIBUTORS THAT ARE CERTIFIED WITH AT LEAST ONE CERTIFICATION
FROM AN INDEPENDENT THIRD PARTY VERIFICATION, SOURCED DIRECTLY FROM RESPONSIBLY MANAGED FORESTS. WE ALSO
MAKE ONGOING EFFORTS TO REDUCE OUR CARBON FOOTPRINT, REUSE ENERGY AND RESOURCES, MINIMIZE WASTE DURING THE
MANUFACTURING PROCESS, AND RECYCLE 100% OF SCRAPS, TRASH, CARTRIDGES, EQUIPMENT, AND SOLVENTS WHENEVER POSSIBLE.
WE ARE A FAMILY-RUN BUSINESS, LOCATED IN HUDSON, NEW HAMPSHIRE.

Tommy

The one who attains unity with nature rides the clouds and wind, life and death do not alter them. Such human beings don't know start from finish.

Zhuangzi, 4th Century BCE

Preface & Postscript

The crows bobbed high in the cottonwood as they watched a human stumble to the top of the ravine, punctuating progress with mocking caws. Red dust rose in a cloud around the man, blending in with the protective coloration of his clothes. With a practiced adjustment to his spine he stood upright in a pillar of amber light, shielded his eyes, and guessed the time by the sun over the mountains. It was late.

He squinted and imagined a point. He imagined it expanding, stretching out across the sky and enveloping the horizon. He felt the electric currents of his body course through his cells and synapses, then flow out into the world, joining the soft rush of distant streams where pebbles bounced down craggy peaks, his breath a high whistle through the aspen leaves. There was nothing he was not a part of. Grape tendrils. The majestic elk. Magpies, ravens, crows. Yes, even the crows. He absorbed the sound of the canyon wren's song and made it his own. Along the creek he sponged up the beavers and muskrats and the long-legged insects that stood upon the water. As he bloomed with wonder at his surroundings, he felt a sudden shock of doubt crack open his core like an egg.

"What're we doing here?" he said out loud, startling the crows into flight.

He heard the hawk before he saw it. It screeched then banked overhead before landing hard on his shoulder. The red-tail ruffled its wings and lifted one prehistoric claw, then flexed it before setting it back down, digging into boney flesh with the careless disregard of an apex predator. The bird smelled of ash and ponderosa pines. Its eyes focused on the faint movement of a distant creature with such acuity it made human vision seem like a sorry afterthought. With a tight contraction of muscle, the hawk pushed off the man's shoulder and flew over the charred foothills in search of its prey. The man's consciousness, such as it was, attached itself to the hawk by a tender thread then rose up with a jolt, erasing the space between them. Skirting the treetops, they veered sharply down into a canyon that raged with water, not knowing if it was a lethal trap or a new beginning.

Book One

August, 2019

Chapter One

Pavement heat crawled up Shelley's bare legs like some hairy animal as she circled the old Accord, airing the wretched thing out. Leave it to her to choose a car in Heat-Retentive Red. As she opened the doors, dragon breath lashed out. Inescapable, but by no means unavoidable. It's not like she forgot to unfold the sun deflector and put it in the windshield, she just thought she'd be back in no time. And no time was what she had to get her final chore done, rushing around King Soopers with the List, scooping up anything that hadn't already been delivered over the long course of the shopping day. When Mimi needed something, she needed it now. Even this tub of kitty litter, which did not often go on sale. Back in aisle eight, Shelley had wrangled it up to the kid's seat of the shopping cart to make it easier to load into the car, but it didn't seem so easy now. Plans made in air-conditioning didn't always pan out under the sun, especially not with this vile wildfire smoke drifting into town, making it hard to even breathe.

Locking both hands on the yellow tub's handle, she gave her wonky back a heads up, and lift! Lift! Over and down, into the Accord's trunk with a thud. She wasn't as strong as she used to be. She was sure as shoot not as young. The 24-block of toilet paper was unwieldy but pliable. It could be squeezed to almost any shape and still bounce back, so she forced it next to the tub. Then in went the bottled prunes, shredded coconut, spiced almonds, and a two-pack of ammonia, all of which fit into one of the hundreds of reusable bags that Mimi had acquired over the years and insisted Shelley use when shopping. "For the environment," Mimi explained.

Shelley removed the meatloaf dinner she'd picked up for herself and tossed it in the front seat. Then, with one hand she slammed the trunk shut and with the other aimed the empty shopping cart towards the cart corral. It missed. "Damn," she said. Her aim was usually so good her carts rarely even brushed the metal sides as they rolled on in. She blamed the pavement, which was hot enough to melt the tires. A teen in a red King Soopers smock was pushing a train of carts nearby and stopped to stare right at Shelley. Her eyeglasses reflected the yellow sun like an insect.

Fudgesicles. Shelley hadn't turned away quick enough. After a brief check-in with her better self and already begrudging the amount of sweat it would cost her, she walked over to set things right. She was halfway there when she nearly got run over by an overflowing cart at take-off speed. The woman propelling the cart was rushing down the aisle, talking on the phone while fussing with a baby in the child's seat. It was too hot to be moving so fast, but it was not Shelley's business to tell her. As it was, the woman never even looked up as she rushed by. Parking lots were as dangerous as highways these days with everyone so distracted. Shelley retrieved her empty cart and maneuvered it between the metal guards, then paused for some recognition from the King Soopers' teen. A friendly nod would do. But no. Just that insect stare. Even as Shelley walked away, she felt the girl was still looking at her. Maybe she was afraid she'd lose her job if everyone was a good supermarket citizen who returned their carts. Skin was about as thin as a soap bubble these days.

When Shelley got back to her car it seemed hotter than before, like it had sucked up the parking lot heat instead of releasing it, making the vinyl insides smell like industrial fluid. She rearranged a bath towel under her bum to protect her tender pink thighs from the heat. She didn't usually wear shorts to work. She tried to look professional, like the manager of an estate and not some domestic worker, but by the end of the summer she really didn't give a hoot how she looked, and neither did Mimi. The engine started with a loud cough but held steady. The air conditioner was cranked up high but didn't do a whole lot except stir the heat so she opened the windows as well. The weak AC was on her own to-do list but there was never enough money. As much as she liked her title of house manager, the salary was just meh. If she got paid on commission she'd be rolling in gold. Even one percent of Mimi's purchases would make for a considerable take-home check, even half a percent, but since that wasn't the case she had to wait until things broke down completely then decide if they were worth replacing. Body parts too. There was an empty space in her pie-hole where a tooth should sit. She choked on her own spit when a dentist told her how much an implant cost. Even a bridge was beyond her budget.

It would all have to wait, wouldn't it? Her house, car, and mouth, all held together with spit and string. Before she drove off she sent a text to Mimi to let her know she got everything on the List, then took a photo of the receipt and sent that to her as well. Shelley immediately got back a screen of pounding heart emojis, and her job here was done. As she backed up, she had to inch along because that shopper who almost ran her over was in the spot next to hers, putting her groceries away. She had all the car doors open, and was trying to load stuff with the baby carrier in one hand. A paper grocery bag was ripping even as she lifted it from the cart. She should be using reusable bags. Tough as nails.

When Shelley finally got on the road, shadows were spilling

across the city as the sun began its long, slow dive behind the peaks. The western sky did not look well, all washed out in yellow and black, what with the soot clouds in the air. She rolled up the windows but the Accord's pathetic AC could not filter out the smell. Still, even through the haze, the very sight of the Front Range stretching across the land was eye-blinking as always, with its draping slopes and protruding slabs of rock. If she squinted just so, the formations looked like turrets, towers, pyramids, and castles, a city of legend rising from the prairie. You could project any life you wanted on them. It was why everyone wanted to live in Boulder, the sweet spot where the Rockies hit the American plains. Horses and cows still grazed along the foothills, making you feel like you were living in the Wild West and not some New Agey college town where every other person was some vega-yogatarian. The peaks drew low thoughts up and made you feel good about yourself no matter what else was going on in your life. Even if all you did was stay inside and watch TV, you knew the mountains were only right out there.

Not that she could see them from her house on Arroyo Circle. To see a mountain you had to have some distance. Some perspective. Hers was in the armpit of the city, too close for a mountain view, and, except for morning, almost always in the mountain shade. It was what made the house affordable when she and Keith went looking for one, must be close to twenty-five years ago now. That and the steep gully behind it, with a trickle or torrent of creek depending on the season, and the foreboding noise of human habitation year-round. In spite of the name of her street, the creek was no arid arroyo, more like a damp ravine of tangled vegetation and debris, but city planners were partial to names with Western flavor. It seemed half the roads were named after Native Americans, like Arapaho or Cherokee, the people forced off their land so the city could be built in the first place.

The creek was nearly a city unto itself, with folks camped out along the twisted length of it, as if they'd fallen into an open wound, out of reach of basic human comfort. One of them cut through her yard all the time. "Les," he called himself. "One 's', please." It was not the most direct route back to town but he seemed to know where he was going, walking along in his cloud of ditch dirt. Sometimes he had empty milk jugs clattering behind him like a brood of ducklings, tied to his waist with lengths of perforated fruit bags, presumably headed for some recycling bin. There was no money in it for him. It was just looney. Her friend Betty-Ann told her she should put up a fence, but who had that sort of cash lying around? And who cared really? Les never asked anything of her in spite of looking like he needed everything there was to be asked for. Shelley was no Boulder Buddhist counting her karma, but she felt she owed the world something, even if it was just letting some homeless guy walk on through. What goes around comes around, as her mom used to say. Shelley's throat still got a little tight thinking of her.

Out of sight, behind the Flatirons and Devil's Thumb, well beyond the trails she used to hike when she first arrived from Baraboo, Wisconsin, rose the mighty Continental Divide, visible only at the most eastern edge of town, tucked as it was behind the Front Range. What must the first pioneers have thought of this looming sight after a thousand miles of flat prairie? Higher altitudes were usually snow-capped the year round, but the spring had been too dry and the summer too hot, so peaks were bald for the first time in her memory, over thirty-five years of living in Boulder. Not much more than a teenager when she got there, now in spitting distance of sixty. How did that happen?

Just as she was pondering her life and counting years, she saw a helicopter off in the distance, hovering over the creek in a dirt-red storm of dust. It looked to be practically on her house.

"Sweet Baby Jesus in swaddling clothes. What now?"

Chapter Two

Amanda Newell was running late. She trotted across the parking lot pushing the cart in front of her with one hand, the other on the yellow baby carrier balanced sideways in the child's seat to keep it from jostling. Little Freddie's eyes flickered. "Almost done, baby cakes," she said. It was so hot she'd just put him in a onesie, leaving his arms and legs bare, but then, of course, the supermarket was too cold and she'd had to cover him with a light swaddle, the blue one dotted with yellow fire engines. She should never have told people she was having a boy. Her baby shower was a flood of blue, with half the teeny clothes covered with trucks, like this one. Is that really what you wanted your kid to bond to? An emergency vehicle? She took it off him and stuffed it in her bag as she kept moving forward. Free of his blankie, Freddie stretched his dimpled arms over his head and scrunched up his face in pre-cry mode. She adjusted her ear buds and asked Siri to call Ilana at the office. She had to show a house in an hour. Her first client since maternity leave. Freddie sputtered soft infant complaints, so she put the binkie in his rosebud mouth when Ilana picked up. After a few sucks, Freddie closed his eyes and went back to sleep. As exhausting as it all was, he was a good baby. Her baby.

"Ilana, can you call the Calhouns and tell them I'll be twenty minutes late?"

An acceptable amount of time to ask for. No one would hold twenty minutes against her, not with notice. "I know, I know. But they're flying back to California tomorrow and they wanted to see this last one before they go. I've heard they haven't made up their minds yet, so they might jump on it. I just hope these wildfires haven't turned them off from moving here altogether." A big commission so soon after coming back to work would set them back to rights again. Who knew babies were so expensive? The cost of diapers alone was enough to bankrupt a queen. This baby carrier, part of a complicated module system which conveniently snapped into the car seat base as well as the stroller, had to be jointly funded by a half dozen baby shower guests. Convenience costs. "Tell them the truth. I have a new baby and can't get out of my own way. I forgot half the things I came for because I couldn't find my shopping list. I probably used it to diaper Freddie before leaving the house." They laughed, because, really, what else could you do but laugh? As Ilana rattled on about call-backs and new listings, Amanda's mind raced ahead to what she had to do in the next hour. Her sister was right, it was a young woman's sport. She shouldn't have waited so long to get pregnant, and she really shouldn't have waited until the end of the day to do groceries. Everything took so long with an infant. It was not just the fussing, it was everyone wanting to 'ooh' and 'ahh' as she walked down the aisles. Of course he was the cutest thing ever, but it took time she did not have. How nice it would be to have someplace to leave him for a couple of hours while she did chores like this. There was her sister, but she had to save her for emergencies, which were often enough. She couldn't afford any day care until commissions started to flow in again, so she could only show houses at night after Devin got home from work.

Amanda struggled to find her car keys while pushing the cart, rummaging through the diaper bag, her pocketbook, and the pockets of her skorts before finding them in her hand, clutched against the shopping cart. Ilana continued to talk and she made listening noises. She knew she should be paying attention to the new listings Ilana was describing, but she could only designate part of her brain to the conversation. She was so tired. Freddie was up half the night. Between her and Devin, they probably got two hours of sleep. She knew Ilana would send all this information to her by email later, so she'd read it tonight, after Freddie fell asleep. If he fell asleep.

She unlocked her cherry-red Camry with a chirp, picked up the baby carrier by the handle, then walked around the car, opening all the doors to air it out. It was still too hot to put Freddie inside, and she dared not start the car to cool it with AC for fear he'd breathe in the exhaust. Besides, she'd never put him in a running car without her. She clicked open the trunk and attempted to load groceries with one hand, but the very first bag ripped and she almost lost the contents, all liquid, all breakable. Not only that, the smokey sun was shining right on Freddie's worried face. A bad dream? Did babies dream? He was such a wonder. She briefly set the carrier on the ground, then envisioned a car swerving out of control, and picked it up again. She kissed him on the forehead, then put the carrier in the trunk where the open hood shaded him from the glare.

As Amanda began to load the car she wrapped up her conversation with Ilana. "Get on the line with the Calhouns and tell them I'll be there at 6:20 on the nose. I'll be home soon, then all I have to do is put the perishables away before heading out. I wish Devin could do that too, but he'll have Freddie and he can't do two things at once yet." She laughed. "He'll learn. I'll call you later and let you know how the showing went."

She slipped the phone in her skorts pocket and continued loading. The three soft cases of diapers used all the room in the trunk next to the baby so she had to use the back seat for the other bags of groceries, and then, because the baby seat base took up most of that, she filled up the passenger seat with bags as well. She had no time to pump so Devin would have to feed Freddie a bottle of formula. At least she remembered to pick up a case of Similac. Breastfeeding was such a struggle. Her milk was more like a trickle than a fountain, as everyone in her mommy yoga group kept yattering on about. It made her ashamed to already be supplementing with a bottle, but she had to keep Freddie's weight up or suffer a lecture about New Age Neglect from his pediatrician. She thought the expectations in the real estate world about how she should look and how she should act were tough until she became a mother. Now she was supposed to be both Earth Mother and efficient CEO of her household, ready and rested to go back to work three months postpartum. She did not feel ready, and certainly not rested. When she bent over to put a bag on the passenger seat she glanced at herself in the rearview mirror and saw a madwoman, as if motherhood was a form of insanity. Her hair had fallen out of its clip and she'd never had time to put on mascara. Before meeting with the Calhouns she'd have to do something with herself so she wouldn't look like a bag lady. A shower was out of the question. She'd call Devin and ask him to take her yellow striped shirt out of the closet, find her pearls, make-up kit, and hair spray, and leave it all by the door for an on-the-fly makeover. It was the best she could do.

She was almost finished loading when the phone vibrated against her thigh. She looked at the screen. Devin. "What? I hope you're calling from home because I have to run as soon as I get there."

"Bad news."

"Oh no." Amanda bent down to arrange the groceries on the floor of the passenger seat, trying to fit one more bag in. Devin had his defeated dog voice on, the one he used to convey that he was helpless in a situation, like fixing a screen window or putting

Freddie to sleep. He gave up so easily. He had no fight in him, like now, as she listened to him stumble over his explanation why he couldn't leave the shop until his boss returned. Devin managed a tech repair store downtown, and the owner always took advantage of his good nature. That would have to stop. They were on baby time now.

"I hope he'll be back soon," he said. "But maybe not soon enough. I don't even know where he went. He's not answering texts."

"I'll have to bring Freddie to the store then." When Amanda stood back up she felt sweat running down her back. "I can't show the house with a baby on my hip."

"I can't wait on customers and watch Freddie too. Larry won't like it. Can't you make the appointment a little later?"

She wiped her face with a tissue that smelled of baby spit-up. She hated always being the one expected to rearrange her life, but they could not afford for Devin to lose his job and the health insurance that came with it. "I already have," she said. "I can't move it again. You know what? Nevermind. I'll call my sister and see if she can meet me at home and watch Freddie til you get there."

"Sorry," he said. "You know Larry. He walked out before I knew he was gone. What could I do?"

"Really, Devin. You should have told him this morning that you had to leave exactly on time today. Everyone's got to learn to give a little."

"I know, I know."

"Just try to get there as soon as you can." With one hand she clicked a number on her phone and started closing all the car doors, already talking to her sister as she jumped in the driver's seat and sped out of the parking lot, leaving her empty cart behind.

Chapter Three

The flapping wings of chaos sucked the dust from the earth and spewed a whirlwind over the cottonwood, jolting Les conscious with a cough. A *Chiindii?* The word plopped like a turd into his brain pan. *Chiindii*. Navajo for dust devils. A mystery, the cells that survived. He wasn't even Native, was he? No. His was an invasive species of the first degree.

He scanned the heavens with a salute, protecting his retinas from a smoldering sun ninety-two million miles away. Roaring, rotating blades, no dust devils. No angels neither. Just a police whirly whipping its way through billows of wildfire clouds drifting down from the canyon. The flying blues patrolled the creek overhead in sporadic fits to disperse dreck like him, show the neighbor-people they were doing something. All show. Just show. The blues didn't want creek dwellers like him wandering around town. No-no-no-no. No.

To escape from the swooshing taunt of the 'copter—*coming for you, coming for you*—he rolled across the ledge and under the coyote willow, feeling bone-on-bone in hips, the crunch of dry twigs, the points of broken glass through pants. Was he wearing pants? Yes. Yes he was. Ready to go. Ready to begin the daily resurrection from his afternoon nap. First, provisions for the journey. A bread bag with a half a burger roll in the bottom of his jacket pocket. Check. On the ground, ripe *Vitis riparia*, the riverbank grape. Food for the gods. Into an inner pocket some go. Check. He shook his empty Tito's for drops, just in case, just in case. Into a top pocket. Glass was heavy, but just hot sand after all, no nasty petroleum product. No bottle bill in the land neither, but buddy Ralph paid a quarter for every hollow Tito's, making one-buck shot glasses for the college crowd on the Hill. The closed circle of his drinking habits. No such circle today for the milk jugs and soda bottles from the morning's creek sweep. Most days he dragged them to a recycling box where they were certainly not recycled, but at least he tried. No time now for even trying. He found his battered Marlboro box with three decent butts inside. The rest of his things, if he could call them things, if he could call them his, he crammed into his black trash bag and tucked it away in his hidey hole behind a boulder, while the jeering of metal blades crept closer, *coming for you, coming for you, coming for you.*

"Alright already. I'm moving." First the aching bladder. He maneuvered his pecker out and got things flowing but his pee-stream nearly drowned a digger bee on the ground. It crawled to the safety of grape leaves. It needed the sun to orient itself, but the old star was full of smoke today. As he relieved himself, he watched fellow creek dwellers pack up, hiding tattered blankets, taking inventory, wandering up to the street by the main path. Gathering children. Traveling in a pack was nervous-making so he traveled a path of his own. That Shelley woman let him cut through her yard. Not in so many words. Not in any words but a nod and howdy-do now and again. Goes to work, comes home, goes to work, comes home. Lived life on a low flame that gal. One of those who protects the brain by not paying attention to the world around her. He was tempted to snooze in her garden shed when weather was wet and thunderous, curl up with a lawn mower as bedmate and plastic pot for pillow, but his little ledge always won out. And not for nothing, but Shelley would surely call the dark blues if she found him in the shed.

As others disappeared to the upper world, he put away the pecker and burrowed under the dry scrub to his path, breathing in ground dust. Death by dust. Dust to dust. Taking the slow, careful steps of a sherpa, he made it to the top of the path and bent over for labored air. Breathe it in, breathe it out. Spit. Hack it up. Spit again. Blood. Hmmm. Never good. But what is? A good question. He ratcheted himself straight and looked around, nearly falling back down the embankment in shock. Armed blues in front of Shelley's house? He slipped behind the garden shed and pondered. Could he remember the night before? No. Had he done something bad? Who was to say? What was bad? He was just down at the creek harming no one but himself.

"You! Don't move!" One of them, a fitful male, loomed towards him. No angel this, but blue-winged and power-mouthed. Coming from the front yard. *Coming, coming, coming for you.*

"Where do you live?"

"In possibility," Les said, hunching his shoulders forward to protect his underbelly.

"Possibility? What's that? A new shelter? What're you doing here?"

Then Les saw Officer Sokos, one of the blues always moving him along on Pearl. Why bother changing Pearl from a street to a pedestrian mall if all they were going to do was herd people around like cattle, he always asked her to no avail. Now here she was, crouching behind one of the police cars with a gun. Shoot out on Arroyo Circle. She turned to look at him.

"Lester," she shouted over the sound of the helicopter. "Get out of here. Go on."

The first blue lost interest and loomed back to the others. Les was not the one they waited for. He was not the one. He shuffled over to Sokos. Her red hair looked to be sweating liquid brick out from under her cap. "What's up?"

"Leave."

"Something happen to Shelley?"

"You know her?" she said.

"Depends on whether you believe reality rises from a yes or no question."

"Stop it. Do you know her?"

"Know her name, but not her. So yes and no."

Sokos adjusted her blue sunglasses against her face. "Stay over there, out of the way. We could have questions. Don't think I don't know about your path behind this house. Maybe you've learned a thing or two."

"Is she okay?"

Sokos had gone back to staring at the street as if some miracle was about to spring up from the pavement. "We have reason to believe she's kidnapped a baby."

Les fondled the Marlboro box in his pocket and looked around. "I doubt she even likes babies."

Chapter Four

Shelley wondered if the helicopter had something to do with the homeless again. Maybe a body, dead or dying. That happens. An overdose. Exposure. Violence. Sometimes nothing to do with the homeless, like in the spring when the snowmelt arrives like a bullwhip and college kids go tubing in the white water. She'd done it herself, those years when Keith kept chasing an outdoors rush, always dragging her along. Every year there was always some poor soul getting snagged on a fallen tree and held down till dead. Mishap by adventure, they called it. But it'd been months since the creek had more than a trickle. Even a complete nincompoop needed water to drown.

She'd find out soon enough when she got home. It was too late in the day to drive back up the hill to Mimi's, but Mimi knew that. For all her grasping panic that she'd run out of something, she always calmed right down as soon as Shelley assured her that all was in her possession, down to the bottled prunes. Mimi could then toss the day's List off her mental worries, and begin her sleepless night on the computer, deciding what to put on the next day's List. Having a document to work from made her feel secure. She used that word a lot. Secure. It wasn't, "Did you buy the prunes?" It was, "Did you secure the prunes?" Mimi had security issues, by god. She had plenty of issues, period, but Shelley loved her for all her neediness. It made her feel needed. But she knew how fragile people could drain others dry so she kept her own boundaries strong. Mimi was one of those people who tied you to them early on by telling you an ugly personal circumstance or two. JonBenét Ramsey was one of those odd circumstances, which only went to show how far-ranging Mimi's problems went. She was not a healthy woman.

Then again, neither was this weather, all clogged up with heat and smoke. She'd unpack and stack first thing in the morning when it would be cooler and maybe even clearer if they ever got that fire under control. There was nothing that required refrigeration. Certainly nothing that Mimi and her family would need overnight. Or ever. There was a pyramid of kitty litter containers in the garage for the one spoiled cat, Spree, and enough bales of toilet paper in the basement to last the family to doomsday. Ammonia? Lined up by the dozen on stairs and closets with all the other cleaning staples, as if there were still surfaces left to clean. Edibles that didn't need refrigeration, like the spiced almonds and shredded coconut, were stockpiled in Rubbermaid bins in what had once been the family room. Other rooms held clothes, or small, useless appliances, like bread machines and egg poachers. Toaster ovens and air fryers, still in their boxes, had a walk-in closet of their own that spilled out into the hall.

Over the years, Shelley kept thinking Jeremy would put his foot down, either reining Mimi in or giving Shelley the authority to make real change, but he just retreated deeper into his business. He put on a black Stetson, bolo tie, and cowboy boots every morning like a ranch hand at a square dance, but she knew he did some vague financial thing in the cattle industry. Whatever it was, he must be pretty good at it to afford this massive consumption. But that was not her business. Neither was his relationship with his wife. Even though he slept on the third floor, she knew he visited Mimi once in a while, crawling through and over the stuff like an obstacle course. If her mess bothered him he kept it to himself. He seemed to tolerate her the way the Romans put up with a petulant goddess. You don't cross her. You make your offerings and hope to be spared.

As for the children, they had Louisa to drive them around and see to their care. At this point they rarely visited their mother anymore, and had even stopped replying to her texts and emails. Now it was up to Shelley to give Mimi news of her family, what little she knew. In spite of that, Mimi truly seemed to love them all, booking restaurant birthday parties she was unable to attend, and ordering presents for every occasion and non-occasion, but stuff, physical stuff, was the driving force of her life. It was what gave it meaning and Shelley was hired as the instrument to that meaning.

It was what it was. Shelley's own home, a single level with a somewhat finished basement, was clean and orderly, arranged over the years to fit her like a shell. She could not wait to get there and switch on a fan and the TV and watch an old movie while she ate her meatloaf. She wouldn't mind a cool Coors either. Turning into Arroyo Circle, Shelley saw a police car in her rearview mirror. No, two, three police cars. From where? To where? It was a dead end street, no longer than her arm. Where were they all going? In a typhoon of dust, the helicopter swept over the street.

Four or five police cars jammed the turnaround at the end of the street, behind the grassy circle where her little house sat next to where the land dropped off to the creek below. A cruiser blocked her driveway so she pulled up to the curb, where she was abruptly caged in by other cruisers. A dozen or more officers crouched on her lawn. Armed. *Armed?* When she rolled down the window to talk to them, they were like blue bees swarming down on her. "What's going on?"

"Don't talk," said an officer, a tall gal with hair the color of red mud. Her sunglasses had blue reflective lenses so all Shelley saw was herself, in another, darker, world. Behind her, two other cops were holding guns. Holding. Guns. "Take your keys out of the ignition."

Shelley had trouble understanding what she said. What did those words have to do with her? "What is this?"

"Open the door and step out with your hands up, Ma'am, with the keys."

Shelley's hand shook as she removed her keys. The cops all stepped back when she stood, like she was some threat. She felt sick, but if she bent to vomit would they shoot her? She looked around, but even her own home looked unfamiliar. "I don't understand. Are you sure you have the right person?"

"Hands over your head, Ma'am."

"Okay already." Her arms were as weak as noodles when she raised them. The next door neighbors stood at their screen door looking as confused and alarmed as she did, like she was an actor in someone else's messed up life. She shrugged at them and they turned away. She'd become a danger to know.

"Go to the trunk of your vehicle," said the redhead.

With shaky legs, Shelley walked to the back of the Accord and the blue hive moved with her.

"Open the hood."

Shelley backed away from her own car. "Is there someone in there? Is something going to jump out at me?" No answer. "There's nothing in here but groceries. I've got a receipt for all of it." Still, no answer.

"Open the hood, Ma'am."

"Is there an escaped prisoner or something?" Her fingers trembled as she clicked to unlock, so she had to give it a few tries. By the time it popped open an inch she almost screamed.

"All the way."

She had a sudden urge to run. Why was that? She hadn't done

anything wrong. But did that even matter if they thought she did? "Me? Why me?" The guns seemed to lurch at her, so she sprang open the hood with one hand and jumped back. She couldn't breathe, and she wouldn't look. The cops moved in closer and stared into the trunk.

"All this yours?"

Afraid of what she might see, Shelley peeked. It was the same batch of groceries she'd loaded back at the store. What the sweet bejesus was going on?

"I'm a house manager for a family up on the hill. I was picking up a few things for them on my way home from work."

"Remove the yellow container with the handle," said the redhead.

"The Tidy Cat?" Shelley asked, but no response. When she lifted the pail the compressed toilet paper expanded with a sigh, relaxing into the empty space. It took some effort to land the pail gently on the ground. Pain rippled through her lower back.

"Open it."

"I'll need a screwdriver," she said. No one moved. The helicopter above made so much noise, she thought maybe they couldn't hear her. "To take the tab off?" she shouted. Nothing. They did not offer assistance of any kind. She could slice it off with her trusty box cutter, but she was afraid if she reached into her pocket they might well shoot her. Instead she pried the plastic top off with her sweaty bare hands and broke a nail in the process. She felt dizzy. Out of nowhere a police dog rushed towards her. She scrunched up and covered her head. She could smell her own sweat. This was it. This was how it would end, and she wouldn't even know why.

But the dog ignored her and sniffed the cat litter. Its tail did not go up.

"Is that a drug dog?" She stood up slowly to not alarm the animal or the cops. "Or a bomb dog? Do you think I have a bomb?"

"Search and rescue."

"Search what? Rescue who?"

"Okay, thank you."

"Thank you? Wait, what did you think I had in there?"

"A baby." The redhead was putting away her gun and didn't even look at Shelley.

"A *baby*? I don't understand. What does that even mean?"

The redhead finally looked right at Shelley, annoyed. "Someone at King Soopers reported they'd seen you put a baby in the trunk of your car and drive off."

Shelley snorted a laugh out her nose so hard she almost burst a sinus. She looked around at all the expressionless faces. No one was laughing with her. "You're kidding, right?"

"Wrap it up," the redhead said to the others, turning her back on Shelley. "Let's get out of here. No kidnapping today."

"Wait," Shelley said. "Don't I even get an apology? Aren't you sorry?" She looked over at her neighbors, who immediately shut their door. She spotted that homeless guy, Les. Even he looked away.

"Thank you for your time, Ma'am," said the officer, getting into her patrol car.

"You can't do this," Shelley shouted. "Who reported a kidnapping? How about arresting the jerk who made the false report?"

Not a single officer even pretended to listen, which only made Shelley shout louder. "I'll bet it was the girl over at King Soopers who had some sort of problem with me when I returned my cart. What about scaring her half to death now? This can't be legal!"

One by one the cruisers drove away, leaving her alone in the street, frazzled, angry, and hot. In an explosion of dust, the helicopter made a final swoop over the house then disappeared. Fine brick-red particles fell like ash from the sky.

Les shuffled over like his legs were chained together. "Oh, great," she mumbled. They'd always kept a polite distance, but now he saw a kindred spirit in her, someone the police knew. And yet, who else but someone like him to understand how she felt? She'd been unfairly accused and practically assaulted, and she wanted justice.

"What do I do?" she asked.

Les looked up at the smoke-streaked sky. "Depends on whether you think systems can organize themselves without any conscious input."

Shelley stared at him hard, then beseeched him with open hands. "I don't even like babies."

Chapter Five

Shelley needed to get to the bottom of the injustice flung on her, starting with the cart girl. As she drove back to King Soopers with Les by her side, she worked herself into full battle fury. "I can't believe they thought I kidnapped a baby! Me!"

"Even chaos has rules," said Les.

"What?" asked Shelley.

"You weren't randomly chosen," said Les. "The strange attractor is at work here and must be found."

"What? Who's strange?" asked Shelley.

Les had asked for a ride into town in her "metal cave" as he called it, and in her rage she didn't even consider the safety issues of being alone in a car with a homeless guy she knew only by sight, and not a pretty one at that. And the funk. The man was so fragrant she could smell him over the wildfire smoke. But she'd wanted an eyewitness with her, so she rolled down her car windows and brought him along. Just as she was thinking she should let him out at the next light, he started chanting "Find the cart girl!" and she joined right in. They were having a grand time, but then, with the shopping center just ahead, Les quieted down like a parakeet at sunset.

"I'm not really allowed at King Soopers," he said, so, whatever that meant, she dropped him off at Baseline Liquors and he wished her luck. For a minute there she'd felt stronger having him with her, but it was just as well. It wouldn't further her cause to be seen with a guy who had cracked sores at his mouth and a matted braid down his spine. Not that she looked so good herself. She should have taken the time to change into something more managerial to put a little fear into Cart Girl. Long pants. Jacket. Scarf. A speck of jewelry. But too late for that now. She turned into the supermarket lot and trolled the aisles in the darkening light. Then again, she knew this parking lot so well she could have driven it blind-folded. She'd spent a lot of her work days here when she wasn't at Mimi's, slicing open boxes from Amazon or eBay or local delivery services. When she displayed the contents to Mimi, her employer got pos-itively giddy, becoming the delightful woman that lived beneath the blighted surface of her personality. Inevitably though, Shelley had to shut the circus down with talk about where things should go. Mimi wanted everything to stay in her bedroom but that was out of the question. There wasn't enough space in there to fart. As it was, any package wider than Shelley's hips couldn't fit through the bedroom path anymore.

Every day was a struggle to find a square inch of storage some-where, anywhere, and by the end of the week, there were towers of flattened boxes leaning against the house for support, waiting for recycling pickup. Perishables were a constant headache. A small country couldn't eat its way through them before rot and rats won the day. The pantries and refrigerators were so con-gested it took her the better part of the morning to help Claudia, the cook, sort through them to find what was needed to make the day's meals, from a menu that Mimi texted to both of them before dawn. Mimi's food got labeled and laid out in the refrigerator in her room, where she used the microwave next to her bed to heat things up. Meals for Jeremy and their two tame teenagers, Harper and Winnie, waited for them whenever they passed through the kitchen. The food was almost always untouched when Shelley arrived in the morning.

"Don't worry about us," Jeremy told her early on. "I usually have a big old steak downtown for lunch, and you know kids, they snack all day at school. You just take care of my princess." For a long while, when the children were young, she worked with Claudia and Mimi to come up with meals they might eat. Chicken fingers, mac n'cheese, burgers. Ice cream. But one day she realized it wasn't the food, it was the constipated surroundings. What swallow reflex could function in such a place? Not hers, for sure. The children were clearly afraid of being smothered. Louisa, the nanny, padlocked the children's doors while they were at school or camp so Mimi couldn't fill them with crap, which she most certainly would. Eventually, Shelley found out Louisa fed the kids out in the world after picking them up from school or activity, then they locked themselves in their rooms, sanctuaries from the chaos. When Shelley began working there, Jeremy had already moved out of his princess's bed to the third floor, in spite of his professed devotion. He had a padlock too.

It was a moot point now. Mimi had gotten too big to do much but use the walker to get from bed to toilet to refrigerator and back again. The family was polite, but did not confide in Shelley or ask anything of her. She belonged to Mimi, along with all the rest. There were times she felt positively complicit. The house was congested when she signed on, but had gotten much worse under her care. She was hired for her considerable organizing ability and had welcomed the challenge, but she hadn't been able to keep up as Mimi's retail appetite grew. It was, after all, not her job to say no to Mimi. Her job was to say yes, to do what she was told. There was a time she tried to work around her. Since expiration dates meant nothing to Mimi—she claimed they were a corporate conspiracy—food was not allowed to be thrown away until it was in an unidentifiable, semi-liquid state, or pressing against the sides of cans with gas. For a while Shelley snuck aging groceries to the local food pantry, but then Mimi had security cameras installed everywhere, even the garage and basement, so she could admire her scattered bounty from a laptop. That was the end of Shelley's smuggling operation, but it was some comfort to know that if she got buried under an avalanche of crap, Mimi might see it on her computer or phone and send for help.

"There you are," Shelley said out loud. Her prey was around the corner of the building, smoking a cigarette. Cart Girl. The tip glowed in the shadows. "You can't hide from me," she said as she pulled into the alley to block her in. The police had taught her that much. The girl looked at her like she didn't even know who she was. Cool as a cucumber, that one.

"Hey, you," Shelley said, slamming her car door for effect. "What the hell?"

"What?" the girl said. "I can smoke here. It's my break. It's still a free country."

"Don't make believe you don't know what I'm talking about. I was here a little over an hour ago. Either you didn't like that I returned my cart or you didn't like that I didn't. Remember?"

The girl looked behind her and at the car. "Ma'am, I don't know what you're talking about. I just move carts from one place to another."

"No! You called the police. You called the police on me and told them I put a baby in the trunk of my car."

"Oh yeah," she said, perking up. "I heard there'd been a kidnapping in the parking lot. Wait a minute."

"There was no kidnapping." Shelley followed her to the employee's door. "It was a tub of kitty litter, not a baby carrier."

"Dave!" the girl shouted into the building. "You'd better come out. The kidnapper is here."

"I am not!" Even as she defended herself—her very innocent

self—a flush of fear went through her that they would call the police. She could not go through that again.

The manager stepped outside just as the parking lot lights began to come on. Shelley knew who he was. She remembered when he was a cart kid himself. Over the years he'd worked his way up, one of the few people of color in management in the city's supermarkets. Because, of course, she knew all the supermarkets intimately, knew their sales days and their layouts, knew whether their produce departments smelled like onions or lemons, and what time of day they cleaned their fish bins. "What?" Dave said, wiping his hands on a paper towel. "What's going on?"

"The kidnapper here wants to know who reported her," the girl said.

He pointed the towel at Shelley. "You're the one! I saw you put the baby in the trunk."

"You saw no such thing. You called the cops on me?"

"No, Ma'am. They called me. They'd had a report of a kidnapping or some sort of child abuse involving a car trunk and asked me to go over our surveillance tape, see if I could get a license plate number. That was you. Middle-aged white woman. Dark hair. Red Honda, Colorado plate. I forget the number, but I remember you." He waved the towel at her car. "You took a baby carrier out of the cart seat and put it in the trunk. You can't do that. Not in this heat."

"Oh dear lord. It was kitty litter. Go look at your tape again. You know me! You've seen me here almost every day for years. Have you ever seen me with a baby? Your employee made it all up. She had it out for me and called the cops."

The girl put her cigarette into a butt caddy by the door. "I didn't do anything," she said. "I'm just collecting carts. And I've got to get back to it."

Shelley felt her heart in her throat. All she wanted was for Cart Girl to admit what she'd done and apologize. She'd been wronged and she wanted some sort of justice.

"You go, Trudy," said Dave. "I'll take care of this."

Shelley couldn't believe what she was hearing. "*This? This?* Do you mean me? I'm a steady customer. Maybe your best customer. I have a receipt!"

"You were definitely lifting something plastic and yellow with a handle," said Dave. "I know what I saw."

"You saw a thirty-five-pound bucket of Tidy Cat," she said. "Go into your store and look. Aisle 8, bottom shelf. $18.99, on sale. Ask the police. Ask their dog! They almost killed me over it."

Trudy turned and walked away.

"No!" Shelley grabbed her by her sweaty smock. "No. You can't just do this to people. Trudy? Trudy what? Afraid of losing your job because people like me return their carts, aren't you? That's it, isn't it?"

"Hey," she said. "You're going to break my glasses."

Shelley let go. This wasn't like her. Or maybe it was and she'd just never been so unjustly accused before. The police were one thing, but the supermarket was supposed to be her people.

"Ma'am," said Dave. He stuffed his towel in a pocket and moved towards her. "I'm going to have to ask you to leave the premises. You can't abuse my employees."

"I'm the one who's been abused. Me! She knows she did it. Ask to see the log on her cell phone. I'll bet there's a call to the police on it."

"That's not necessary," said Dave.

It was necessary. How else to prove fault? Shelley turned from him and followed Trudy into the parking lot, with Dave on her heels. "Let me see your phone!" she screamed. "You know you did it! Admit it and say you're sorry. Maybe the sun was in your eyes, or something. Say you made a mistake. Just say it."

The girl stopped and turned to her, then pointed at the smoldering mountains. "I was probably looking at all the smoke. I don't know. But I sure as shit wasn't looking at you." They all turned to look at the western sky as if it held the answers to the problem at hand. Tucked in the purple billows of smoke, red flames flickered up from behind the ridge. That couldn't be good. The three of them just stood still, forgetting for a moment what they were doing there.

"Ma'am, I'm calling the police," Dave said finally. "Unless you get in your car and leave right now." He took his phone out of his pocket like a gun and stared her down.

Shelley was sick to her stomach down to her toes. It was too hot for this. She was not going to get any satisfaction here. She took in a deep breath. Then another. Breathe it out. Let it go. She refused to let her temper get her in trouble. As Betty-Ann once pointed out, she had a real talent for turning misunderstanding into anger. It was how she lost her job at McGuckin's hardware, where she'd run inventory. One day, she snapped at her boss over some stupid question. It wasn't the first time, but the Great Recession was still in full swing and he must have been looking for a reason to cut staff so out she went. She was unemployed well past when her benefits expired and her nails were bitten down to the whites. Then, through a friend of a friend, Mimi hired her on the spot when she saw the words "inventory control" on her resume. Shelley should have realized then that was what her job was going to be, trying to control Mimi's stuff, not managing a household. But what did she know or care? It was a job. And she was appreciated, even loved. She could not let this stupid episode escalate to being banned from King Soopers, one of Mimi's favorite supermarkets. Mimi would not be happy. Shelley might be loved, but it was a love tied to doing her job.

"Okay," she said, in defeat. "Okay, I'm going."

She got back into her car and slowly drove back to where the problem began. Her parking space was still empty so she turned in. Between the smoke and the sinking sun, the sky was as dark as a plum. She looked around, then up, and spotted a security camera on top of the light pole across the aisle. She'd been wrongly accused by a long-distance, grainy, stop-motion piece of video. But who called the police? If not Trudy the cart girl, who? Did she really look like a kidnapper? The rearview mirror showed her as a stressed-out woman no longer young, with a mouth too big for her face and white roots seeping from her scalp like she had a skunk on her head. But was it the face of a baby snatcher? Really?

Some days she didn't know who the hell she was. For years she'd worked as the office manager at Flash, an electric supply company, her first job when she got to Boulder in the 80s. She took some night classes at the University but not nearly enough for a degree. That was pretty stupid of her. A life of half-assed jobs because of it. After ten years she'd had to go take care of her mother as she was dying back in Wisconsin. Flash would not give her a leave of absence, and when she returned a month later her spot had been filled. In short order she joined Flash's competitor in town, and in even shorter order married the boss, Keith.

That was a little reckless. She could see that now. Her love for him was all wrapped up with her grief and she shouldn't have made a life decision so soon after her mother's death. In one of their last chats, in between hospice nurse visits, they had talked about Shelley having children someday. "You would make a good mother," her mom said, squeezing her hand. There was no strength in it.

"Only if you stick around to be a grandmother," Shelley said. "I'm not going to go it alone."

"I'll try," her mom laughed and coughed. "I'll try."

She was dead three long days later. Shelley always felt she had failed her mother by moving away. She must have thought she was going to have another chance at family by marrying Keith, joined together in a world of their own making. She was well into her thirties by then, and after a haphazard attempt at children, they threw in the towel. Keith wasn't sure they should burden the planet with another human, and she wasn't sure she wanted to burden herself. For three years she worked inventory in Keith's office, and they hiked or kayaked on the weekends, and seemed like a normal enough Boulder couple. She thought they were happy. She thought this was what marriage looked like, like a calm pond. Then one day he announced he was selling the business and moving to Crested Butte with Alan, his best friend, to start a wild river rafting company. They were in love. He was sorry. He was so sorry. He signed the house over to her, paid off the mortgage, and said goodbye. And sorry, once again.

That was a long time ago. Almost twenty years, and she still couldn't wrap her head around it. She supposed he had to follow his heart, as he put it, but how had she been deceived about where his heart was to begin with? Or hers. She hadn't trusted herself since.

Time to move on. She had to get back home before her meatloaf went bad. It was in the back seat now, rescued from Les sitting on it. At least it was something salvaged from the day. She stuck her head out the window to see if it was clear behind her, her exterior rearview being so sooty from the wildfires she could write her name on it. She shifted the car into reverse and backed up with a quick glance at her interior rearview. Too late she saw a horrified face, not her own. She braked, but not before bumping into a train of carts, which caused a violent chain reaction, heaving Trudy to the ground.

Honey-sucking duck feathers.

Chapter Six

It was the time of great calming. Subatomic particles were speeding to the stars with lighter helium leading the way. Daytime beasts had gone to ground. Tiny canyon bats swirled into the alpenglow, sun-red clinging to the smoky mountaintops after the dimming of the tableland. The emergence. A few hours of dark, then horizon-glow. Then disappearance. Hello and goodbye, hello and goodbye, over and over into infinity. Les remembers emergence as a systems-theory. Decisions will happen naturally. Night creatures emerge at dusk with no conscious input. But what about animals he sees skulking around who shouldn't be up all night? The melancholy coyotes now nocturnal to avoid humans. Bears too. That's a pretty conscious decision. Someone or something decides. The invisible hand. Or claw. Where an animal simply acts, a human first decides what it wants. But there's no limit to what we want.

So emergence, a failed systems-theory like all the rest.

Les sat on the curb and continued to watch the full moon rise, that bright reflector of our light and desires, a mishmash of planetary debris from earth's collision with Theia, a hypothetical planet. Well, weren't we all hypothetical? Parabolas of night-clouds and fire-clouds drifted across the stars as smoothly as it rose from his hand-rolled cigarette, tobacco poking out of the end like nose hairs. The keen wind rattled through the dry-brush. Wait, no. Not wind, not wind, but the mumbled hoot of the flammulated owl. *You-uu, You-uu, You-uu.* Smoked out of the burning canyon and into Shelley's yard. Forced from home. Forced from life. The world painfully out of joint.

Smoke-stink from the canyon getting stronger with the hour. Not for nothing, but his sense of time passing was now more acute than the cesium atomic clock down the road at the Standards building. They reconciled cosmic and atomic time but always fell short. Not so him. Astrophysics 101: There is no absolute time the whole universe obeys. Time is defined by what happens around it and by the distance between points. He'd done his business in town and came back. That was some time ago and Shelley still gone. The gal was a bolt of lightning looking for a place to strike and he guessed she'd found it. Gone, gone, gone. So was the tobacco, which had finished its transformation from dried plant in his hand to volatile gasses in his lungs to nicotine receptors in his brain. What he liked about night was that it shut out overrated sight and enhanced the other senses. Touch, smell, hearing, and all those many senses that had no name. He shredded the remains with bitten fingers and while he was not one of those highly attuned creatures who could hear a leaf land on asphalt, he could sense the tobacco shreds fall to the pavement like an echo in the dark cave of his torso, the way he could sense the gravitational rush of a grape as it fell from stem to earth. What a release that must be.

Grapes? Where? He patted his pockets. No, not grapes but a soft curve of a doll-sized bottle and a sigh of contentment. A sip and a sigh. The bottle a black hole where time curled into itself. He went back to looking for grapes and found a warm, soft bag of goodness. He ate a few, sorting out the pits from the flesh in his mouth, then spit the seeds into the grass and pressed them into the soil. "Good luck," he said to them. Time for an after-dinner aperitif. Another sip. Then it was gone too. Timed out. Dead. Where did they all go? He looked up until his neck bones ached, then sprawled out on the dry grass on his back to behold the heavens. More satellites than stars. Nocturnal dung beetles roll their dung by the light of the Milky Way. Used to be a straight path, now with all the for-profit crap in the sky, they pile shit every which way. One of a world of consequences. Scanning the punctured black sky, he found the old familiar pinch of stardust through the smoky haze, the Pleiades, those hot middle-aged stars, the most obvious to the naked eye, as familiar as home.

You-uu, You-uu. Wrong time of year for mating, it seemed to him. A lost mate, or a lost mind? There was a slash of feathers in the trees and he saw a bird land on the gutter of Shelley's roof, a dark-eyed insectivore as big as his hand. A secretive species. Flammulated, flammulated. Flamed. Flame-shaped markings.

You-uu, You-uu.

Little guy shouldn't even be here. A refugee from the mountains of smoke. A refugee from life. Well, weren't they all? The northern boundary for Great Plains birds had shifted three hundred and fifty miles in the past forty years. More distance than he'd covered in that time. It was all falling apart faster than he could think about it. The great snake was unwinding, and the daft demagogue in D.C. does nothing. If it wasn't fire it was flood. Ancient Taoists texts predict a flood that will result in drowned people roaming the land as vengeful ghosts. "What can be done?" says an early fifth-century scripture. "The people are to be pitied."

Les considered the owl's mind reflected through its saucer eyes. Why hoot, wee one? Kicked out of the nest, still begging for food? A disgruntled nestling. The parents silent. The parents gone. Les knew all about that. He wondered where the other nest mates were, but didn't want to think about that. Death a blind broom. The little fellow so upset. Anxious. Eat why don't you? Eat! Eat while you can. There are insects to be had for the taking. Not bad tasting. Moths are a little dry, grubs gooey, but crickets like fried chicken, crunchy and oily. Could use salt.

Let's eat! And we're off. Feathered ear tufts twitch, wings open wide, and they soar, searching for sustenance with a vision humans have lost, the night now dazzling and holy. Their wings large for body mass, good for slow flying, slow, slow, as little as two miles per hour. Glide-flying. No loud flapping. Free of earth, free of gravity. Made of air. We are not trapped inside our suits of skin! Les feels the night through their feathers and they open wide the serrations on their wingtips. The James Bond silencer effect for stealth hunting. *Sh-whuuu. Sh-whuuu.* Every creature gets what they need, no more, no less.

"Let's glide, teeny owl." They put their arms out and down they flew over the roof on the updraft of the house, then swept through the crossed maze of branches, looking, looking. Where are the long pole pines of old? Long gone. Gone, gone, gone. No natives? Even the invader trees are not well, some closing up shop until some later, wetter time. He knew the feeling. But it was good to be flying again, wings adjusting altitude as they passed through the crackling leaves of the linden. The air currents lifted them above the canopy, then in a jerk, they head down so fast Les worries they can't pull up in time. On a collision course with Shelley's car drawing quickly up to the curb, just about to hit Les—Les!—with an animal screech of brakes and two eye-beams of light. There is a swoosh of wind against his cheek as the owl snatches a grasshopper off Les's chest with its talons and disappears.

Les bolted upright.

"Raptor!" he shouted to the fleeing owl, and felt himself in a state of rapture. Seized by force, prey carried away, caught in the talons. Gripped, elevated, and devoured. Gone. "Rapturous," he said, and slapped his chest with the calloused palms of his hands.

Chapter Seven

"Hey! Hey, hey, hey." Les was bathed in Shelley's headlights, magnifying the day's dust that drifted from his clothes as he stood. The driver's window was down and Shelley was looking straight ahead. "Near about ran me over," he said.

"I didn't see," she said, without turning to him. "How was I supposed to know the carts were behind me?"

Les reached in and turned off her headlights, then breathed in the darkness he'd created.

"I couldn't see the carts," Shelley continued, this time with a little heat. "I had no idea Trudy was pushing them up the aisle."

Les took a fresh sip out of his pocket and drained it.

"Trudy," he said, smacking his lips. "Cart Girl? She okay?"

"Trudy's friggin' fine," Shelley said with a sob that almost strangled her. "The carts just bumped her. I think she set the whole thing up." She looked right at Les. "I mean, what are the chances? I go to find the girl who called the police on me and all of a sudden she's pushing carts behind my car? Really?"

"The dark blues come?"

Shelley's eyes dribbled. "Oh, the police. The police came alright. They surrounded me for the second time in an hour. I had to be bailed out. I paid a bail bondsman $200 that I don't have. I have to go to court. I might go to jail. I'll lose my job."

Les put his hands in his pockets and found a warm grape. He offered it to Shelley. She shook her head. "It'll be in the paper tomorrow, for sure. Woman runs over shopping cart attendant after suspicion of kidnapping a baby."

"Need help with the groceries?"

She held her hand up. "I need help, but not that kind. The groceries aren't even mine. I was just doing my job, buying the kitty litter. Just my job."

"You going to eat that?" He pointed at the clear plastic to-go box on her back seat.

"The meatloaf?" She turned to pick up the box and gave it a tentative sniff. "It's probably gone off by now sitting in the hot car so long."

Of course, the one item she'd bought for herself was now garbage. Mimi would have gladly paid the $5.99 for Shelley's slice of meatloaf, but Shelley always kept their transactions separate. Mimi would light up like a can of Sterno any time she found something on a receipt she herself had not put on the List. It made her feel in control of her purchases. There would be an awkward interview by Mimi's pillowed lair. "Was it a checkout mistake, Shelley, or had you bought it for yourself?" Knowing full well she'd bought it for herself. Mimi would refuse reimbursement and would accept only the most cursory thanks. What she really wanted was to re-ingest the meal with Shelley. She'd inquire about the quality of the ground beef, ask about the exact texture of the withered green beans, and wonder if the mashed potatoes were instant or made in house. "And the gravy? Any lumps?"

No meal was worth that. Not even a free one.

Les reached in and took it from her hands. "I have a pretty good immune system." He stood there a minute, then reached back into the car and turned off the ignition.

"Thanks," she said. "I just need to sit here a little longer."

"Night, then."

He shuffled into her backyard, toward his path that led down to his ledge along the creek. Just as he tucked under a bush to make his descent, Shelley felt as if she was the one entering a dark space, not Les. She wiped her face with her shirt and got out of the car.

"Wait! Les. Wait a minute."

He reappeared and looked around the yard, as if seeing it for the first time.

"Tell me," she said, thinking of something to say, anything that might keep him for another minute. Anything to ward off her sense of something hurt and hungry looming just outside her line of vision. "Why do you sleep down there? There's a shelter in town."

"The walls," he said. "The shelter walls keep coming at me."

"Aren't you afraid of animals? Mountain lions? Rats?" She'd seen an odd creature the other night. Earless thing, bigger than a small dog, smaller than a big dog. But it wasn't a dog. It stared red-eyed at her from where she stood at the kitchen window. It had a humped back and an enormous bushy tail, then it turned and loped into the brush. It was sure as hell not from around here, whatever it was. An evacuee from the fires in the canyon she supposed. What else might start showing up? Who else?

Les took a butt out of one of his pockets and examined it. "I'm only afraid of the super predators. Humans."

"I hear you scream sometimes," said Shelley. "Is that to keep humans away? I shouted at one today and now I might go to jail."

On a hot, sleepless night earlier in the summer, Shelley heard sounds out back, like a hurt animal. She wandered into her yard and looked down into the creek and through the brush could see shadows of Les waltzing the dance of a madman. Swinging around, fighting, cursing, and praying to unseen beings. His relation to reality, was, she had to say, different. She guessed he was a leftover from the 70s acid scene in town. Fried brain did not scare her, but the homeless were untethered and unpredictable. Maybe the police knew he lived behind her along the creek and that's why they took the call about the kidnapping seriously. Maybe she'd been too kind to someone like Les.

"Nah," he said. "I shout at the damn angels. It's like this, they're not what they seem. Some of them are real pricks, and powerful too, with wings like cast iron gates. You've got to shout at them just to keep them where they are. I've got a shepherd's crook that washed up in the creek a few years ago. I use it to fish plastic bottles out of the creek or bags in the trees, but I do battle with it as needed."

"Shepherd's crook?"

"Hooked pole. Shepherds still use them to catch sheep by their necks. People now use fake metal ones like mine for hanging plants because they've cut down all their trees."

"If you need a weapon, maybe walls are safer than these angels."

Les gave a little shudder. "Nothing's worse than walls. Can't sleep in shelters with everyone's baggy dreams floating around the building. That won't happen here, outside."

"Won't it?" It seemed like years since she'd had a dream. Why was that? "Anyway, it's sad to have no home." She looked at her small, one-story ranch and her heart grew warm. Even the name of the street made her feel toasty. Arroyo Circle. Not a street, not a dead end, but a circle. She remembered the day she and Keith bought it, feeling that she was finally stepping into the circle of life. Of course, that circle crumbled like a cookie when Keith ran off with Alan, but she had the house. It had held her together. Yet, here she was, delaying going inside, the one place where she might shut the world out. She had a vision of herself sitting alone in that house when she was seventy, without so much as a cat.

"I have a home," Les said, and he pointed to the gully.

"I mean a real one," she said.

"It's realer than this," he said, and motioned to her house. "That there keeps you walled off from life. You can't depend on a house. It's not a home. It's a fleeting thing. The land is home! Look at it. Right here, mountains. The mansions of Earth." He swung his arms wide and spun in a circle, and Shelley worried that the meatloaf was in danger of being flung into the street. He stopped at the sound of a small explosion. They looked up at sparkling tongues of flames rising from the ridge, like the Fourth of July. "Looks like the dragon is creeping its way to the ridgeline," said Les.

"The paper said not to worry," said Shelley. "The updraft won't let the fire come into town."

Les snorted and spit. "Embers are heavier than updraft. They'll fly through the air with their black flapping wings, dropping out of the sky to burrow for food, pyrogenic as a flame thrower. Not enough city water for everyone to spray down their homes against them, and no one does the smart thing of clearing. Boreal forests are born to burn baby, burn. We have to let them."

"That's bonkers. You have to put out fires. Fires kill."

"Fires kill if we're in the way and we are in the way in a big way. Putting out fires only makes things worse, making the trees and brush bigger for the next burn. Can't suppress something for too long or it will explode and be more than you can handle. That goes for a lot of things. Better pray for a long hard rain. I'm sure they're praying over at NOAA."

"NOAA's not in the way of the fire."

"We're all in the way," said Les. He paused. "I used to work there. Good old National Oceanic and Atmospheric Administration. We parted ways, but that was inevitable. It was started by Nixon."

"You worked at NOAA?" said Shelley. "What did you do?" She assumed janitorial, maybe cafeteria.

"You know. What they do. Study the atmosphere. I was in charge of Nephology."

"Neph?"

"The branch of meteorology devoted to clouds."

41

Shelley laughed. "Are you shitting me? You were a scientist?"

"I am a scientist. Having a job or not doesn't change that." He shrugged. "Didn't suit me. I went into it because Thoreau said they couldn't cut down the clouds, but he couldn't see what was coming. Morons trying to cool the planet with talk of solar engineering, with cloud brightening and thinning, anything rather than change our lives."

A howl of human voices came from along the creek, and Shelley started. It seemed there were more homeless in the city every year. During the day, she saw them hanging out in the park downtown, sitting under wispy trees, surrounded by piles of their belongings. Some of them had young children. Children. Dear mother of mercy.

"Got to go," said Les. "Got to go."

Shelley stood there, watching him disappear again. Out of the corner of her eye, a small blurry thing shot through the branches overhead and with a flinch she thought "bat," but then she heard the mournful hoot of an owl.

You-uu, You-uu.

Without looking behind her she walked slowly to her door, and then she ran.

Chapter Eight

After moving a towering stack of unread books out of the way, Shelley opened the door to Mimi's bedroom and waved a FedEx box over her head. "I'm here, Mimi!" She jumped up on her toes so her boss could see her. There would come a time when she would be too old for this, but that was not today's problem. Right now she had to negotiate the path that twisted through the unstable trash canyon to the bed, all the retail shit that had accumulated in the room over the years. She could hardly remember what was beneath it all, except that it had been pretty nice at one point. Behind the mountains of stuff, the walls were a creamy white, dotted with vague yet sunny paintings Jeremy had brought with him from California. There was probably an acre of pale, cushy carpet in the house, almost none of which was visible anymore except along the worn paths, and even then, most, like this one, were covered in a slick of glossy magazines and newspapers. The bedroom had long ago been abandoned by the housecleaner, Patti, who arrived every day with her cleansers and vacuum, did the kids' rooms and Jeremy's third floor room, cleaned what she could in the kitchen, then left in disgust. There were so few surfaces. Mimi even managed to fill the ceiling. A crystal chandelier hung in her bedroom like a lost galaxy, tilted from the earthly weight of hanging clothes. It might as well be of some use as a clothes rack since it no longer worked as a light, the wires strained thin with worry. She and Mimi talked about creating a spot for a ladder so the electrician could come, but it was just talk.

And yet, from the street, you'd hardly suspect a thing. The mock Moroccan was like a stop on a Homes of the Hollywood Stars bus tour, with stucco walls of whispery pink, arched doors, and scalloped walkways. All it needed was a couple of palm trees. Mimi told her it was built by a professor of Middle-Eastern studies at the University back in the 1930s. Mimi was that rare item, a Boulder native, or as native as a white person could be, meaning her people had arrived in a covered wagon sometime in the late 1800s, staying in the Mild West of the foothills rather than continue the dangerous trek over the Divide. Mimi would have preferred an Arts & Crafts bungalow like the house she grew up in, but Jeremy loved this odd pink duck. He had come from L.A., so his tastes ran "a bit on the Disney side" as Mimi joked, not thinking about what that said about her. He was part of the reverse Gold Rush that happened after every earthquake, folks leaving California all atremble, arriving in Boulder with fistfuls of cash, paying too much for houses and sending the prices to Pikes Peak. Locals exiled themselves to the flat outburbs, clutching some of that cash and raising those prices too. If it wasn't the earthquakes, it was the landslides, if it wasn't landslides it was the wildfires. In spite of what Les said about the weight of embers, fire danger was fairly minimal on the Front Range. Minimal, but not impossible. There was enough risk that the landscaper kept telling her that the pines and chaparral along the back of Mimi's property needed to be cut down to create a fuel break. Mimi said no. "I don't want hikers to be able to look into my yard."

"Mimi," Shelley explained, "they've got a view that stretches out to Nebraska, they don't want to look into your old yard."

"Of course they do!" Mimi said, and she would know. She'd grown up in the neighborhood farther down the slope and had felt the eyes of the higher community upon her. Shelley tried another tack.

"You don't want to lose the house over a few trees. You've got to think of your safety."

"Use your eyes, Shelley! This house is made of stucco and tile. It's fireproof."

"Fire resistant, not fireproof," said Shelley.

Mimi did not answer and pouted for the rest of the day. Shelley never mentioned it again. It was not worth losing her job over. It wasn't her house.

"Shelley!" Mimi called out from the far depths of the room. "Did you secure the FedEx box that was just dropped off?"

"Got it! I'm coming." The journey to the bed was an ever-narrowing situation, so she had to consider an exit plan even as she worked her way in. Anything in her way, and there was plenty of anythings, had to be moved just so, or else she'd get trapped if the sides caved in. She couldn't grab hold of anything for support because it was all so unstable. She had to find her balance without putting her weight on any one thing. If Mimi wanted to leave her bedroom, which was rare, it might take Shelley hours to widen the path for her and her walker. And since there was no room for both food tray and elbows, Claudia pulled the meals behind her in a small rolling cooler like she was going to a Jimmy Buffet concert. Lately, Shelley could only fit sideways, shouldering through the piles, able to bring along only those purchases light enough to hold over her head. Bigger boxes had to be unpacked in another room or outside, with Mimi cheering her on through FaceTime. But it wasn't the same. Shelley had been glad to see a small package on the steps that morning so her boss would be jollied up before they got down to legalities. Mimi had taken the arrest news well when Shelley called her the night before, wanting to get it over with, wanting her to find out from Shelley herself and not online, the way these things tend to travel. You could find a lot of sordid shit on the Internet. You could also find the truth.

When she turned the last leg of the goat path, she bumped right into Mimi standing next to her bed, staring out the window with binoculars. "Whoa, sorry, Mimi." But Mimi didn't even flinch, used as she was to bumping into things, or things bumping into her as objects obeyed the laws of gravity and toppled off piles. There was not much unobstructed glass, so Mimi held the binoculars right up to a single clear spot of window, looking not out at the view, but down the slope towards her old neighborhood. She wore a distant expression on her dimpled face, and her cupid bow of a mouth was open. Breathing was becoming a chore for the poor woman, but Shelley could not convince her to see a doctor and get an inhaler. That would mean leaving the house. It would mean opening herself up to dark lines of scrutiny.

Mimi brightened at the sight of the package, and found a precarious ledge on a pile for the binoculars. "Oh boy," she said, reaching for her walker. "I can't wait. Is it from Joseph's? Is it the jellied Aplets?" She tapped the few feet to the bed then used the walker as support to lift herself up onto it. This took some time, and while Mimi huffed and struggled with her heavy limbs, Shelley continued on the path to the bathroom and, after moving aside a pile of catalogs and a blender, made sure the shower stall had enough room to enter. She cleared the shower chair of dirty dishes, then checked that the toilet still worked, embarrassed that she still got a little sexual anticipation when she pressed the lever. A stopped toilet used to mean a visit from the plumber, and her body memory was strong. Mimi insisted on the fluffy, multi-layered, quilted, scented, ultra-soft paper that stopped up the plumbing, to the point that Wayne of Wayne's Drains and Shelley were once . . . what? Lovers? Fuck buddies? It was hard to say now, looking back. Impossible to remember how she thought of them when they were together, compared to how she thought of them apart. No matter. As Mimi's house manager, one of Shelley's duties was to be there for the trades people, explain the job, and create access to the project. It took a skilled army of electricians, plumbers, landscapers, painters, and carpenters to keep the place functioning, such as it did, and most of all, it took Wayne, who kept the clogged drains open. The first time Shelley had to call him, her third week on the job, he told her the twisted landscape of medieval plumbing could not handle multi-ply. "I don't mind coming up here all the time," he said, with a wink. "But it'll be a whole lot cheaper for the Crutchfields if they used plain old Scott. Flushes right on out. Easy peasy."

Well, when Shelley told Mimi, she almost lost her job before she'd barely begun. Mimi whimpered, "I can't, Shelley. I just can't." Her words tumbled down around her like a stoneslide. "My bottom gets so sore. He doesn't understand. I'm in a great deal of pain."

"Moira," Shelley said, with a sympathetic touch on her boss's arm. "It's okay. I understand."

"Mimi," she said with a shy smile, wiping off a bead of mucus on her upper lip. "Call me what my family does. Mimi."

Alright, then. As time went on, Shelley had to contact Wayne so often they started going out for drinks, then post-drinks sex, then just sex. The man knew his plumbing. It—the relationship—was solidifying nicely, but Shelley hadn't understood what a snoot she was until Betty-Ann asked what he did for a living, and her throat clogged right up. Shelley couldn't tell her she was dating Wayne's Drains. The words would simply not form in her mouth. So that was the end of that, even though they stayed pals. He was the best snaker in town after all, and it behooved her to maintain good relations with the professionals the house depended on. When the time came—and it came hard on the heels of their breakup, that's how ripe he was—she even went to his wedding. She had many regrets about her life that day, but when she woke up the next morning dust-brained and cactus-mouthed she was glad to be alone in her house. Her own house where she could do as she pleased. Being lonesome now and again was the price to pay.

She gathered up some soiled clothes with the dishes to bring downstairs. After finding a towel buried under a pile of shampoos and soaps, she shook it out and found an inch for it on the rack. It was scary how fast something could disappear in the maw. She'd brought that towel up only yesterday. The bathrobe was on its hook, under some baggy shirts and a purple caftan, which she put on a hanger for later. If nothing else Mimi took a shower every day, sometimes two, so she could use all the cleansers and ointments she'd ordered that week. Shelley listened for the running water for a chance to change Mimi's sheets, or at least sweep up the crumbs.

"Well let's get it on open!" said Mimi, scooting her butt over to the middle of the bed, moving folders, moisturizers, and her laptop as she went, then arranging the pillows for two. Shelley climbed in. There was nowhere else to go. The first year they'd held their morning meetings at a sitting area in the bedroom, in front of the stone fireplace. When the sofa disappeared under piles of clothes they sat at the bay window, with its magnificent view. But that too got filled with stuff. For a long while, Shelley had a small folding chair next to Mimi's bed where she'd sit to chat about shopping plans for the day, the bedspread their desk. Then one day, there was just too much crap to move off the chair and nowhere to move it to, and Shelley did not have the thigh muscles for squatting. So the bed it was.

"Ready?" asked Shelley, clicking open her box cutter with a grin. She kept it in her pants pocket at all times, like a gun. It was not just any box cutter either, not some cheap Stanley from McGuckin's, but a wood-handled, stainless steel Craftsman, a present from

Mimi early on in her box opening career. It was heavy and curvaceous, and fit right in the palm of her hand. Her companion in crime.

"Of course!" said Mimi, clutching her hands together. They had developed this teasing little dance over the years. "I hope it's the jellies. I've been thinking about them for days."

"Okay then," said Shelley. She slit the packing tape in one practiced swipe then popped open the white FedEx box revealing a flat candy box. Mimi clapped.

"It is the Aplets!" cried Mimi. "Happy us!"

Mimi lifted the jellies out like a tray of diamonds, and Shelley moved the shipping box out of the way to bring downstairs for recycling. Another job made difficult by Mimi's unbridled purchases. Recycling pickup was weekly, so by the beginning of the week the flattened boxes formed a teetering skyscraper of cardboard, and by the end of the week Shelley arranged a second tower to support the first. Some weeks, especially around the holidays, or when they were behind in pickups, like they were now, there was even a third.

"No one will ship chocolate in this heat, but Aplets won't melt," said Mimi. She carefully removed a jellied fruit from the container and placed it on her tongue. "Mmmm. Sweet, but not too sweet. And all natural!"

Shelley gave her some time to enjoy the first jelly in uninterrupted pleasure, but when Mimi reached for the second, she began. "So what am I going to do?"

Mimi nodded in thought as she rolled the jelly around in her mouth. "We have to win this thing. We want you to be a citizen in good standing so you can go back to King Soopers. I miss it already."

"It's only been a few hours, Mimi," said Shelley. "You'll survive."

"Not if this keeps up I won't. The first thing we have to do is order presents for the manager and the girl you ran over."

"I didn't run over her! I bumped the carts she was pushing and she fell. You want to give her a bribe? Is that legal?"

"The presents will come from me, not you. I want them to think kindly of me, no matter what the future brings. As for you, call my lawyer, Frankie Angstrom. He's a shark. He'll get them to lift the restraining order against you right away. You have to be able to shop their canned goods sale next week."

"I don't have the money to pay a lawyer," said Shelley. "I had to put the bail on my credit card."

"Have him bill me," said Mimi. "You're part of the family." With that, she held out the tray of Aplets for Shelley to take one, and that's when she knew she was going to be saved. Mimi rarely, if ever, shared her food. Shelley took one, even though she hated wobbly candy.

"I'm worried," said Shelley, looking at the translucent Aplet in her palm. "It was terrible at the police station yesterday. No one believed me that it was an accident. They looked at me like I was a murderer."

"I know the feeling."

Shelley nodded gravely and patted Mimi's sticky hand. Mimi grew up down the street from JonBenét Ramsay and had babysat for her and her brother a few times, and so she, like everyone around the poor child, was cross-examined, everyone—it seemed—but the parents. It took two years for the police to talk to them, which was simply strange. All of Boulder had their own opinion about the grisly murder, all wildly different, from the parents to one-eyed aliens. Shelley always figured it was just some anonymous creep who saw an opportunity. No one ever gave enough credence to the randomness of life. Mimi took another dusty Aplet out of the box and held it to the light. "We used to play dress-up. Billy would come with me and he'd play board games with JonBenét's brother. We were like family."

Shelley always tried to steer Mimi away from the topic, but not this time. "Tell me what your police interrogation was like. Looks like I'm going to need to know."

"Question after question after question. Talk, talk, talk. Detectives, the table littered with cigarettes and Styrofoam cups, lawyers and more lawyers. The room was hot with bodies, but the fluorescent lights made us all look blue-cold. There was a stained coffee maker in the corner. I still can't smell burnt coffee without feeling sick. My lawyers said not to give the police more than they ask for. Ever. You have to remember that. Don't offer any information they don't specifically ask for."

"I don't know that I have any information."

"Frankie can get you a hearing soon," Mimi said, pushing the soft candy from one side of her mouth to the other with her tongue. "Just let him talk and he'll make you a free woman." She took another Aplet.

"I hope so," said Shelley.

Mimi leaned over to the night table on the other side of the bed, which held one of several, partially entombed microwaves in the room, and was able to get the compacted drawer open a bit, enough room to poke under some papers and remove a photo of two teenagers standing arm in arm in front of a house. Shelley had seen it many times. Aside from the folders of shopping site passwords and some financial papers, it was the only object in the house that Mimi could always put her hands on. The first time Mimi showed it to her, Shelley made the mistake of asking who the pretty girl was.

"It's me," Mimi had said, with a hint of offense in her voice. "At sixteen." The other teenager was Mimi's older brother, Billy, but it wasn't their house. There was a little girl in the background, on the front steps of a story-book cottage, where one side of the roof sloped to the ground. JonBenét. Her house. It wasn't really a cottage though, it had been expanded in a really hideous way. The front was so unlike the back it was like the house was wearing a mask. JonBenét stared down at her feet, so it was hard to see her expression. She was not dolled up like she was always shown in the paper, so she looked like the child she was. Just a child.

"Billy loved that little girl." Mimi said, sucking and smacking as she talked. "After she was killed he was never the same. He started dabbling in drugs. You know how it is."

Actually, no. Shelley had smoked some pot in her time, maybe a dot of acid here and there when she first got to Boulder, nothing stronger, nothing that would kill her. Like the brother. That was a story. Shelley had never met Billy, since he died before she started working there. He was a street junkie and never came to the house. Jeremy wouldn't let him in. Mimi had to meet her brother downtown to give him money or food, looking for him in back alleys and in public parks. Then he landed in jail and died of an overdose. Mimi claimed she couldn't bear the sight of Boulder streets anymore and had to have others shop for her.

"Did he talk to the police too?"

"No. They didn't ask if anyone had ever come with me to babysit, so I was able to spare him that." Mimi shuddered. "I should've moved far away after high school, leave the whole thing behind me. But what do I do? I fall in love with the new guy in the neighborhood." She flicked her eyes up, to indicate Jeremy's room on the third floor. Mimi leaned over and returned the photo to the drawer. When she sat up she looked at Shelley's closed fist. "Are you going to eat that?"

"You take it," said Shelley, handing her the damp jelly. "There aren't that many in a box, and you're doing so much for me as it is."

"As I said, Shelley," Mimi said as she delicately removed the sweet from Shelley's open palm with two plump fingers. "You're family."

Chapter Nine

Les considered the clouds of black snakes slithering along the creek bed. Mountain spirits in wrathful cloaks, come to punish and slay the ignorant, but in what state of matter will they strike? Solid, liquid, gas? Tic, tac, toe. Gas. No, no, the other one, the one that everyone forgets about. Plasma. Yes, plasma. Or also plasma. Could be both under the right conditions. The world can be understood through natural laws, or it can be understood through the actions of the gods and fate. You choose. Or no choice. If it is a law of nature that energy is never created or destroyed, then it is impossible for the total energy in the universe to change, but he has broken that law many times.

And yet. And yet again. Scrape up another teaspoon of skull jelly from the bottom of the brain jar. We must remember what it is we know—i.e., clouds are a solid, liquid, and gas combined. No need to choose. And plasma? A holy cloud of protons, neutrons, and electrons, it is a ghost, a spirit. A god. It goes where it wants. It does what it wants. A floating blob of blessed electrons untethered from their own molecules and atoms, giving plasma a life of its own. A substance like a dream where you are home, but have never seen it before. Then you are the home. A dream obeys its own slippery logic, like plasma. Plasma obeys its own slippery logic, like a dream. The door swings both ways. Plasma, the extrabiological soul we have been searching for, human essence extruding from a vast physical system. Concentrated human in an atomizer, seductively sprayed on the warm neck of the cosmos. Neuroscientists and astrophysicists are priests holding out a promised afterlife in a heaven filled with Boltzmann brains, an infinite number of disembodied minds materializing in the deep future of space, when the intergalactic universe finally expands to the point of dissolution. Think of it. Bear down. Work that skull jelly till you can spread it on an atomic cracker. The quantum physicians might be batshit crazy but they were rarely wrong. Like flamines, ancient Roman priests with the funny headgear. Birdlike. And when are birds ever wrong?

He saw himself as a canyon bird preening on the ledge below Shelley's house, gazing at the trickle of creek, his body spread out on a living mattress of grapevines. Just him and the ants. A wind-worn cottonwood tree his shade and his companion, its roots anchored to a slope so steep the trunk leans but never falls, tall enough to rise above the embankment. Trees are the earth's grasping fingers, light-catchers that grow life from air. Whitman wrestled oak saplings for exercise. Les had already finished his daily wrestle with the underbrush, and then he took on those belligerent angels. It wasn't until he found his shepherd's crook that they backed off. They don't want to get a wing hooked. It was exhausting, as always, then falling back onto his trash bag to watch cloudy tendrils roll through the gully. Smoke. An inversion. A trap. Most creek dwellers had already gone to town looking for air. Les stayed for some peace. If not peace, then silence. So many living along the creek these days. Used to be just burn-out boys or the occasional runaway gal. Now whole families. The careless work of demagogues. But today it's just him and a few sips to drift through the afternoon, finding faces on a big old swollen cumulus of airborne mountain.

Listen. Instead of silence, he hears the world trying to be silent. He bolts upright but there is nothing, so he takes a sip. Not for nothing, but what else can he do? Every something is an echo of nothing. It from bit. Nothing exists until it's asked a yes or no question. Another sip? Yes indeed. Don't mind if I do. The gods might have made everything out of nothing, but the nothing bleeds through. He falls back and his eyes close and suddenly it feels like he is rushing blindly up the path, breaking through screens of smoke, passing into other zones, stumbling, struck in the face by sticks, feeling hot breath on his ankles, the creature ever closer, not hurrying or panting, just teasing its kill. Testing him. Ecosystems have a biological structure that is largely defined by feeding relationships. Who eats who. No, no. Who eats whom.

Him.

Black and white snowflakes fall from the sky. Ash. The inversion thickening. The trap releasing pent up energy. Dark particles in their neutrino cars, a gray house cat at the wheel. In some versions of this dream, the cat has a GPS chip embedded in its shoulder to lead us all to safety. Lead on. Show us the way. Pray for us. There is a middle way between nihilism and eternalism, speaketh the cat. You have what you have while you have it. While Les contemplates this wisdom, dark spirits try to possess him, entering through his nostrils and ears, blinding his eyes.

He coughs himself upright in a sweat. The air had weight and texture. He emptied his sip to clear out his throat, then fell back, eyes open, reaching into his thought-bag of pareidolia, wherein he finds shape and meaning in the clouds, a traveling circus of supernaturals. We worship gods because they are able to avoid death. As the loathsome shape of end-time rears up higher and darker each hour, the gods hand us wax wings with a smile and tell us to fly. No need of wings themselves, they float through the plasma. They are the plasma. They are both the message and the messenger. They do not fall, but love to see us land on our face. Their sense of humor is earthly. Pity us, pity the planet, all joy gone from this volcanic orb, the katabatic blow pulling the blanket over the earth. It is the mythical drainage wind, draining the canyon into the gully, not rising as it should, forced by gravity down the slope. Sweeping us along in the horrific beauty of the world.

Sublime. The dangerous thing made safe, the wracked ability of dim humanity to engineer its own security. Or so we believed. With each new generation of technological innovation, we dance mindless into the prehistoric slime, empowered by what we think is power. And that's when they'll strike. Clever. The gods, they are so very clever.

Through the smoke Les senses a stunning golden eagle above, swooping and searching for small creatures forced out of hiding from the encroaching doom. There is no choice, and yet a choice has to be made. Les chooses the eagle and goes for the ride, traveling above the smoked-out world, then above the suns, the earth a smudge of blue. So beautiful. So ephemeral. Avian and human life soaring together in violation of natural law. It's our law now, brother. Earth doesn't want humans here anyway. An experiment gone haywire.

A fuzzy critter far below stirs. A rat? It is sluggish and confused. "Easy pickings! Go!" And with a violent swerve they dive recklessly into the chaparral. Down! Reptilian feet first, feathered toes spread open. One hundred, one-hundred-and-fifty miles per hour they drop! Then snap and rise, a small soft thing trapped in an unnerving grip. The rat struggles in blood-red talons as it is lifted into the heavens. Screams. Screams. Who is screaming? Les wakes up screaming. The human animals are screaming, they are all pointing, pointing up. Look, look. The flames of the forest fires are on this side of the ridge. That which we have been waiting for has arrived. It is here. Our ancient god, fire.

And all we have to save ourselves are these lousy wax wings.

.

Chapter Ten

When the roar came out of the steep canyon above Boulder, it was like a flame shooter aimed towards town, sweeping Shelley in its hot embrace. Not that a single spark touched her, but she got sucked into the conflagration nonetheless. Just as her court hearing over stupid cart girl was going her way, word of the fire on the eastern slope spread like the flu through the courtroom. It was here. That which was not supposed to happen had happened. An aide whispered to the judge, an angle-eared rabbit of a man, who lifted his nose as if testing the air for smoke. And then he looked at Shelley with an appraising eye. He motioned Frankie, Mimi's oily lawyer, over to the bench. She could not wait to be done with him.

"Community service," Frankie told her when he returned. "Trudy and King Soopers won't pursue any action, and the court will drop all assault charges in exchange for a couple of days working with volunteers, handing out water and roll-ups to the firefighters."

"What happened to a stern talking to and on my way?" said Shelley.

Frankie shrugged. "They need all hands on the fire line to keep it from moving down the foothills and into town. They've even called in the inmate fire crews. Look on the bright side. I hear those fire-fighters are hot." He laughed at her misery like the devil himself.

"I don't get paid for days I can't work," she said in defeat. "But I guess it's better than a whopping fine."

"Or jail time," Frankie said. "Jail was always a possibility."

"Was it?" But he was already packed up and trotting off to his next client with the bit between his teeth.

So here she was, with hot air burning her throat and stinging her eyes, stationed on a slope at the bottom of the ridge handing out donuts, wondering if a bit of jail time might not have been the better deal. A thin coating of ash was on everything, including herself. Sweat trickled down her back like there was a spigot under her baseball cap. She could see Canyon Road from where she worked, and it was so dark from smoke the cars had their headlights on.

"Damn," she said as she lugged another case of water out of a truck and onto the folding table, which was beginning to buckle under the weight. As was her spine. She arched backwards to ease the pain, then used her T-shirt to wipe her face. A sludge of sweat and ash had formed under the bandana she wore to keep the smoke out.

"I don't even bother trying to cover my face anymore," her supervisor said, cheery as a golden retriever. Shelley gave her a crooked smile, but had no strength or breath for conversation. The supply line never slowed. Supermarkets from all over the county were sending up crates of sandwiches and snacks.

"You're just out to get me," Shelley said, as she opened a case of donuts from King Soopers with her little knife. Who knew when she was young that this would be her special talent, opening boxes and displaying the contents.

From her work station she could see humans moving in ant-like tandem with the line of fire creeping down from the ridge. Behind the fire line were black mats of burnt grass and clumps of sparking sage. Below, houses. The fire was searching for a meal, and kiln-dried lumber used in construction was dinner. If those flames got close enough to Mimi's, they would smell the packed meat of a hoarder's home within. She did not like leaving Mimi alone. The kids were back in school, and Louisa refused to come to the house until it was time to bring them home. Patti was volunteering as a supply driver for the front lines and Claudia was out shopping for Mimi because Shelley could not. Jeremy had gone off to work, even though Shelley expressed some dismay about that when she called him that morning. "Will Mimi be okay by herself?"

"She'll have to be," he said. "I have an emergency at the office. Bad timing for you to get in trouble with the law." Jeremy was usually even-tempered, but the days of smoke and impending fire made them all tense and irritable.

"I called the landscaper to come and hose down the yard," she said, raising her voice to be heard over sirens blaring up and down the canyon. "I hope the neighbors are doing the same. Someone has to start widening the path in Mimi's room in case she has to evacuate."

"Who?" he said. "No one's here except me, and I'm out the door."

"I'll see if I can find someone," she said without conviction, wondering if Mimi's friends would be willing, but there were no friends. No one but family, staff, and contractors had been inside the house for years. Wayne might be game, but Mimi would balk at what it would cost. She'd gotten funny about money lately. She wondered if Les was physically capable of clearing a path for a few bucks, but she didn't even know how to contact him.

"You and Mimi created this problem," said Jeremy. "I hope you've thought about how to solve it." And then he hung up without so much as a goodbye.

"Us?" Shelley said to the dead phone. It was his house. His and Mimi's, not Shelley's. She didn't have the power to make change, but he did. And then she realized with a shudder that he could use that power to fire her, making her the scapegoat for what he let happen. All she could do was pray Mimi would intervene. More supplies came in, so Shelley went back to stacking and opening, stopping only to answer Mimi's calls.

"Can you come by during your lunch break? UPS has been here twice already and I see boxes down there. Claudia doesn't answer the phone or texts."

"Mimi, you've got to think about getting out of the house until the fire is under control."

"It's far away. I can barely see the smoke from my window. And I keep telling you, we're stucco and tile."

"Did the landscaper come to water down the yard?"

"He did, but he called to say there was just a trickle of water coming from the hose. He said he could piss more than that, so he left."

"I'll see if I can get a water truck up there during my break, but we're all pretty much under the gun here."

"Okay, I'll try Claudia again," pouted Mimi. "She can bring the boxes up when she gets back, but I know she's going to make a fuss. I wish you were here!" Shelley heard an air-kiss then silence.

With a flex of her aching back, Shelley picked up another case of water and slit the plastic off with a swipe, handing the bottles out two to three at a time. The water was warm, but it was wet. The first bottle got squirted on the face. The second down the back, then the third down the throat. Hundreds of firefighters came by in flame-retardant shirts and yellow hardhats, Pulaskis and shovels hanging from their packs, smoke-stained and freshly filthy from digging ditches and clearing brush between homes and the hot red line. They had raspy throats and not a few were coughing up black spit. When they talked at all, it was to compare this fire to other Boulder fires, especially the Fourmile Canyon fire years before. That had been a living hell, for sure. And the Hayman, which produced so much ash it looked like a summer snowstorm down in Denver.

She kept asking if anyone thought it would spread to Mimi's neighborhood. "There's no telling," one firefighter told her. "It'll leap to where it can find fuel. It's a hungry bastard."

Shelley thought of Mimi's yard. The brush. The trees. Fuel. She should have had the yard cleared in spite of Mimi's protests. She should have gone around her and talked to Jeremy about it. But there was no point dwelling on that now. The firefighters were smudged and tired, in a dark dream they could not shake, looking so wrung out Shelley unscrewed the bottles for them. And yet after a rest and a refill of their camel packs, they had to go back, and back again. At noon, just as truckloads of roll-ups arrived from the Red Cross, the wind suddenly shifted and the entire front line had to reorganize. Everyone looked strained and worried as bright orange flashes started popping up in new places on the ridge. As she helped break down her relief station to move it closer to the action, she thought about slipping away in the chaos to check on Mimi. Just as she was plotting her escape, she felt her phone vibrate in her back pocket.

"Shelley, there's smoke in the house! What do I do?"

"Look out the window, Mimi. Are there flames in the yard?"

"I don't know what happened." She was gasping for air. "I don't understand. The fire's still way up on the ridge, but the recycling piles, somehow they're on fire. You've got to come."

The boxes. An ember must have blown down from the ridge and landed in the stacked boxes by the house. Her stacks. Twice as much as usual because the recycling service failed to pick up last week. It was on her list to call them and raise hell.

"Mimi, listen to me. The smoke is probably just seeping in through the windows. You have time. I'm sure the alarm company has called the fire department by now, but I'll tell them too. You just go. Start moving stuff out of the way and get out."

"The flames, Shelley. I can see the fire on the monitor. The flames are so high."

Shelley opened the app on her phone that let her access the security cameras too. It was as Mimi said—the recycling was an inferno. It was horrifying for sure but with any luck the cardboard would quickly burn off and there would be no more fuel. The stucco would blacken but not burn. The stacks were not near Mimi's window. The only danger was if the box towers torched high enough, flames could reach the wooden eaves.

"Just go, Mimi. Go."

"I can't Shelley, I tried but things kept falling on me and I can't climb over. I don't want to die!"

"I'm on my way," said Shelley. "Keep trying to clear the path. If you can get to the door, it'll be easier the rest of the way. You can do this."

"Shelley, Shelley. I can't breathe."

"Get a wet towel from the bathroom and put it over your mouth and nose. Calm down and get the path cleared."

Shelley did not wait for a response as she headed to the control center, not breathing too well herself with ash swirling around her like a gray blizzard. She texted Jeremy as she ran, telling him about the fire, even though she was sure the security company had already contacted him. The noise was thick with choppers whipping overhead, and the drone of an air tanker spreading red slurry farther up the ridge, like opening a vein. The air and the noise were a single impenetrable solid, yet she found her way to someone with a badge. She grabbed his arm and held on. "There's a woman stuck in her bedroom on 6th Street and she can't get out. She says the fire is right outside."

The captain wiped his face with his free sleeve. "We heard that call come in. A crew is on its way over."

"They'll need a ladder truck," said Shelley. "I'll meet them there to show them the window."

Shelley did not remember how her body got from where she stood to Mimi's street. It was as if she'd lost consciousness, yet somehow in that fugue state she managed to find her keys, her car, and the road. It was a short ride made long by evacuees on foot, vehicle, and hoof coming down the ridge and filling the roads, but she kept pushing forward. The fires along the ridge were creeping farther down the slope and she could see firefighters digging trenches to contain them. But air could not be contained and it was in the air that embers soared, firebrands finding their mark and blooming red. Ahead, she could see the thin pyre of smoke. The recycling pile. From something so small, so random, such destruction. Just as she got to the last turn, police blocked her way.

"Only emergency vehicles," an officer said.

"The fire captain in the canyon said to come and show them where a woman is trapped inside."

He talked into the microphone on his shoulder, and suddenly she was out of her car and into a fire department Jeep. She checked the security cameras again, but the camera on that side of the house had gone dead. Other cameras were still active but were screens of smoke. Mimi did not answer. The voicemail did not pick up. The phone just rang and rang. She texted Claudia and told her not to bring the children home, that she would let her know when it was safe. Claudia texted back that she already knew about the fire, and she'd bring the kids to her own home until she was told otherwise. As the jeep drove up the steep road, they passed neighbors on foot carrying children and laptops and holding dogs on strained leads. One woman, Ella, and her two daughters from the end of the block had turned to look at the devastation behind them, frozen in place. Shelley rolled down her window and shouted. "Ella! Go! Keep moving!" but they just looked at her with open mouths and blank stares as she passed by. Four horses, eyes wide and terrified, galloped across the road in front of them, then disappeared behind a house, heading for the open pastures at Chautauqua. If owners could not trailer their horses, they had to let them go. You could not leave a horse fenced near fire or they would die in terror.

With a screech of brakes she was out of the Jeep and in front of someone directing the effort. The doors and ground floor windows were smashed open and the house oozed contents like it was vomiting a department store. Firefighters worked to shovel it all out of the way—ironing boards, hair dryers, boxes of Christmas lights, bike tires, books, baking pans, plastic bins—and yet there was still no more than a few feet of clearance into the house from any opening. She could not even see the main stairs inside the front door. She looked up. The fire was smoldering inside the third floor, right where the towers of recycling boxes had stood under the eaves. Except for Jeremy's bedroom, that floor was crammed with crap too. The good news was it was packed so tightly there was hardly any oxygen, and that might slow the fire down. But just as Shelley was reassuring herself, flames broke through one of the third floor windows and reached out for air, sucking it in like a jet engine. In seconds, the heat sent sheets of stucco falling to the ground in shatters, and her body began to tremble.

There was still hope. Mimi's end of the house was untouched. Full of smoke maybe, but not in flames. Shelley grabbed the officer by his sleeve and pointed up. "It's that room, right there. She might have passed out with an asthma attack."

"The window packed with stuff?"

"Yes." She inhaled a bit of floating ash and began to cough.

"And this is how that all ends."

"There's another set of stairs in the back," she said, but even as she spoke she saw a ladder truck maneuvering in the sloped yard. Farther up the ridge, a crew was goring a trench into the hill with excavators, but firebrands sailed across the break on rafts of wind and landed in yards. On either side of her, neighbors and volunteers armed with shovels smothered them with dirt, then ran to the next, a deadly game of whack-a-mole. That should have been her, putting out the little fires and waiting for it to pass after she'd gotten Mimi out. But no. The smoke thickened and sparks began to fall like burning rain. She opened her mouth to yell at the captain, but only a ragged cough came out. "Mimi's not far from that window. She can't go anywhere else. She's a big woman."

The captain spoke into his mic again. "Her name is Mimi. Start shouting her name."

A TV truck pulled up to the end of the driveway and began to set up their camera, ready to expose them all. Shelley felt protective of the house and Mimi. Just as she was about to chase them away, her phone rang. Jeremy. "I'm in the car," he said. "Did she get out? She doesn't answer her phone."

"They're trying to get the ladder up to the window now," said Shelley. Her mouth filled with smoke.

"She's still in her room? Do you see her?"

Shelley shook her head but could not say the word "no."

"I'm almost there," he said. And then the line went dead.

Shelley fumed. Where was all this concern this morning when he walked out the door? She had no choice but to be elsewhere, but he did. He was the boss for sweet heaven's sake. Hand the office emergency off to someone else and take care of your damn princess.

Shelley pulled her bandana up over her mouth and watched the third floor as the blaze appeared first at one window, then another. Part of the floor collapsed with a roar and for the first time she saw it on the second floor, eating its way through the mountains of crap towards Mimi's room. The heat rippled the air outside like a haunting. Over the turbulence of sound, she listened in on the captain as he gave orders to break the windows at the end of the second floor hall, away from Mimi's room to lure the fire away from her. Shelley stopped trying to call her. The phone was dead. Her eyes stung from smoke and her forehead felt like hot skin on a done chicken. She should move back, away from the heat, but she stayed to watch the ladder truck try and try again to reach Mimi's window, but the yard was too steep and tight to maneuver.

"You'll have to try from there," the captain said into his mic. He looked up at the foothills behind them. It was coming. Shelley had not been keeping track of the main fire, she'd been so intent on the house. A long arm had gone around the firebreak. Smoke barreled towards them, fronted by leaping flames. Stones the size of heads skipped down the hill. Through the smoke she could see upslope homes behind the firebreak scorched but standing, the dry grass around them hissing, oily shrubs smoldering. The fire had passed quickly through those properties. They had not invited it to linger with a pyre of shipping boxes, as she had. And when that fire hit Mimi's yard it would gather more energy with the trees and chaparral that stood waiting for it. A bulldozer had arrived to tear it all down, removing all that Mimi had not allowed to be removed. The captain was right, they could not stay between the two fires for much longer. Behind the police line down the street stood the TV crew, surrounded by people taking videos of the fire with their phones, so greedy for excitement they put their own lives at risk. She felt violated. She felt violated for Mimi.

Jeremy's Land Rover braked to a stop near her, pelting her with gravel. He must have gone off road to get around the blockade. He jumped down from the car, wearing his cowboy hat and bolo tie as if he'd come in off the range and not from his office. Even though he was a big man, all barrel-chested and long-armed, he seemed so small as he looked at the inferno that was his home. They were all so small next to this.

"Where's Mimi?" he asked, looking like he might hit her.

Shelley lowered her bandana, but it was impossible to draw an unprotected breath without coughing. She shouted over the noise of the fire and the equipment. "Still inside. They can't get through the crap in the house so they're trying to reach her with ladders."

They looked over at the firefighters scrambling at Mimi's end of the house with one piece of equipment or another. The ladder truck was as close as it could get, and a firefighter stood at the top, brandishing a long-handled hook. More crew were maneuvering a free-standing ladder right up to her window.

"Can they save her?" Tears came to Jeremy's eyes and he seemed to crumble in on himself. Then he turned on Shelley in a rage. "How did you let this happen? She's going to take everything with her." He grabbed her by the shoulders. "Where's that folder of hers?"

"The shopping passwords? Are you crazy?"

He looked up at the house as he pushed her away from him. "We've got to save her," he said, then backed away. Before Shelley could make sense of his words he ran, heading around the building to the back door. He took off his cowboy hat and used it to shield his face from the heat. He'd snapped.

"No!" she shouted and made a step to follow him, then felt a hand on her arm.

"He's not . . ." a firefighter said, as they watched him disappear behind the house.

"Porch door, back stairs," said Shelley. "He's going in."

"Moron," and then he was off after Jeremy. She almost followed, but just then a plane released water on the flames and created a hot ball of steam that knocked her back. That seemed to make the fire angry, and it picked up speed. The water truck turned its hose on the window of the room next to Mimi's, breaking the glass, trying to lure the flames outside. Smoking debris fell to the ground and Shelley saw it all as if in slow motion, floating in the smoke rather than falling. Apple cores, chopsticks, old snapshots, doll heads, egg cups, greeting cards, a skull mug, trolls, a typewriter, novelty cocktail stirrers. Bathrobes, shirts, shoes. Shoe inserts. Mimi had loved it all. Her wall against the world, gone. Shelley heard the back porch collapse at the same time the firefighter staggered back into view, at his heels a small dark animal that flew into the chaparral.

"Spree!" she shouted, but it was too late. She was losing them all. Even if they got the ladder to the bedroom in time, there was no way anyone was going to be able to lift Mimi up and out. Just as the free-standing ladder reached Mimi's window and a firefighter scrambled up with a hatchet, she saw a figure inside Mimi's bedroom. Jeremy. He must have climbed up the porch trellis and into a back hall window, an area still untouched by fire. Even though he could not possibly have seen shit for the smoke, he must have crawled his way over crap in the hall, then navigated the goat path in her room. He visited her enough to feel his way across the room on top of all the stuff.

Why hadn't she done that herself? She knew the way too. She knew every object by touch, the danger spots, the safe place to shift some weight. She knew it so well because she's the one who stacked it.

The firefighter smashed through Mimi's window and a torrent of stuff fell to the ground. Jeremy's sweat-lined face appeared as he pushed it all out the blocked window, and more again, raining down onto the life net below, where firefighters braced for Mimi, holding the net hand to hand like a prayer circle. But instead of a human, garbage. Shelley recognized things she hadn't seen for years, lost iPods, figurines, CDs, toys, an old toaster oven. When finally the window was cleared of shit, she expected to see Mimi next, ready to jump or be pushed. Instead, she saw Jeremy again, who flung two laptops and an iPad down to the life net. The firefighters flung them right out onto the ground and screamed at him to stop. Where was Mimi? Where? The next time he appeared at the window he held an armful of loose folders and he tossed them out, hundreds of sheets of paper like a flock of doves soaring through the smoke-filled air, rising up on winds of heat pouring out from the other windows, combusting as they rose, then fluttering down in white ashes, like snow, over the firefighters. The empty box of Aplets blew out of the window on a blast of heat, igniting and dissolving as it flew across the yard. Shelley's eyes followed the box until it caught in a tree, releasing red ash. The ground moved beneath it. Rattlesnakes.

When she looked back at the house there was a commotion at the window. Firefighters on the ladders outside and Jeremy on the inside all struggled with a massive, limp body, trying to pry Mimi out of the window. The firefighter on the ladder truck had long tools for pulling, and the firefighter on the other ladder had her by an arm. The smoke cleared enough for Shelley to see Mimi's face, upturned eyes white against skin gray with smoke. Jeremy struggled to raise her up as the firefighters worked to pull her out far enough to fall on the life net. But it was too late. The fire had caught up with them. Shelley could see the flames inside the bedroom now, slithering up and over and around the piles of shit.

"Get out, Jeremy!" she called. "Jump! Save yourself!"

The firefighters yanked Mimi to the windowsill, filling the space. As they pulled, Jeremy gave a final shove, collapsing from the effort, arms hanging empty as Mimi tumbled out into the world.

"Dead weight" were the words that went through Shelley's mind as she watched Mimi fall, her blank eyes open, flying fearlessly through the clouds of smoke. Free. She was free of it all for one, two, almost three seconds before a hard, mean landing on the pummeled net full of her possessions. If only she had wings. Big, glorious wings to keep her airborne forever. But it hardly mattered now. Even as Shelley ran to her, she knew, it hardly mattered now.

Chapter Eleven

Les sat cross-legged under eerie orange skies like on a distant planet, watching the pyrocumulus clouds billow from the vents of hell in the canyon, rising up over the foothills, the fire now forming its own weather. No, not a distant planet, but our own grim future, here at last. He heard mangy street dogs barking up and down Pearl, defending the indefensible. High noon and street lights flickering on. A Hindu Purana falls into his brain pan: When this era comes to an end, the world will be set ablaze by the sun god, then drowned by centuries of unbearable rain.

"Fitting end for a species fueled by fire," he announced to an ant head-butting the grape seed he'd wedged in a pavement crack. Flame on demand was a hot idea back in the Ice Age, as they—we—squatted around the first human fires. Such delicious warmth, and portable to boot. Put humans on the move, expanding their niche north, taking their own hot sun with them. Keeps the saber-tooth beasts at bay too. One day a hunk of bloody mammoth meat fell in the sacred fire, starts the glands salivating. Cooked food! Predigested by heat, begets the fat human brain and skinny gut.

Energy goes to thinking, not digesting. Modern humans not possible without combustion, now combustion about to make humans impossible. What goes around comes around and around. The more it burns, the more it will burn.

In a pocket the discovery of a crumpled cigarette, ignites it with a match. Breathes it in. Blows it out. Instant dragon. Starbucks cup out on the pavement in front of him. A service to the community, not a beggar, as Officer Sokos calls him. Certainly not a vagrant. He has a home, it is all around him. He stares into middle distance, not trying to catch eyes, third eyes or otherwise. As a rule, he lets earthly existence happen to him, although, since he needs his sips, he has to give it a little nudge now and again. A hand-scrawled sign is neatly propped up against his knees, "I am the Lily of the Field. I am the Bird of the Air."

Passersby smile and toss pocket change, missing the small target of the cup since no one wants to get too close. Dimes and quarters hit pavement and bounce, rolling off a little distance. Les does not go after them, letting coins gather round his person as if he were a golden idol. If other homeless come to collect, let them. It was all one. But a dollar bill, hands off. He'll make a grab for one before it gets airborne. It would be like letting a sip blow away, especially on a day like this, the katabatic winds coming sideways on the slope. One house near Flagstaff Mountain was smoldering, spewing billows of suppressed energy up into the troposphere. The sun cut through the smoke in slanting rays like a scene from the Old Testament, and not in a good way. It was probably never in a good way.

Judgment Weather. There was a lot to be judgmental about, but on a deeply personal level it was a good day for sips. Everyone walking past—college kids, shoppers, tourists, and god bless them, the Buddhists—all had one eye on the flame-breathing dragon creeping down the foothills and the other on their mortality. They gave Les offerings to placate the beast, knowing deep

72

down that the dragon was sent not by the gods, but by drought, beetle kill, and human carelessness, all accelerated by global warming. Fire was not the enemy. The gods were not the enemy. We were the enemy. We were the dragon to be tamed, and an offering to Les was a shortcut to cleansing the soul. Anything rather than change their lives.

He counted his gelt. Five Tito's. He folded up his sign and flattened the cup, storing both in the vast inner folds of his jacket. Time for the long walk to Hazel's. He still grieved Liquor Mart, an easy trek, but now a forced march to 28th. Sometimes he took the bus, The Hop the city called it, trying to sound hip, but walking was good for the old body. Kept him alive, for what it was worth. Alive and drinking. So much better than meditation. Inebriate, don't meditate. He'd used that sign to great effect. He could always find food. Soup kitchens, dumpsters. Even the cult deli if he could stomach religious predation for free food. But alcohol, like any spiritual enhancer, had to be sought. It had to be earned. Vodka transformed his sense of self into a long luminous present, and gave him a blessed moment of immortality, a fast horse running through the hills named Nothing. He didn't get drunk, he got disembodied, just like the gods.

When he came out of Hazel's he downed a sip for a quick start out of the gate. A better view of the ridge this end of Pearl, everyone staring up at Flagstaff. He marveled at the speed with which the dragon was sprinting through dry vegetation, racing, leaping, climbing. Junipers going up in flames like fireworks, splitting and twisting, then collapsing in a spray of sparks. The house that had been smoldering in dark veils had ignited, fully engaged, blossoming into a million scarlet petals of a single flower where a roof had been, the walls cupping the flame like hands. Incineration could be felt to the bone. No eyes could turn away. Some were crying. He could feel the synergy of fear in his gut. The vodka soothed it with numbness, feeding his inner dragon, and from his placated brain rose the words of the Buddha in his Fire Sermon. "Everything must burn, my monks," Les said out loud. And here we are. Finally. The world a burning house.

Not for nothing, it didn't look as if the fire would make it any farther down the slope. The one house a fluke, the target of a high-flying firebrand. The home must have been a tinderbox, or it must have been cursed. The dragon itself was still moving but getting tired, breaking up into segments all over the hills, a slow procession of dying particles.

Well, weren't they all a slow progression of dying particles?

As he walked back to his spot on Pearl he passed a cluster of Naropa students and they bowed to him. He bowed back. It was the polite thing to do. The students, who'd come to Boulder to be taught by the Buddhist monks, sometimes came to sit with him and other homeless on the mall like they were sacred beings, from whom something could be learned. The students said nothing, but sat in silence. Sometimes they took notes. They always left an offering.

Les stopped when he heard their conversation tumbling into his ear. Someone has died in the fire. Two someones? The home owners trapped in their home. How did it happen they didn't have time to evacuate, the students asked one another, thinking they would have gotten out in time, thinking that with determination and the right frame of mind they would have escaped that fate.

Pity the poor charred souls, thought Les. Not only did they have to forbear their hot transformation into carbon dioxide, dragged to the heavens, they had to endure the ridicule of those left behind. The students should know by now. No one escapes. No one gets out alive.

Les reached for another Tito's. He knew Shelley worked in one of those houses, but she was safe today doing her community service. He had watched her storm off early that morning, heading up to a relief station. He sipped. Above the burning house in the smoke-dark sky, turkey vultures circled, their feathers tuned to the currents of the air. They waited. Life must be stirring on the ground. The prehistoric birds sensed the dying whimpers of animal consciousness. A small creature up a tree? A raccoon? A cat? Beneath a burning bush, Les feels the pain of rattlesnakes writhing in the heat. One escapes, only to lie long and flat on the driveway, widened by wheels. The turkey vultures move in and out of the smoke on open wings, watching seared bodies carried away, waiting for their chance.

"Les, put that bottle in your pocket or I'm going to knock it to the ground."

Officer Sokos was standing next to him. He wondered how long she'd been there. He gestured at the fire with the sip. "Whose house?"

"No one you'd know," she said.

"I might." He downed the sip and put it in his pocket.

"We've got enough on our plate today, stay out of trouble." And then she walked away to harass other panhandlers, not appreciating the soul-cleansing service they performed for the community.

"No, really," he called after her. "Whose place is it? The gal you accused of stealing a baby, she works up on the ridge. A house manager, she calls herself."

Sokos stopped and assessed him through her blue sunglasses, even though the day was too smoked over for them. "I don't know the names, but both homeowners died," she said at last. "An employee was there, but I don't know who it was. I just know they had to pry her off one of the bodies. I heard it was . . . she was . . . it was sad."

They were both quiet for a moment, then she walked off, and Les went back to his spot. Shelley. He was sure of it. Shelley. He pondered going back to Arroyo Circle and checking up on her. But no. There was too much work to be done here. He set up his cup and his sign, and settled down for a busy evening. People would be feeling very emotional. They would want to give away their money. They would want to buy their way out of this dark, smoking hell. He had to be here for them. It was his job.

Chapter Twelve

"It gets so hot in here," Amanda said as she pumped up the air conditioning in the nursery. She adjusted the blue swaddle around her neck, wearing it like a scarf. It was his favorite, the one with the yellow fire engines. She liked to carry it around because with a little baby you just never knew, but right now she needed her hands free in order to tidy the room up a bit. There was always so much to do. She reached behind the rocker and shut the blinds against the scorching light of day. There. Cooler already. She opened the top drawer of the bureau, the sleek Scandinavian one that matched the crib, rocker, and changing table. The set had cost her, but it was built to last a lifetime.

She arranged, then rearranged Freddie's clean clothes, shaking out the onesies and rolling up the miniature sweat pants with the Denver Broncos logo. Some of Devin's friends had gone a bit overboard on shower gifts of team regalia, as if infants were teeny fans-in-training, but navy and orange was a nice change from all the pastel blues and yellows. She folded long-sleeve shirts into squares, with the little arms neatly crossed and tucked under. Some outfits were still new in their packages, warmer fall things and clothes he hadn't grown into yet. But it wouldn't be long. It all goes so fast. She arranged the piles in the order of size, then closed that drawer and opened another, pulling out a fresh, dotted sheet.

She changed all the linen in the crib, leaning over the rails and feeling the blood rush to her head. Drop-down sides would make this job easier, but they had been banned years ago for safety reasons. This was a solid, modern crib. No one was going to get hurt in this baby. With both palms, she smoothed a yellow blanket over the sheet, straightening out the pattern of dancing hippos. Silly. But it was only for show. You'd never put a blanket in with an infant for fear of suffocation. Freddie's pediatrician was adamant about that. Still, she'd gotten a few of them at the shower from aunts and other older women who hadn't gotten the memo, so why not make the room look cute?

On the rocking chair, she arranged the pillows and picked up a plush animal that fell on the floor. The Heartbeat Bear. She felt for the switch behind its purple neck, and listened. Nothing. The battery must be dead. A heartbeat was supposed to be a soothing sound to put babies to sleep, but the heart was attached to the outside of its fuzzy body. That was no place for it, unprotected like that, vulnerable to the dangers of the world. A beating heart was a precious thing. She pressed the trash can open with her foot and tossed it in.

The changing table was a mess. How did that happen? She stacked the diapers in their basket, then arranged all the wipes, and powders, and ointments into another. The rash cream tube was nearly full. She squeezed a small amount into her palms and rubbed them together. Her eyes fell on the baby monitor. That had to go too. It didn't work. It never worked. All these expensive gizmos meant to keep babies safe were useless. She picked it up and threw it in the trash with the stupid bear.

The diaper genie. She popped the pail open and was surprised to find it empty. She pulled down a new liner anyway to keep things fresh and tied the plastic tight against leakage. It was amazing how many diapers a little baby could go through in a day. The cost! She closed the top and patted it. Then she felt a little wobbly on her feet, like she was standing on water. She put one hand on the wall to steady herself, and with the other opened the diaper pail and vomited into it. Just some mucus and a little dark liquid, but her body kept retching in dry heaves. She wiped her mouth with the swaddle, then slowly went to ground on her knees, balancing herself with her hands. She tried to hold still but for some reason she was shaking. The sun forced its way through slits in the blinds, filling the room with bars of cold light. She knelt on the rug for some time, watching the shadows creep across the floor. She pushed her hair away from her face and smelled rash cream on her hands.

A ticking sound. She sat up. That clock with its cow forever jumping over the moon was so loud. Was it always this loud? She unplugged it from the wall, then yanked the cord out of the back just in case. Where to put the cord? She wouldn't want Freddie to get a hold of it.

Devin appeared in the doorway. He stared at her for a moment before turning off the AC. Then he gently pried the cord from her fingers and put it in his pocket. She laid her hands on the swaddle as a warning. Don't even try.

"Whatever you want it will have to wait," she said. "I've got too much to do." And with that she went over to the bureau, dumping everything out of the top drawer and began to fold Freddie's clothes again.

Devin sat in the rocker and leaned all the way back, staring at the ceiling. "We've got to get out of this house," he said.

"Yes, you're right, it's time to move," Amanda said, rolling up a onesie into a tight sausage. "It's not really big enough anymore, is it? I'll have a look at the listings, see what's out there. It's my job, after all. It's what I do. But first I have to walk Freddie. He needs the air. We all need a little air."

Chapter Thirteen

Someone—Shelley thinks it might have been Betty-Ann—had come to collect her from Mimi's. Someone had led her gently away from the devastation and back to her own home, stripped her of her smoke-soaked clothes and left them in the yard. Someone washed her down with a soapy sponge and a cool trickle from the hose, brought her inside, dried her off, slipped fresh pajamas over her body, and made her lie down. But Shelley would not lie down. She had failed. She had failed at the one thing she thought she was good at, household management. Now she knew, she was never good. She was a danger to the world. She'd been hired to help Mimi and she'd been no help at all. Help would have been finding a way to save her instead of catering to her. Instead, together the two of them constructed a labyrinth of material goods from which Mimi could not escape. She died trapped under the weight of her beloved things, fighting for breath. The EMTs said it was a lost battle even before she flew out of the house and onto the net full of her things, a scorched, wingless bird, propelled by Jeremy. She was already dead from smoke inhalation. Jeremy should have known it was too late to save her. At a certain point, you can only join them as they go down in flames. Exhausted by trying to lift Mimi, he could make no effort to get out of the window himself, and as the firefighters reached for him they were attacked by fists of fire that blasted out with a punch so abrupt and powerful she could not say if Jeremy even had time to scream.

"I built a ladder of death with the boxes, with these two hands," she kept trying to explain. "These hands."

Betty-Ann gave her two pills and had her wash them down with a Coors, then sat by her bedside, waiting. If they talked, Shelley could not remember the words. She heard "Ssshh, ssshush," over and over, as she rose in and out of consciousness, jolted awake by the memory then shocked back to sleep. The fire inspector came knocking sometime during the night and Betty-Ann let him in. He asked Shelley a couple of questions, then turned to Betty-Ann and said he'd be back some other time when Shelley was more lucid. She heard Betty-Ann apologize for giving Shelley the pills, but the inspector understood. He understood too well. Shelley felt blessed with understanding. "Thank you, thank you," she'd mumbled, then disappeared inside a fog of agony.

Some sort of eternity followed, but eventually a hazy sun rose up over the distant plains, sending splinters of light through the shades into the room. But it was not the light but the smell of smoke that woke Shelley in a panic. She lurched upright and looked around, then put her arm to her nose. It was her. It was everything. Her throat was scorched raw and she couldn't swallow. She rolled out of bed and ran to the bathroom, just in time to vomit up a bit of sludge in her stomach. She stayed on the cool floor for a minute, clutching the toilet bowl, thinking hard what to do next, as if Mimi's death was a puzzle to be solved. But her brain was flooded with the stench of burnt, charred flesh. She stunk of Mimi. When they pulled her off of the body she had felt the skin peel off Mimi's face and onto her own.

When she returned to her bedroom she realized that Betty-Ann was no longer dozing in the chair where she'd been all night, pushing her back down on the bed with two soft hands every time she shot upright, trembling in horror. There was a note on the night table. *Had to get to work. Will check in on you later. Hang in there. XXBA*

"Hang in there," Shelley said out loud as she opened the shades. The sun was up. A sunset and a sunrise had not undone a thing. The fire had come and gone, taking two lives and leaving her behind. She saw Les sleeping on the front lawn, curled up near her front door like a watchdog.

We all have our place, she thought. We all have a job to do. And she had hers. Now she had to see it through to the end, doing that which she was not allowed to do before. Bulldoze everything into a massive pile and get rid of it all. Bring it down to ground.

Where were the children? Who was in charge of them? She could not remember if they had shown up at the fire. She hoped not. She had no idea who told them the horrific news. Did they see the firefighters struggle to carry their mother's body away? Did they see their father's sheeted body laid out on the lawn, cooling down enough to be put into the waiting ambulance? Where was her phone? She spun around the room in a panic. God bless Betty-Ann, it was charging on the bureau. She went to unplug it and was startled at the sight of herself in the mirror. She had to turn around to make sure there was not someone else in the room. But no. It was her. Wild-haired and smudged along the edges. A changed woman. A changeling.

She tried calling Claudia and Louisa, but nothing. Then the kids. Texts. More texts. No answer. They were being taken care of, she hoped, by someone. If not Louisa, then who? Mimi had no family that she knew of, her parents and brother having died long before, and Jeremy's were in California. She called Louisa again and left a message to say she'd be going up to the house soon, maybe she'd see her there? Then she remembered her car, still on the road where she'd been stopped by the police barrier. She went to the kitchen and found the coffee thermos filled. "Thank you Betty-Ann," she said, and poured herself a cup. Then she poured another and went to the front door. Les was awake and sitting up on the stoop picking twigs out of his braid.

She handed him one of the cups. "How do you sleep on the ground like that?"

"We evolved to sleep on the ground. Our spines can be fitted to the earth's contours like a puzzle piece."

"My back hurts enough as it is. Everything hurts, inside and out."

"Thought I'd come with you," he said.

"What makes you think I'm going anywhere?"

"We all keep appointments we did not make." With that, he drained the coffee in a single, long gulp.

"It's my job, if that's what you mean." She sat down on the stoop with him. "I guess you know about . . . Gone." She could not say the word *dead*. She could not say *Mimi*.

He contemplated his empty cup. "Not for nothing, but matter and energy are never gone."

"True. All the crap up at the house, that's not gone. Burnt, but smoldering in a mess like one giant disgusting thing."

"Stuff lets us avert our gaze from what lies ahead, knowing that one day we'll wash into the waters of time with all the crap. Extinguished. Now even the fire is freed from its need to consume."

"The kids. I don't even know where they are. I've got to make sure they're safe. I have to track down relatives. I have to do so much. The cat. Spree is missing. I've got to call the insurance company. I've got to talk to the fire inspector, I've . . ."

Les raised a finger to his mouth. "Listen," he whispered. "An angel is passing over."

She took a breath and looked in the sky, but there was only a big, scraggly bird, and it flew off into the smoke-filled mountains. They sat for some time on the stoop, staring straight ahead at the sun hanging bloodshot over the city.

"The standing dead," Les said later, on their way to Mimi's in an Uber. He pointed at the blackened skeletons of trees and touched his forehead in a salute. They were heading to Shelley's car, and the higher they got, the more charred the landscape. Lawns and homes were singed where the fire had passed quickly by, and scorched where it lingered. Even in untouched areas the vegetation was curled in upon itself, like it was protecting its innards. Many buildings were blackened by smoke, but none had been annihilated like Mimi's, because no one else had left a funeral pyre of boxes leaning up against their home.

"It all looks so different," she said. "Like we're on another planet."

"A static landscape is only in our minds," said Les. He rolled down the window and threw out a few grape pits. "Along with everything else."

The Uber driver cleared her throat and spoke. "*The Camera* says the fire was started in the canyon by some idiots using exploding targets. Remember the big fire in Denver a few years back? Started by a fire ranger burning a letter from her estranged husband on a red flag day. What's wrong with people?"

"All things physical are information-theoretic in origin, and this is a participatory universe."

"Over there," said Shelley. "That's my car."

The Uber driver pulled over to the curb. Les and Shelley had barely got out when the car sped off. Les had that effect on people. Shelley wondered if she'd made the wrong decision in bringing him. She was long on wrong decisions these days.

"Air it on out," she told Les, opening all the doors of her car before getting in. She was wondering how she was ever going to get the smoke stink out, but that turned out to be the least of her worries when she tried to start it up. The old Accord was dead.

"Particulates in the filters," said Les, as they listened to the engine straining to turn over. "Ashes to ashes."

"Let's walk," said Shelley, closing all the doors they'd just opened. "I'll deal with this later."

There was no shade going up the hill and she had not prepared for the heat. Heavy shirt. No hat. But she mindlessly trudged behind Les like a pack animal. She did not understand how he wore that denim barn jacket of his in this heat, but she'd never seen him out of it. When he stopped suddenly she bumped into him.

"Not here," she said. "A little farther up."

He didn't seem to hear her, but walked down a stranger's driveway. There had been some burning in the backyard, but the house was fine. The garage was scorched but standing, and leaning against it was a beehive. One of the legs was burnt through so that the whole thing had fallen to one knee. Les opened the top. He stood still, just staring, then he closed it, made the sign of the cross, and returned.

"What?" She stood still, panting. The air was unbreathable.

"Dead beehive," he said. "It's one thing to burn your own house down, but it's not right to burn down the homes of others."

"Why didn't they fly away?"

"They'd never leave their queen, and she can't fly. Only ones disoriented by the smoke that couldn't make it back to the hive might have been saved."

They both stood there for a lost moment, then a rush of wings made them look up. Two large, ugly birds floated above them on an updraft.

"Must be nice to just coast," said Shelley.

"Vultures," said Les. "The natural order of things has returned."

"We'd better keep moving so they don't think we're dinner." Shelley turned and headed up the hill.

"Wait," he said. "A little offering." She watched him take a grape from one of his pockets, suck on it, then press the seeds in the edge of the lawn under his feet.

"Why?" asked Shelley.

"Burnt soil is receptive ground for seeds," he said. "This is the beginning of a disturbance regime."

"The disturbance is in your head. You don't really think grapes will grow here, do you, by the side of the road?"

"He who plants a seed, plants hope."

"Here's hoping we get to the damn house before dark," said Shelley, and she started walking.

"Life is a numbers game. We might get wiped out, but some vegetation will survive. Why not my grapes?"

"Right here," said Shelley, as she turned onto 6th. Before she could see Mimi's house, she saw gasps of smoke rising above it. As they walked they breathed in air thick with particulates, as Les called them. Particulates. A fancy word for pieces. Pieces of trees, pets, wildlife. Humans. Jeremy. His particulates must still hang in the air. Shelley coughed as she walked, but went silent when they got to the house, a brittle shell in a yard layered with rubble and broken glass. Sharp objects poked out at every surface. Wet, sodden pieces of cardboard and paper melted on top of the debris. The watering system had melted and curled up from the lawn like giant alien worms.

"It looks like a war zone where both sides lost," said Shelley. "It was a beautiful house, once."

"You know what Thoreau says," said Les. "What's the use of a fine house if you haven't got a tolerable planet to put it on."

There were a couple of firefighters on duty with rakes and hoses, watching that hot remains didn't flare up, what with all the constipated surprises the house held. Shelley and Les moved closer, feeling the heat. Les groaned. A red-headed police officer was standing guard at the taped perimeter.

"Sokos," said Les. "Our old friend."

The officer turned around at the sound of her name, and briefly registered Les before making eye contact with Shelley.

"Ma'am," Sokos said.

Shelley felt a wave of anger rise to her face just looking at her again, all tall and poised and perfect, with eyes shielded from the world with those blue glasses of hers. Hiding.

"These people," Shelley said, pointing at the ruins, "they were my employers. You know me. You accused me of kidnapping a baby from King Soopers."

Sokos nodded. "We were working with the best information we had."

"Because of your 'best information,' I wasn't here to help Mimi out of the house and she died. And her husband wouldn't have gone in after her, and now he's dead. *Incinerated.*"

"I heard you went back to King Soopers and tried to run over an employee," said Sokos. "That's what got you sent to community service, not me asking to see the contents of your trunk. Besides, I might have saved your life. You could have died trying to save your boss, like the husband."

"Saved for a purpose," said Les.

"A purpose," said Shelley. "Yes. Finding the cat is now my grand purpose in life. Remember the kitty litter in my trunk you thought was a baby? That cat ran out during the fire."

"He's not lost alone," said Les.

They heard neighbors shaking bowls of kibble, keening the names of pets, calling them home. When they'd evacuated the day before, most people couldn't bring their animals, and simply let them loose and prayed. She remembered the horses galloping over the hills and through the streets, Spree flying through the air to safety. The cat seemed to be the only one in the family who knew how to save himself.

"I'll go ask around if he's answered the call," said Les. "What's he look like?"

Shelley paused. "He's a gray and white long-hair. Or was. Who knows what he looks like now. Probably all gray with soot. He's got extra toes. Or did."

After Les wandered away, Sokos spoke. "Who is Les to you?"

"Nothing. He lives along the creek bed behind my house. He wanted to come along."

"Be careful," said Sokos. "He can be volatile."

So can I, thought Shelley, and then took a deep breath. She needed to play nice if she wanted to stay. "Mind if I poke around a bit?"

Sokos nodded. "I don't see you."

Shelley slipped under drooping police tape and paused in the shadow of the ruins. Most of the tiled roof had fallen in on itself, crushing the floors beneath, but some of the stucco walls still stood. Probably because so much of Mimi's shit was propping them up, baked into solid supports. It was so sad, that something so beautiful should end like this. When she first arrived on that doorstep, the house had seemed the pinnacle of domestic civilization. She wanted to be part of it. At times, it even felt more like hers than Mimi's, confined as her boss was to her bedroom, a prisoner of her own making. She saw twisted metal remnants in what had been the small appliance room. Having twenty-two toaster ovens must have given Mimi the idea she'd live long enough to use them up.

She took a step closer and felt herself getting faint. So much stuff to which so much had happened. Sour fluid rose up her throat and she threw up a bit. She was dizzy, but she stepped carefully over hot debris to the kitchen, where the exterior wall had fallen away, revealing the gross contents, warped, black and flattened with the pressure of water, condensed to a few feet of grocery muck. All that food could have fed the hungry. Now the rats and scavengers will come as soon as the coals were cool enough to walk on. Every can, every swollen box, every broken spice jar, immersion blender and bashed-in bowl, it had all mattered so very much once, first to Mimi, then to her. All those hours spent gathering it in. A lot of her own life had disappeared in that fire. She and Mimi, the ultimate scavengers.

The basement was exposed in places and she could see the bales of toilet paper at the bottom of the stairs, soaked from the fire hoses, exploding from their plastic wrappers, disgorging a paper slime. She had stacked those bales herself. Revolting. It was just revolting. She remembered she still had the one bale in her trunk. Of all things spared.

"Shelley."

Louisa stood on the other side of the tape with the two stricken teens behind her, Harper and Winnie. Their loss was so much greater than her own. They'd lost their parents. Mother and father, gone forever. Their home, their childhoods, gone. Shelley ducked back under the tape and opened her arms to hug them, but they both stepped back. Winnie had tears on her face, and said, "Fuck you." Harper looked like a pillar of rage.

Louisa put her arms around them and whispered, then herded them to the garage, which, since it was not attached to the house, had survived. "Go see if there's anything useful to take along," Louisa said to them. "Luggage? Maybe there are even clothes or toothbrushes in that mess."

"I don't understand," said Shelley. "Why are they mad at me?"

Louisa shook her head as if she was dislodging water from her ears, then gestured at the house in disbelief. "What do you think? This. Now they are orphans."

"Me? I didn't do this. That was nature."

"It was a tragedy waiting to happen, and you know it. You created it."

"Mimi created it," Shelley said, and wiped her eyes. She was so very tired. "Not me."

"The kids were at school, *Gracias a dios*," said Louisa. "You must have been   somewhere safe too. The one time you could have been a help and done some good, you're gone."

"What? I didn't have a choice. I had to do community service."

"The kids think you encouraged Mimi so you could have the thrill of shopping without having to pay for it. You certainly didn't try to stop the spoiled thing." She took a tissue out of her pocket and wiped her face. "The poor *aniñados*."

Shelley knew that word. It's what Hispanic workers in town called the rich Anglos. Childish ones. "But there was no stopping her," Shelley said. "My job was to do what she told me."

"Your job was to manage the house. Now look."

"Louisa, I don't want to argue with you. Tell me what you know. Whose job is it now? Who's in charge?"

"No one. The kids stayed with me last night, and I'm putting them on a plane to Jeremy's sister in L.A. in the morning."

"Has anyone called the insurance company? The lawyers?"

Louisa looked at the ruins with puddled eyes. "Go ahead. Call. But there's no money to pay you to do it. It's why Jeremy ran into a burning building for a woman he did not love."

"He adored her," Shelley said.

Louisa shrugged and looked right at her. "He adored her money. He adored her family's name in town. She talked him into doing things, illegal things. Fraud. They made millions then lost it all. Indictments are being handed down any day."

"Indictments? For what? What are you talking about?" Everything she thought she knew about the world was falling in on itself, and for the first time since she got to Boulder, she wished she had never left Baraboo. She remembered wild scarves of starlings over field after field of oats, the sense of being part of the world around her. She couldn't even imagine anyone saying the word "indictment" there.

"You are so blind," Louisa said, the tears now streaking down her face. She looked over at the garage to make sure the kids were not around, then lowered her voice. "I've been sleeping with Jeremy for years. Years. I'd go through his text messages to make sure there was no one else. That's how I knew about the business troubles." She made a gesture of disgust with her hands. "I'm going back to Mexico, to my own family. I should have gone earlier."

"I just don't believe it," said Shelley. "I would have known. Mimi couldn't have kept something like that from me."

"You, you see what you want. Ignore the rest. Makes life pretty for you."

"If you thought I was doing such a rotten job, you shouldn't have stayed silent."

"Believe me, I told Jeremy what I thought. He said you were the only person in the world to put up with Mimi's crap."

Harper called to Louisa from inside the garage. "Spree is here. He's alive!"

"That's who God chooses to save?" said Louisa, shaking her head. "He takes both parents and leaves them a cat?"

"Harper, a cat carrier is on the shelf by the side door," Shelley called. She turned to Louisa. "Let me help. I know where everything is in there."

"If you want to make yourself useful," said Louisa. "Bring Spree to the shelter. They can't bring him to California. The sister is doing enough as it is."

"I can't do that," said Shelley. "Mimi loved that cat."

"Mimi loved everything she owned. All the stuff. The cat. You."

Harper came out of the garage with a duffel bag over his shoulder and a cat crate in his hand, and carried both to the car.

"Harper," Louisa called. "Spree has to stay here. Your aunt said she can't take him too."

"What?" he said. Tears ran down his face, and he wiped them away in anger. "No, Spree comes with us or we're not going,"

Louisa did not argue with him. She just looked at the ground in front of her. Harper put the crate down on the scorched lawn, then stood there for a minute before crouching to look in at Spree. He said something to the cat that Shelley could not hear, then turned quickly towards Louisa's car and slammed the door. Winnie carried an armful of clothes from the garage and put them in the trunk of the car, then walked over to the crate and picked it up. Louisa approached her with a hug, then said something in a soft voice that set Winnie into tears. She tried to pull away, but Louisa wrangled the crate from her. Winnie stared at the house, her mouth open in shock. She looked like an old woman at sixteen. Shelley tried to choke down tears, which made Winnie glare at her. It seemed as if she was going to say something, but broke into gulping sobs instead, then ran to join her brother in the car.

Louisa wiped tears from her own eyes and put the crate at Shelley's feet. "Try to do a better job with him than you did with the house," she said, and walked away.

"I can't bring him to a shelter," Shelley said. "What am I supposed to do with him?"

"Eat him for all I care," said Louisa, without looking back.

Shelley's smoke-filled head was spinning. When did they all turn against her? Had they hated her all along? Maybe they were just overwhelmed with grief right now. Shelley watched Louisa back the car up, almost hitting Les, who was leading a pale, sweaty horse down the driveway. When he got closer, he stooped to peek into the cat crate.

"Back half of its fur is singed off," he said. "Looks like Sekhet, the lion-headed goddess."

"It's a boy cat."

"A goddess can appear in any form she wants."

"Why do you have a horse?" Shelley asked. "No, really, why? I ask you to find the cat and you bring back a horse."

"The horse and I found one another. Sokos is pulling up the missing animal report."

"What about Spree?" Shelley knelt down to have a look at this boy goddess, and the cat looked back at her. Les was right, a lot of its hair was burnt off, but hopefully nothing worse than that. "He's not missing anymore, but no one wants him. Now what?"

"We live on the surface of a gas-covered planet going around a nuclear fireball. That's our base normal. Bring Sekhet to the vet to be healed."

Shelley stood up. The cat was her responsibility, at least for now. "I'm calling an Uber," she said, pecking at her phone. "Les, can you grab a tub of kitty litter from the garage, and some kibble?" She lifted up the cat crate with two hands, ignoring the pain in her back, and lugged it to the road. She passed Sokos on the way out and they nodded.

"The owners are coming by with a trailer," Sokos told Les, putting away her phone and taking the lead from him. "They said to stay, they have a reward for you."

Les sniffed the air. "During cremation, the mercury from dental fillings are volatilized into the atmosphere. I gotta go."

"A reward, Les," Sokos said. "Money."

He waved her away. "Not for nothing, but even money will be swept away by the wings of the destroying angel." And then he went into the garage and emerged a few minutes later swinging a tub of kitty litter in his hand and cradling a bag of kibble in one arm like a baby.

Chapter Fourteen

Overnight, Shelley had become a cat lady against her will. A middle-aged, unmarried, childless, unemployed woman with a bald, frightened cat. She had the Uber drop Les off at her house with the kitty litter and kibble, then she continued on to the vet clinic where Spree was given IV liquids and a boost of oxygen, which seemed to perk him up. Shelley wouldn't have minded some oxygen herself. She had a memory of a firefighter putting a mask over her face after they'd pulled her off Mimi. She must have passed out. When she came to, an EMT was fussing over her, and Mimi's body was gone. The fire was more or less under control by then and Shelley sat up to look, just in time to see firefighters lower Jeremy's charred, smoking body from the window, and then her brain went dark again.

All that death, yet this little critter survived. His singed fur was shaved down to his skin, and he had tight rubber booties on his two front paws to keep him from licking the burn liniment. The vet was sympathetic about the fire, but did not waive a penny, so she had to put it on her own credit card. None of Mimi's cards worked. Was Louisa right? Was there really no money? Shelley kept her receipt and hoped she could get it back from the estate soon. If nothing else, there was house insurance. But who would it be paid to? The kids? Their custodian? When she got home from the vet, she wanted to fall flat on her face, but she had to get Spree settled first. She found bowls for water and kibble, a box for the kitty litter, then laid everything out on a mat in the corner of the kitchen. Spree ignored it all. Shelley collapsed on the sofa in a pile of self-pity, where Spree found her and meowed to be lifted up.

"Can't jump yet, Spree?" she said. With a sharp ping in her back, she leaned over and lifted him up. She let the cat arrange itself on her lap, and then she called Frank, Mimi's useless lawyer.

"Who's in charge?" she asked. "I'm owed salary, and I just paid Mimi's cat's vet bill."

"Poor Mimi," said Frank. "And Jeremy. Shit. But you knew the situation better than anyone. It was a fire waiting to happen."

"Was it? No one let me in on the secret. What happens now?"

"Don't know. Jeremy's sister in California is the executor. I called and offered my services, but she said she'd hire the Devil himself before she'd take me on and then she hung up. She must think I was in on whatever shenanigans Jeremy was up to. I knew the business was in trouble, but not to this extent. Sounds like that was a fire waiting to happen too."

Shelley very much doubted Frank was all that innocent. "Why didn't Mimi tell me?"

"You'd have looked for another job, wouldn't you? You were important to her, and she was trying to hold on to you and every-thing else for as long as she could." He paused. "If there are any assets, they might be impossible to recover. Mimi asked me about crypto and the law a while back. I told her there was no law and all she said was 'goody'."

"I don't understand any of this." Shelley petted Spree's bare body. Who knew there was so little of him under all that fur?

"I don't suppose you have any of Mimi's passwords?" asked Frank. "You were pretty deep into her personal business."

"If I knew anything about her business I wouldn't be calling you, would I? I know the debit card PIN, for all the good it does me. She used to keep a messy collection of papers in the nightstand drawer, but that's gone now." She remembered watching all the papers Jeremy threw out of the window dissolve into ash on the hot air. He must have thought they were important enough to save them, using precious seconds he didn't have. They might have cost him his life. But whatever they were, Jeremy wouldn't be needing them now.

"Oh well," said Frank, and he sighed deeply. "The details of their troubles will be in *The Camera* tomorrow and we'll both learn more then. Jeremy's sister better hire good criminal counsel to get the house extricated from the mess so those kids can get something."

"And me," said Shelley. "I'd like my last paycheck. And the vet bill."

"Go file for unemployment and I'll call you if I find anything out. She owed me money too, if that makes you feel any better."

"I'm so sorry for your loss," said Shelley, and then she hung up.

She sat for a long time, trying to sort things out in her head. Mimi had her juggling the credit cards lately. "There's been some fraud activity," Mimi had told her. There sure had been, only the fraud was apparently hers and Jeremy's. "How could I have been so blind, Spree?"

He had nothing to say about that. She forced herself to eat a little dinner, and then she tended to Spree's wounds before going to bed. In the morning, after a sleepless night, she went online and found *The Daily Camera's* article about Jeremy and his company. The indictments that Louisa had mentioned had been opened, even though the indicted were now dead. It was bad. Jeremy was a real con artist, and had been from almost the beginning, selling shares of cattle ranches that existed only in photographs so fake they looked like movie stills. He sent out annual disbursements financed from a constant stream of new investors. Jeremy sold a vision of the West, and everyone wanted to own a piece of it. It fueled their image of themselves as rugged Americans, real Westerners, images as false and fabricated as Jeremy himself. No one looked too closely at what he was actually doing, which was stealing and lying. And Mimi had been in on it, indicted right along with him for fraud. If Louisa was right, it might even have been her idea to begin with. She was the one who needed all the stuff, all that stupid, disgusting stuff.

It took Shelley a while to absorb it all. If she'd been a real house manager, she would have been in charge of the bills herself, checking them over then paying them from a household account. But she was no manager, she was just the personal shopper for a spoiled rich thing, helping her spend her ill-gotten gains. She was as gullible as Jeremy's clients, wanting to believe in a story of wealth and bold, entrepreneurial spirit.

When she pulled herself together that night, she searched through her contacts and found the number for Tina, Jeremy's sister in California. She had to find out what happened now, and how she should go about getting her money.

"Hi Tina. Remember me? Shelley Price? Mimi's house manager? We met a couple of times when you came to visit."

"What do you want?" Tina asked. "I'm at the airport waiting for Jeremy's kids."

"I'm so sorry about your brother."

"That woman killed him," Tina said in a voice that could lift paint. "I knew she'd bring him down one way or another. She was a monster."

"A monster? No. She was just needy."

Tina laughed with a snort. "For someone who helped her create that disaster of a house, you don't know much about monsters. And that brother of hers, a total pervert."

"Being an addict doesn't make him a pervert."

"No, but feeling up children does. Good thing Jeremy found out because Mimi wouldn't have done a thing. It was easy enough to get him busted for drugs. Even easier to have him die in prison. Mimi knew. She and Jeremy had each other by the balls. What a marriage."

"That's not true," said Shelley. "Mimi said the kids were too young to remember their uncle."

Tina made a sound of disgust. "That's just more bullshit falling out of her mouth. I'm going to hang up now."

"Wait, wait. I called to find out what to do. Should I stay on for a while and help manage the property until it can be sold?"

"Jeremy said it was your job to keep her sickness under control, and you failed. You are to do nothing, do you hear me? Nothing."

"Then Jeremy might have freaking well told me it was my job. In fact, you know what? He encouraged her, and hired me to help her spend it." Tina made a sound, but Shelley cut her off. "You know why? It just hit me. Because as long as Mimi was the one with the problem, no one would look too closely at what he was doing. He was the bigger hoarder in the end, hoarding all the money."

Shelley could hear Tina breathing, and when she spoke her voice was flat. "She was a sick woman and she pulled him into her sickness. She pulled you in too, and you know it."

"I don't know what I know. I just know I need my last paycheck and vet bills for the cat, who got burnt in the fire."

"He's not the only one who got burnt. Jeremy owes me a bundle he borrowed just last week. He said he was trying to straighten some things out, that the monster had talked him into some sort of 'financial experiment' and it got out of control. Now here I am taking their kids with no money to raise them. I don't want to hear about your last paycheck."

"I don't understand," said Shelley. "What's going to happen to the house? Do we all just walk away?"

"That's exactly what we do. My lawyer said it was about to be foreclosed on anyway and to move on as if the bank already owned it, not to even clean the site. As if that place could ever be cleaned up. The insurance company will work it out with the bank. I think it's already impounded by the feds for back income taxes. Who knows?" She was crying now. Shelley could hear the airport sounds behind her, the closing of gates, the announcements, people shouting.

"I'm so sorry," said Shelley, although she didn't know why she was apologizing. "What about funerals?"

"The bodies are being cremated in Boulder—whatever's left to be cremated—then they'll be buried here in California. We'll have the joint service next week. I'd say come if you'd like, but the children don't want you here."

Shelley heard the airport loudspeaker crackle in the background. "I've got to go," said Tina. "They're about to land. Good luck with your life, Shelley. We'll all need luck." And with that, she hung up.

Shelley sat and looked at her phone for some time, long enough for Spree to jump up on the sofa and stare at her. "What's going on, Spree? How could I have not seen this coming?" Spree kept staring without seeming to blink. "I know, I know. I didn't see because I didn't want to. Is that what you're saying?"

The room darkened and they both turned to the window when a car turned around in the circle. The headlights swept across the room. It was late. The days were getting shorter. How long had Mimi and Jeremy known the noose was tightening? She wondered if they had a plan and if that plan included her, or if they were going to just skip out of town and leave it all behind, let other people clean up their mess. It hurt to think of how she was an unwitting part of it, helping Mimi spend money that wasn't hers to spend, helping to destroy people's dreams, with Mimi and Jeremy making money off of ranch land that existed only in their heads. Money to buy all the stuff, then money to let it all burn.

Chapter Fifteen

The thirst. The trembling, heaving thirst. Struggling neurons firing out of control, the iron taste of blood, dry ashes where teeth once stood. Les, the unlucky endling, trying to squelch the ravenous dragon of the gods with the only weapon on hand, his treasured Tito's, but they only fed the flames. The dragon morphed into a single organism oozing over the planet, devouring it, licking it clean with scarlet tongues flickering from its mouth. Slobbering with fire. According to the *Book of Revelation*, after the breaking of the seventh seal, an angel will hurl a censer filled with fire down to the earth, causing blinding lightning, deafening rumblings, and a globe-splitting earthquake.

Gotta go! Les abandoned his body, soaring outside the Virgo Supercluster of galaxies before looking back at Earth, seeing the monster whole for what it was. Us. The dragon was us. He knew what had to be done. A sacrifice was called for and his eyes flashed open in horror. It was coming.

The sun was already hiding behind the Rockies, the continent's primordial spine, staining the graveyard with a reddish western light. Weeds and parched flowers came into focus. His gray braid sprawled near his face and he saw his hair moving. He squinted.

A yellow spider was spinning a web in his braid, working its spin-nerets, strands of silk shooting out its bristled bottom. White markings on abdomen, a cross. The crowned orb weaver. *Araneus diadematus*. Les snapped his brittle hairs from the web and pulled his head away, leaving the web draped on some prickly weed. The spider bunched up all its legs for a moment, then relaxed them, continuing its work of survival, repairing his damage.

Day after day, arachnids woke up knowing their job, their short lives driven by purpose, but Les woke up several times a day know-ing only chaos and disorientation, even in this place of solemn silence. His first awakening back at the creek had been filled with wild noise and panic. A skin-stretched cow had stumbled down the embankment, a refugee no doubt from a smoked-out foothills ranch, her thirst driving her into the trap. She never reached the trickle of water to be found.

"Mithra," he'd said when he found her. An old Roman cult believed that the struggle between good and evil would end when the great bull Mithra appeared on earth to reawaken humans to life. Now, instead of a great bull, a famished cow. Another sign of the times.

After a number of scrambles and dusty falls, the withered beast simply lay down in the ruthless sun and offered herself up to the deerflies. Why hadn't a rancher gone looking for her? Even old sick cows were worth money to pet food companies. Maybe she was an escapee from a trailer on its way to a meat processing plant, pre-ferring to die under the open sky instead of the abattoir. Les gath-ered folks from along the creek, but no coaxing, pulling or pushing could get the cow back on all fours again. Three times, folks went to town for more help and never came back. One gal, two tea-colored children clinging to her legs and her belly distended with another, collected water in a bowl and offered it to her, but no. Too late. Her eyes gaped up, searching the clouds.

"You can only help those who want it," said the woman. She

carried the bowl away, her children dotted with splash. One by one, the others gave up and left. Les stayed. Death was inevitable. Dying alone was not.

"We are in this together, Mithra." He stroked the fur on her head, and brushed the flies away from her open mouth. "The truth is, we're all just a few steps behind you."

Les sat crouched on his heels by the cow's side for an hour or more, a human presence, the very smell of which kept coyotes at bay so they would not eat the old girl alive. Not that it looked like she'd notice. The gaze in her dark brown eyes was far off. And yet the ribs continued to rise. Soon, the heaving breath moved from the ribs to the throat, first struggling, then imperceptible, then gone. The big circle had turned a notch. He could not explain his tears, but someone had to pony up for this magnificent creature, someone had to stand in awe at the ceaselessness of life and death. The coyotes paced in the shadows of the dry brush, waiting for him to leave. Farther up the creek he saw men with sharp knives, women with high hopes. He left them to it.

Not for nothing, waking up sucked. Yet because of the sedating power of Tito's he had cause to wake several times a day. Les rolled his body over to his heart side, then hauled himself to a sitting position with pained effort, coordinating elbows and knees, finding leverage, gaining altitude, until he felt his upper body press firmly against a headstone then let his head fall back to open the airways. Look. The sky. Still there. The quilted cirrocumulus stretched low and thin above him, tinged with mango light. It was a thing to witness. A fleeting wonder in more ways than one. It would not be long before climate change annihilated not just all cows on the land but clouds in the sky, burning them off in a warmer atmosphere. No more shafts of divine light falling through the billowing cumulous, a sad end to the biblical concept of God in the heavens. We are the destroyer of gods. Zeus was right, humans could not be trusted with fire. Prometheus deserved to have his liver devoured—over and over—for giving us the flame, a pathetic species destined to abuse its power.

Les looked down and watched the spider work, feeling his own limbs swept up in creation. The first web the orb weaver spider makes in its lifetime is perfect, a thing of beauty and destruction, then the more it makes, the sloppier the webs get, as if the world teaches them to expend only the bare minimum necessary to survive. "You got that right, little weaver." He watched a dark moth flutter about, then brush against the sticky web, getting its wing snared. In its struggle, it got the other wing stuck as well. The spider felt the vibration and came running on all eight legs, proving the universe is composed of vibrating strings. Superstring theory in action. The spider produced more silk from its bottom, shooting it around the moth, around and around. The moth continued to fight, and unless Les intervened, this was it. But he was no god. He let the spider do its job and looked away. Death was Nature's friend since it allowed the wheel of life to roll on. The spider had to eat and drink too.

Drink. He patted his garments for the familiar pint, took a sip that sent warm blood through his dry veins. He'd gotten out of the science biz just in time. Knowledge cannot help us with what we are about to experience. He pulled up a pants leg to examine his latest sores and scabs. He bruised as easily as an old peach these days. He couldn't be trusted on pavement, but he had to work on Pearl if he wanted his sips. It had been a good day in that regard. An excellent day, even though the street had been lousy with buskers. Tough to compete with a contortionist who could fold himself into a small, clear box, but Les had a new sign: "The universe provides. Be the universe." Soon he had enough for more than a few sips, then a whole pint, sending him off to where he sat now, Columbia Cemetery, for a bit of charnel ground meditation to check in with his impermanence.

He took a long swig and swished it around in his mouth before swallowing, letting the burn linger on his tongue. The world gets mad at the drunk for not being able to change the behavior that might kill him, yet the world is unable to change the behavior that is killing itself. He tucked the bottle away in a pocket and felt a small stone. A fossil he'd scratched out from the dust waiting for Mithra's demise. The faint impressions of a trilobite from when the Rocky Mountains were at the bottom of the sea, before two ancient tectonic plates collided and became one, under God, indivisible. Les licked the stone for a clearer image of this ancestor to the pill bug, the little guy that curls up in a ball when disturbed from his job removing harmful metals from the earth.

He placed the fossil tenderly on top of the sunken gravestone next to him. He read the inscription. *Infant Kettery, Aged One Day, August 1870.* No given name. No gender. He turned to read the stone he leaned upon. Not a Kettery. No other Kettery around. The baby alone. A transient. Well, babycakes, aren't we all? Infant Kettery was probably conceived in the East only to be born here during the westward expansion. Maybe too soon, what with all that bouncing in a creaky wagon. An unsustainable burden. Weak. Needy. The mother forced to make a harsh assessment of time and resources needed to cross the Divide before winter, and decided, no. No. The survival of the family unit had to be considered. Other families were giving each other the eye. Her husband turned his back and looked up at the stars. All their energy had to be directed to the difficult crossing, where, on the other side, land awaited. Pulled by a sweating team of oxen, they were eager to start claiming it, devouring existing nations in their path, replacing the wild with crops. The milk never flowed. The infant cried, whimpered, then went silent. Digging took no time at all. Prayers were swift, then the family continued their migration, moving up and on, climbing the Divide, leaving a small, still bundle in the ground behind them. No looking back. No looking inwards. There was only looking ahead. This was America. The future beckoned.

He pulled his bottle out of his pocket, emptied it and closed his eyes. Wet with tears. He heard the flapping of powerful wing-beats pass overhead and looked up. Nothing.

He turned to the weaver. "Why?" he asked. "This grieving, this constant grieving. Why?"

No response. Not a single one of the spider's eight eyes looked his way. It was busy doing its job, mummifying the moth, who was twitching under its tight swaddling of silk, still thinking it had a chance.

Chapter Sixteen

Officer Sokos slowed down as she drove past Columbia Cemetery on her way to the station and saw someone sitting up against a gravestone. She stopped the cruiser to have a look. For what were supposed to be peaceful places, cemeteries were hotbeds of illegal activity—the usual underage drinking and sex, legal-age drinking and sex, pagan rituals, grave defacement, and public defecation. This was the closest cemetery to town, so it had more problems than most. And there he was. Lester. Crying, of all things. She'd never seen him do that before, and wondered if he was visiting a grave of someone he knew, or just on a jag. She pulled her cruiser over and got out to check on him.

"Lester Blake," she said. "What are you doing here?"

He coughed and wiped his face with his sleeve. "I'm fighting gravity as I spin around the sun, a temporary collision of two energy waves."

"I don't want you sleeping here," she said. "This is sacred space."

"It's all sacred space, officer." Les waved his hand around. "All of it. Besides, the ancient Greeks called cemeteries the sleeping place, so I'm just following orders."

"Find another place," she said. "Go."

"Are you aware that dreams have become shorter and more fragmentary? Which means they are a cultural as well as neurobiological product?"

"Now."

"I'm going, I'm going." Les stood up with some effort, one hand on a gravestone to steady himself. "I'm mourning the last of my Tito's anyways, so it's time to move on."

Iris turned to go, then paused. Someone was walking down the sidewalk, past her cruiser. The new street person. Oblivious, in a daze. "Who is that?" she asked Les.

He shrugged. "She just sort of showed up. Not sure she's homeless, since no one's seen her sleep anywhere." They both watched her shuffle along, her head down. "I've said hello, did she need anything, and she said no, she had to get home to her baby."

Iris nodded. "Does anyone know her name?"

"You know Hattie? She chased that woman down Pearl the other day and kept shouting Who are you? Who are you? You know how Hattie can be. The woman started crying and said Mandy. Mandy Newell. Don't know if it's her real name or if she was just trying to shut Hattie up."

"I'll see if I can find anything out about her," Iris said. "See if she needs services, or something."

"Or something," said Les, and they both headed out of the cemetery by two separate exits.

When Iris Sokos got back to the station, she looked up Amanda Newell in the database. A real person, with a real address. A husband, no children. Iris pulled up her driver's license and there she was. The photo showed a vivacious woman with frosted pink lipstick on a mouth slightly parted in a practiced smile. Dark blond hair, freckled face, and heavily mascaraed blue eyes. On the street, she was a tired version of that person, but it was her. She wrote down the address. On her way home she had a few minutes so she swung by for a wellness check. It was a tidy house in a neighbor-hood of tidy homes. Two cars were in the driveway, one red, one white. She knocked on the door, and a tall man answered. He had pale skin and dark hair, wore thick glasses, and was so perilously thin it seemed he swayed.

"Is something wrong?" he asked, panic all over his face. "Is it my wife?"

"Maybe you can tell me if something's wrong," she said. "Is your wife Amanda Newell?"

"Yes, Mandy. I'm Devin Newell."

"Devin, I'm Officer Sokos, and I've seen your wife wandering around town lately. She seems pretty out of it. I wanted to make sure she has a place to sleep, and that she's alright."

"She has a home," he said. "This one. But she's not around much these days. I was just going out to look for her. We've—she's had a terrible loss," he said. "She's taking it hard."

"She mentioned a baby. Is there a baby in this household?"

He looked away and shook his head. She waited to see if he wanted to talk more about that, but no. She guessed there'd been a stillborn, maybe a miscarriage or failed IVF. Some event to plum-met the hormones into oblivion. She remembered that depression all too well, both hers and Carol's in their efforts to create their family, taking turns being the designated carrier. There was so much heartache surrounding that, so many miscarriages or failed implantations. It was nearly unbearable. They almost gave up until a zygote finally took hold in Carol, and then a couple of years later in Iris. It was a process that bordered on insanity. She took a few brochures out of her pocket and handed them to him. "Sounds like she could use a little therapy. Here are some agencies in town that might be able to help."

He shook his head. "There's no helping her right now," he said, but he took them. "She says she doesn't need therapy, she's just tired."

"I'd be tired too, if I walked all day long," said Iris.

Devin pulled a business card out of his wallet and gave it to Iris. "Here, take my cell phone number if you need to reach me. I work downtown at the computer store, and I can come and collect her if she's a problem. Her old workplace friends stop in now and again to see if she's okay, but everyone's so busy. I can't afford to hire someone to watch her every minute I'm not here."

Devin looked at his feet and Iris was quiet. Mental health issues were tough on families. There was so little help for them.

"Don't hesitate to call the station if there's anything we can do," she said.

"Thank you. But I'm hoping she'll snap out of this and get better on her own. Doesn't that happen?"

Iris shrugged. The assumption was that material things like computers needed attention and repair, but that people could take care of themselves.

"Time heals," she said, with no conviction whatsoever. From what she saw on the streets, time usually made things worse.

Chapter Seventeen

Shelley turned into Arroyo Circle, driving her own car again. While her credit card still worked, she had a tow company bring it to a repair shop and had the ash-filled filter replaced. She needed a car to look for a job, and she hoped that job came along soon. As she pulled into her driveway, she passed Les taking a long package out of her mailbox. She should have known. He'd probably been stealing from her for ages. Not that she could think of anything missing. She'd never had to track a package meant for her, although she did it all the time for Mimi, who became unstable at the teeniest suggestion that a package might be late, or, God forbid, misdelivered. Even now, her own heartbeat rose at the thought. Why was that?

Shelley parked and got out to stare at Les. He reached back into the mailbox and pulled out a few bills and flyers. "Here," he said. "These are yours."

"I know they're mine, they're in my mailbox," she said as she took the bundle from him. "And I'm guessing that's mine too," gesturing at the package.

"Nah, that would be a bad guess. This is mine."

"Yours? In my mailbox?"

"There's no mailbox in the creek, is there?" He waved his arm in the general direction. "My address is the world, but I gave an old friend more of an address than that so she can mail me smokes once in a while."

"Cigarettes?"

"Won't send me money, because she knows I'll spend it on Tito's. But she doesn't know that smokes are currency on the street, like in prison. The thing is, I have no release date and slim chance of parole." When he laughed, a small twig fell from his head.

"How long has this been going on?"

"Long as I've been living along the creek." His face darkened as he seemed to work his memory, and then shook it off. "You've been dependably gone, including most Saturdays. Some Sundays. But even when you were home, you seemed pretty oblivious to your surroundings."

She looked at her house and struggled to keep from tearing up. "I guess I'm going to find out everything that's been going on around here now," she said. "I'm not sure when I'll be working again. I've just come from the unemployment office trying to straighten things out. There's some sort of screw up with my account so I don't even know when I'll start collecting." She looked down at the mail in her hand, as if there might be some relief there. But no. "Great. A bill from Frank, Mimi's attorney. He didn't waste any time directing it back to me. Bastard."

She stood looking at the envelope, and suddenly there were tears running down her face. Soon she'd be peeing herself in public if she didn't get better control over herself. Les tore open his package and held out a Marlboro. "Here," he said. "Brand new."

She wiped her face and felt her skin hanging loose about the jaw. "I don't smoke."

"It's not too late to start."

"Mimi said she'd pay my lawyer's fees because I was family. Just like family."

"If it's any comfort, our base family consists of a bacteria-like microorganism that appeared in the seas about four billion years ago." He put the unlit cigarette in his mouth, tucked the carton of cigarettes somewhere on the inside of his baggy blue jacket, and headed for his path behind the house.

Shelley watched him disappear into the brush and listened as he stumbled down the steep path to where he camped out. Back to his people. Where were hers? She had a house, but he had a community. If she wasn't able to find another job soon, she didn't even have family to fall back on. She only had Henry, her younger brother back in Wisconsin she hadn't seen in years, with grown children who barely knew who she was. She'd made friends over the years, but there was lots of churn, Boulder being a somewhat transient place. Some were work buddies who'd fallen away with every job, others were mutual friends from her marriage, gone with the wedding ring. Then there were those who had arrived in Boulder when she did, and had bonded over drinks at Potter's, united in their common search for exciting lives. Their friendships had formed when their possibilities were endless, and any reminder of those days made them all too sad. They rarely saw one another now.

But Betty-Ann was still a pal. Shelley didn't know how she would have gotten through the first night without her, but she was in no position to help, financially or otherwise. She had a grandchild now, a darling boy who kept her preoccupied with babysitting when she wasn't working. In truth, for the past few years Shelley thought of Mimi as both friend and family. What a hoot. She'd been so involved in Mimi's life she wasn't taking care of her own. She was a community of one.

She went into the house and tossed all the bills on the coffee table. Spree meowed. He no longer needed his little rubber booties, but she still had to give him expensive meds. She closed the curtains, and the afternoon light filtered through the fabric, shimmering, like she was standing in water. The days were getting shorter faster and she felt it keenly. Time was closing in on her. She measured out Spree's pills and crushed them in the kibble bowl. He brushed up against her legs as she worked. It was startling to have another living thing in the house, but she had to admit he was some comfort after a difficult day. She and the fire inspector had finally connected. She'd been trying to put him off, but then he just showed up at the door that morning. She had to go through a blow-by-blow of what happened the day of the fire, Mimi's texts, the phone calls, the camera footage of the recycled boxes catching fire. She couldn't control her shaking as she recalled the events.

"That was some massive pile of cardboard outside where it started," the inspector said.

"Yes. Recycling didn't come to collect it the week before. I don't know why."

"They didn't come because the Crutchfield's didn't pay the bill. Same with the monitoring service. Neighbors called the fire in, not the service. That might have cost them their lives," he said.

He went on to ask a lot of questions about the hoarding. Had Shelley tried to stop it? No. Had she ever talked to her employers about the obvious dangers? No. Had she thought of reaching out for help? She shook her head, no.

"I'm sure you did your best," he said, and then stood up to leave with a few mumbled words of sympathy. "If you ever find yourself in that situation again, please reach out before it becomes a danger."

Shelley sat there for a long while. She had not done her best. She had done nothing. Mimi ordered the shit, but it was Shelley who whisked the evidence away. Stacking the flattened shipping boxes was her way of keeping order. Some order. Now she was unemployed with no savings. She had to scramble to pay bills until unemployment kicked in. Maybe she could borrow against her pension. She wondered if there was anyone still working at Jeremy's company to ask about that. Along with the bill from Frank, there was a notice that her health insurance through his company was canceled too. She hoped Colorado had some form of Obamacare. One more thing to track down. More phone calls, more hours online.

"It is the transitions of life that are the most dangerous," her father had said, as he closed the door behind him forever. "They leave us exposed and vulnerable."

Or they just leave us, thought Shelley, as her nine-year-old self watched him drive away. After he left, she and her mother and brother never had a real home again. Her mother, who worked sporadically as a seamstress, could no longer afford the house and lost it. "Home isn't always a place," she'd said, as she packed up their things. The three of them slept on a lot of sofas, her mother's friends trying to be kind, trying to hide their impatience. Then came subsidized housing, food stamps, and government cheese. It never seemed to bother her mother, who actually seemed lighter after he was gone, in spite of everything, but Shelley and her brother never really got over it.

She couldn't go back to that. But she couldn't get a reverse mortgage for a few more years, and a home equity loan was out of the question until she paid off the one for a new roof. And unlike the roof, that loan would last forever. She could sell her house, but then what? She could never buy back into Boulder again. She would have to admit defeat. Admit she'd failed at life and move.

No. Not without a fight. She'd get on the computer to search for health insurance, jobs, and other resources to get her through this rough patch. Keeping her phone was critical on so many levels. She couldn't even apply for a job without a working phone number. Her cable bill was already late. Nevermind TV, how could she job search without the internet? How long before the electricity got turned off?

"Our world is falling apart at the seams, Spree. We'd better get on it."

She put a bowl of medicated kibble down on the floor and went to look for her laptop in the living room, but when she saw the sofa she threw herself down on it, overcome with fatigue and despair and unshed tears. She closed her eyes, and then she closed her mind.

Book Two

April, 2020

Chapter Eighteen

It was dusk. Shelley stood behind the garden shed and watched the lights come on in her house. The curtains were open and she thought of her heating bill. Thanks to Airbnb, the house was rented out that week by the Watsons, a couple from Durango hoping to visit a sick and elderly parent in a Boulder nursing home. Shelley knew that was impossible. They'd only be allowed to stand outside a window and wave, but that would have to be enough. Like this would have to be enough. Shelley watched as the woman sat down at the kitchen table, Shelley's table, and put her head on her folded arms. The husband came in and looked at his wife, then went to the refrigerator, took out a beer and went into the living room. She saw the man sit on her sofa and turn on the nightly news. The light from the screen flickered through the room, and she felt like she was watching her life as if it were on TV. And it was all bad news.

"What's up?"

She yelped and nearly fell backwards, but it was just Les, his old disheveled self, a red wool cap pulled down nearly over his eyes, grinning his random-toothed smile. "Damn you, Les! Are you trying to kill me?" She looked at the house. No one stirred. She lowered her voice. "I'll get a bad review if they hear someone out here."

"Why aren't you up in the garage?"

"Spree. I wanted to top off his water and kibble. I'm heading up to Mimi's now."

The only thing left standing on Mimi's property was the free-standing garage, and she had the key. It was a four-car garage that never had room for a car until now, her old Accord. She could no longer afford to insure it, but it made a nice bed on rental nights. The burnt-out shell of the house had long ago been bulldozed and the site cleared by the board of health, leaving the sad and ravaged property to wait on a complicated probate, with a ferocious fight among Jeremy's creditors scratching for loose coin. For months after the fire she was hounded by estate lawyers wanting to know about accounts and passwords, along with criminal lawyers trying to determine if she knew anything about the fraud. Mimi had protected her by not telling her anything more important than a PIN code, so she wasn't caught trying to hide anything. She could only express shock that there was so much to hide. She'd always thought Mimi's hoarding was the family secret, but it seemed there were so many other secrets they put the hoarding to shame.

Lawyers had come soon after the fire and ransacked the dense piles of consumer goods in the garage, and walked away without finding anything of value and without changing the lock. The neighbors knew her so didn't question that Shelley had been emptying it of mountains of shelf-stable food and paper products all through the fall, assuming she was still working for the family in some capacity. Soft things, like clothes and bedding, had reeked of smoke, so Les handed that stuff out to the creek dwellers. Everything else got aired out, then sold at tag sales at her own house throughout the fall, cartons and cartons of it, still using her trusty box cutter to slice through the day. It was a pity that the bales of toilet paper had been kept in the basement of Mimi's house and not the garage. What a fortune Shelley could make with them now, with toilet paper impossible to find at the stores at any price. But she refused to think about what might have been. That road was a dead end. After the fire and the deaths and the public shame of being associated with Mimi and Jeremy, she'd spent long days in sorrow and rage but those emotions were luxuries she'd had to put aside in order to survive. She might not have a mortgage thanks to Keith's guilty generosity in the divorce, but she still had house insurance, a home equity payment, water bills, gas, electricity, and taxes. Plus, she had to keep up with internet and phone service, since that's what made Airbnb possible. It was work just to hike up to Mimi's, using both bus and legs, but she was grateful to have somewhere safe to go, protected from the elements and other humans.

"It's late," said Les. "Plenty of room down at the creek."

She opened her mouth to ask if he was nuts, then decided it was a subject best left untouched. "Thanks, but I like the garage."

"Suit yourself," he said. "Consider a hot meal at the Grille tomorrow?"

The Purple Grille was the cult-owned restaurant at the far end of Pearl. The cult believed that in order for Jesus' second coming to occur, they must raise 144,000 perfect male virgins, who would be killed around the year 2070. It was hard to believe they got any recruits with that come-on, but hunger and poverty was a strong preacher. You could dine for free if you were willing to read their religious brochures. The Grille was open around the clock on weekdays, making it a popular spot with college students and the homeless, particularly runaway teens, a cult's low-hanging fruit. She'd heard they moved tables outside to serve customers, in violation of the stay-at-home order, an order which did not address how you stayed at home if you didn't have a home. Or money. She was never eligible for unemployment benefits. In spite of the fact that she had paycheck receipts showing all sorts of deductions,

Jeremy had long ago stopped paying in. She'd be golden right now if she'd gotten unemployment because the feds were supplementing benefits, but since hers never came through there was no supplement. Stupid her, she even believed she had a pension. Jeremy told her she did. He's the one who talked her into it. "Think of your future," he'd said when she was hired. Ha. So even though it would have been nice to have had extra cash in her pocket, every week a small percentage of her salary was transferred into some hollow investment arm of his company, the company that went down in flames with his death. It had been a total pyramid scheme and regular investors like herself were just rubble. There was no "recovery," as Frank, Mimi's shark, called it.

Jeremy. She felt her blood pressure rise just thinking about him. And Mimi. Jeremy's sister had been right, it looked like Mimi knew everything from the beginning. It hurt to know how much she knew. According to *The Daily Camera* articles that ran for weeks after the fire, Mimi's inheritance funded the ranch scam to begin with, and it was Mimi who called the shots. Shelley had a vision of her sitting in her messy nest of a bed, shouting "More! More!" like a monstrous fledgling, her mouth always open.

She shook the image out of her head. She had to think of her own needs now.

"Think the Grille's safe?" she asked.

"They don't kidnap people, if that's what you mean," Les said. "Not for nothing, but they're always trying to save me and I'm still here."

"I'll worship salamanders if it gets me a hot meal," said Shelley. "I mean, is it safe with the virus?"

All those early months of spending days at a time away from home, looking for places to hang out, she had avoided the Grille like the plague. But now that the plague was actually here, she couldn't afford the meager scruples she once held. She'd gotten used to not sleeping in her own bed and getting around without a car, but going without food hurt. Les once told her that living with nature was to live with hunger, so it was best to make peace with it. But all that day she'd eaten nothing but a few granola bars, and was not feeling peaceful about it. She could not seem to live on old grapes like he did.

"Eating outside at one of their tables isn't any different than the outdoor eating we do every day."

"True that," she said, already anticipating the taste of real food. She rarely went down to Pearl if she could help it for fear of being seen by anyone she knew, but since everything got shut down, who was there to see her? "Noon, by the buffalo," Les said, raising his hand in a peace sign as he ambled back down to his path.

The "buffalo" was a bronze statue on the mall, not full-sized, but what you might call fun-sized. Les hung out there sometimes because there were benches to stretch out on, but he was bitter about the statue. "We hunt them to near extinction, then plunk a teeny facsimile on a pedestrian mall to evoke the Wild West. Another victim of human imperialism."

She didn't understand half of what he said sometimes, but whatever this imperialism was, she never looked at the buffalo the same way again. She watched Les disappear in the darkness, and listened as he cursed the ice, slipping down the steep slope to his spot. It was considerably warmer the last couple of days, at long last, but it had been a particularly cold and snowy winter. Here it was—the end of April—and big storms still tore through, and flurries still made regular nighttime appearances. Snow patches were everywhere. Sunny days only packed the snow down like rock. Many creek dwellers, especially families, lived in real tents under the overpasses, the recent ban against tents be damned. Others built makeshift lean-to's, but Les slept rough on a flattened appliance box, pulling an old sleeping bag and tarp over him. Sometimes, from the warmth of her kitchen, on those glorious mornings when she could wake up in her own home, she watched

Les climb out of the gully with his face and braid plastered with snow, a black plastic trash bag draped over his shoulders like the cape of a superhero. He waved off any offer to come inside and warm up, but would sometimes accept coffee out on the stoop before he headed into town. The man had a total disregard for his own wellbeing, but it seemed to make him indestructible, practically immortal.

The outdoors was not for her, but neither would she go to a city shelter, a moot point once the pandemic took hold. Her old Accord in Mimi's garage had been her second home since Thanksgiving, when she could no longer afford car insurance and started renting out her house. She couldn't sleep in her car in her own driveway because she'd get one hell of a negative Airbnb review, and she couldn't afford that. The garage had no heat, electricity, or running water, but was still filled with enough stuff to create a fortress of insulation. The garage also insulated her from harassment by both police and street people, but it could not protect her from debt. Last month, just as she was thinking she might have to let Comcast go and use the library's internet to do her business, the pandemic closed the library and with it, free computer access. She went into reverse Buddhism—total worry. Worse than that, when the shelter-at-home order began, Airbnb cancellations followed. That had crushed Shelley. She'd already spent that money in her head, but soon enough her rentals started picking up, to the point that now her house, a single-family in a quiet neighborhood, was more in demand than ever. When the University closed, so had almost all the hotels, and with offices closed and kids at home, parents sometimes rented the house to take turns getting work done. No matter the reason, the Airbnb money was a lifeline and she held on tight, never saying no.

The only trouble was, she had to walk straight up a hill to Mimi's on rental days. It had been a lot easier to get by when she first started listing her house, back when she still had Betty-Ann's sofa at night and she could park her butt in a coffee shop for hours during the day. The pandemic put an end to both. Not only that, it was harder to come by free food. There were food banks where she could, if she wanted to wait in line all day, pick up some groceries, but she had no kitchen on rental days, and there was only so much she could carry home on the bus otherwise. Harvest for Hope only did dinner now, no breakfast, no lunch, no sit down, and nothing until five when, after waiting forever on a line, the volunteers handed out covered containers of tepid chicken thighs, green beans, and macaroni, or some minor variation thereof. What with the snow, places to sit were scarce, so she and Les often ate standing up in the dark and cold.

Spree came running up to her from wherever it was he spent his rental days, and rubbed up against her legs. She'd set up a little cat house for him behind the tool shed, up on a potting table. She picked him up and felt it in her back. The cat was simply enormous with his winter coat. The singed hair had grown in and then some, adding extra fur and fat for his new outdoor life. Shelley wished she could do that, but she could only wear so many coats and sweaters. They rubbed faces and then she put him down so she could feed him. She quietly lifted the latch to the shed and opened the metal can where she kept the kibble. It was a blessing that Mimi's garage had kitty litter and cat food in abundance, enough to last Spree all nine lives. She could not have afforded to keep him otherwise. The vet bills had emptied her pathetic savings. But when she had to vacate her own home for renters, Spree got the boot too. The first time she tossed him outside she thought she'd never see him again, what with the cars and coyotes. Other than the time he flew out of Mimi's house in a ball of smoke, he'd never even been outside except in a carrier to the vet, but he adapted. He learned to fend for himself, just like she did. She left kibble and water for him next to the cat house and hoped for the best. She worried about him—it surprised her, really, how much she worried—but every time she returned home after a rental, there he was, waiting for her in the yard. Renters never mentioned a bothersome cat in the reviews, so it was working. When a renter was there longer than a few days, like right now, she snuck back to her backyard to pour more kibble. She stored the food in a metal tin in the shed, away from scavengers, then took a water bottle out of her bag and poured half of it in a bowl. It was warm enough it might not even freeze by morning.

"Good night, Spree," she whispered. "See you later."

She tip-toed back to the street, with one more wistful look at her house. The man still sat on the sofa watching TV and the woman had not lifted her head from the kitchen table, as if they were frozen in time. By the time she snapped herself out of it, she had to run to catch the Hop. The bus was on a reduced schedule, and it would be a mighty long wait if she missed it. She tightened her mask and joined the few other riders, mostly health care providers and other essential workers off to start their night shifts. The driver had built a plastic wall around him and all the windows were cracked open. In spite of the warm day, it was a cold ride. If nothing else, winter couldn't last forever, although if there was ever a year where it might, this one was it.

A young woman sat across the aisle from her and looked her way, blinking behind her glasses. It was hard telling who was who these days, what with masks, so Shelley just crinkled her eyes as if smiling and gave a little wave, just in case she knew her. The woman pulled her mask down, gave her a crooked smile, then pulled it back up.

"Trudy," said Shelley. "The cart girl."

"Shelley Price," said Trudy. "The kidnapper."

"I did not . . .   "

Trudy laughed. "I was just yanking your chain. What? No car to run me down in?"

"Out of commission. I'm a little out of commission myself."

"That house that burned down, where the people died? You

worked there, right? I read it in *The Camera*. It was exciting to see someone I knew in the news."

"Not so exciting for me," said Shelley. She pondered whether to connect the dots for Trudy. Could Trudy have ever imagined that because Shelley went back to King Soopers to yell at her, that the tragedy happened the way it did? It seemed too ludicrous to put into words. "You know, I honestly didn't see you when my car hit your carts and knocked you down."

"Ancient history," said Trudy, standing up. "I got more to worry about these days. I just did my second shift in twenty-four hours. Instead of gathering carts, I help keep shoppers in line outside. Only so many in at a time. People scream in my face, some won't wear masks, every minute I'm afraid of getting sick. My parents want me to live in the garage so I don't bring the virus into the house and kill them."

"Is it heated?"

"They said they'd plug in some sort of unit."

At least you have a working outlet, thought Shelley. Over the winter she'd experimented with exhausting the car out a window with a dryer vent and duct tape, just to warm the car up a bit before bed, but the car battery conked out early on. Just as well. A neighbor was sure to see the exhaust and call the police. Thankfully she was usually so beat by the end of every endless day, she passed out before she got cold. The bus slowed and Trudy gathered her bags of groceries. "This is my stop. See you around."

"See you," said Shelley. She watched Trudy from the window as the bus pulled away. She couldn't believe how angry she'd once been at that young gal, as if she'd been trying to pass on the bad energy from the police stop. But she'd had no evidence Trudy had called them. It was all in her mind. Les always said everything was only in our minds. She snorted. If only that were true. She stood for her stop, and as the bus pulled up to the curb, she saw the woman she and Les called the Wanderer. Not wearing enough clothes for the weather but at least she kept her face covered. They saw her walking around town with a vacant stare at all hours of the day and night, and couldn't figure out where she slept. Or if she slept. Shelley had seen her sitting down only once, earlier in the winter, on a bench downtown. She was sobbing into an old rag. Shelley sat with her and asked if she needed anything, but the woman just shook her head. "No, I have to get back to the baby."

"Mind if I walk with you?" asked Shelley, thinking this woman was in no shape to care for a baby.

"No, no," the Wanderer said, standing up with a lurch. "I'd better hurry." And with that, she put the balled-up rag in her pocket and walked away, continuing whatever sad journey she was on. She was a woman who walked in darkness, for sure. Shelley wanted to say something to her, but by the time she stepped off the bus, the Wanderer had wandered away. Shelley stood still at the intersection, a place that should've been bustling with students and commuters, letting her brain adjust to the eerie quiet of the road. Gone. Everyone was gone, like they'd been wiped off the planet.

She pulled on her gloves and headed uphill on the empty street, taking culverts and alleys so people didn't see her and start asking questions, or calling the police. She was like Les now, with her very own path.

Chapter Nineteen

As Officer Iris Sokos cruised Baseline, patrolling the streets, she spotted Amanda Newell up ahead. She had a blue flannel cloth pulled up over her mouth as a mask. All winter long, Iris had seen the thin, slightly bowed figure shuffling around town, even now during the lockdown. Ambulatory psychotics, they were called at the police academy, and she'd seen her share. They were not usually homeless, although they rarely went home. They just kept moving to stay ahead of their agitated depression. She supposed that negative energy had to be spent somehow. They were a worry to the police because they often put themselves in harm's way by walking into traffic, or their obliviousness made them easy targets for muggers and rapists.

Iris drove the cruiser past her twice before she decided to stop and talk to her. Amanda had not, as her husband had hoped last fall, snapped out of it and gotten better on her own. If anything, she was worse.

Iris had recently watched Devin pull up to Amanda and call her name to no effect. He'd had to get out of the car and gently lead her back. She got into the passenger seat like an automaton, barely bending her body. She did not look at him. She did not look at anything. He got in the driver's seat and drove away. Sometimes Iris texted Devin with a heads up where he might find Amanda, but he couldn't keep her from going out in the first place. The computer store was considered an essential business, what with everyone working from home, so he had to go to work every day, leaving his wife behind.

Even though Amanda was unlikely to do what she was told, it was now Iris's duty to tell her to return home, that there was a pandemic. There hadn't been much Iris could do about her all winter, since there was no law against walking, but with the health emergency, Amanda had to go inside not just for her safety, but the community's. She was a potential moving vector of disease. Iris pulled up to the curb, but Amanda didn't even pause in stride, so Iris had to get out of the car to follow her on foot. She pulled up her mask and blocked Amanda's way on the sidewalk. The only light came from a distant streetlamp, which gave Amanda a waxy complexion, as if she'd been embalmed.

"Ma'am, how are you this evening?"

Silence. Amanda looked at her feet.

"Do you need a ride home? We'd like to clear the streets."

"I'm walking. Just walking."

"I'm going to have to ask you to head on home now. There's a lockdown and we don't want people about, catching the virus. You're only allowed to go to the supermarket."

Amanda touched the flannel masking her face. There were little fire engines on it, and Iris realized she'd probably lost an infant, not a miscarriage or failed implants like she'd presumed. She spoke, but her voice was empty, even ghostly. "I'm fine. Thank you. I'm just heading back now."

And then she stepped around Iris and kept on going, not walking anywhere near the direction of her house. Iris watched until she turned the next corner and disappeared. Then she stood a moment longer, staring at the empty space.

Iris was jolted out of her troubles with an all-hands call coming in from dispatch. She had to go to King Soopers and help keep order in the parking lot. Like most supermarkets, the store had shortened its hours in order to clean and disinfect all the surfaces, but the people outside waiting for their turn would not leave. "Disperse the crowd," the dispatcher said, "and good luck."

Later that night, Iris was at her monitor at the station. King Soopers had been like a war zone, and required a dozen officers or more to restore order. Thankfully, it was not up to her to write the report, which would be long and complicated, but she did have to finish her weekly report for the Homeless Outreach Team before she could go home. CDC guidelines encouraged municipalities to allow encampments during the pandemic and to focus instead on access to water and restroom facilities. No one wanted the unhoused to disperse and spread the virus. For the first time, her job was to encourage street people to stay where they were, locking down instead of locking up. As she filled out a request for more porta-potties and sanitizing stations, she wondered what to do about Amanda Newell, who had a home but wouldn't stay in it.

She Googled her name, hoping to discover the secret of keeping her home. Maybe there was a relative besides the husband who could help. A page of real estate links popped up, all homes Amanda had once brokered. A Realtor. Iris scrolled down the page and found a link to an obituary. Iris's heart sank. An infant. They had lost a three-month-old baby. Freddie. Could there be anything worse? No wonder she walked the streets in a daze. Sometimes Iris felt like the most rewarding part of her job was knowing she was keeping the city safe for her own kids. She could still feel them as newborns in her arms, warm bundles pressed against her heart. No cause of death was listed in the obit, but there often wasn't for infants. Babies were such fragile creatures they sometimes just up and died. She looked at the date of death.

"Is that coffee ready yet?" asked Officer Rogers, who walked past her towards the break room without looking up from his phone.

Iris stared at the screen. "Fuck off."

"Hey, I was only asking about the coffee. I didn't ask you to make it."

She pulled up the police log for August 8, 2019. The day she stopped Shelley Price for suspicion of putting a baby in the trunk of her car. And there it was. At almost the exact same time Iris was forcing Price to open her trunk under gunpoint, a 911 call had come in about an unresponsive infant. According to the report, Amanda Newell had pulled the car over to the side of the road, less than a mile from King Soopers. Going in a south-easterly direction on Broadway, a straight line from the supermarket to her driveway. Ted Rogers had been the first officer to arrive at the scene, so she went to the break room.

"You got your coffee?" she asked. "Sorry I was so short just now. Pandemic nerves, I guess."

"We're all a little on edge these days," he said. "Can I pour you some?"

"No thanks, it's almost the end of my shift. I wanted to ask you something though, about the death of an infant last August, over on Broadway. In a car. I just came across the obit and looked up the report. You were the first officer to arrive. Remember anything?"

"Who could forget?" He shook his head. "Christ. Heartbreaking. The mom must've realized something was wrong and pulled over. We could barely pry the kid from her arms. There was nothing the EMTs could do."

"Where was the car seat?"

"The car seat?" Rogers looked around as if the answer was to be found in the break room sink. "On the sidewalk, I think. It was a while ago."

Iris felt moisture rise on her forehead and thought she might be sick. "She took the whole seat out to check on the baby?"

"Who knows?" He shrugged. "She wasn't in her right mind. She's still not. I see her wandering around town at all sorts of hours. Poor soul."

Iris went back to the computer and tracked down the dashboard camera data in the cruiser Rogers used that day. Amanda's trunk was open when Rogers pulled up behind her car. Amanda was on the sidewalk, keening back and forth on her knees with a near-naked baby in her arms.

Iris wanted to reach out and grab the infant from her and hold it tight. But it was too late. When she stood up she felt her stomach in her throat, and ran to the restroom to throw up. She took a minute to splash her face with water. When she got back to her computer, she called the coroner's office. Closed until Monday. Just as well. She had to get home. Carol was at her wits' end with the girls underfoot all the time, having to oversee Tatiana's schoolwork and Sharee's solitary playtime, while trying to do her own job at the bank remotely. The girls were out of sorts as well. They missed their friends. They wanted their world back.

Chapter Twenty

"Slow down," Shelley said to Les, who, as always, walked in a sort of shackled lunge that covered ground fast. "It's hard to breathe with this mask. And my back hurts."

"Not for nothing, backs hurt when you sleep curled up in a car. Your body cries out to be flat on the earth."

"The floor in the garage is scary," she said. "Besides, my back has been in pain for years. I've lugged a lot of groceries and boxes in my time."

"Sleep outdoors. Breathe the healing powers of the planet right into your spine. Let the good earth massage those discs."

"I'm not sleeping outside."

"Good weather," he said.

"Nights are cold." Shelley groaned. "Just slow down." And as she was saying it, she bumped into his back when he suddenly stopped. One of his street buddies ambled over, forearms raised like a prairie dog. Shelley nodded politely and inched herself a few feet away as if she were suddenly captivated by the light hitting the mountains. She was friendly, but not friends with any of the Pearl or creek crowd. Many had mental illnesses, like Hattie, who was aggressively curious and a shouter to boot. Others had addictions which made them unpredictable and scary, but the ones who made her really uncomfortable were regular people, just like her. She did not like to think of herself as homeless, or unhoused, as the city called it. She had a house, she just couldn't use it all the time because she needed the money in order to keep it. What was that called? An oxymoron? A dichotomy? Les would know. He had a word for everything, it seemed. She couldn't keep track of what was in that scraggy head of his. Anyway, she felt hers was just a temporary situation, although she had a sneaky suspicion the others once thought that too. She kept her distance, and now with the pandemic it didn't even seem rude.

Her stomach growled. She turned to catch Les's eye to get a move on so she could behold some of that cult food, but he was deep in talk with his friend who seemed to be acting out every word he spoke under his mask, gesturing with both hands and jumping up on one foot. It was not a conversation that seemed to be ending any time soon. Les had just come from Hazel's, the liquor store, an essential service, so he was in no rush. He had what he wanted. She looked longingly at the restaurants, and wished she had the cash to order anywhere she wanted, then bring it to a warm, dry place to sit down and eat it. All it would take was money.

Even now, in this time of fear and foreboding, the human parade was out shopping. Up and down Pearl, masked shoppers waited in six-foot-spaced lines to pick up takeout or curbside necessities from the few restaurants and stores allowed to stay open. That fall, when she was actively job searching, she had marveled that she could not get work behind one of those counters, considering how much of her time with Mimi had been spent in front of them. The problem was not so much skills, as references. Hers were dead. Worse, prospective employers Googled her name and found out she was Mimi's house manager. Her name often appeared in the many *Daily Camera* articles about wildfires and climate change, always mentioning the house and lives lost, often casting blame on Mimi, and soon enough, disgrace on Jeremy when his company's dissolution came to light. "Shelley Price, their house manager, could not be reached for comment," was the constant refrain, implicating her in the hoarding. Once she saw it in writing, who could not think so? A house manager who let the house fill up to the rafters with flammable crap, and then created cardboard box pyres outside of it? Not to mention the King Soopers incident so easily found in police and court notes. Now she had to wait until the fire and her name faded from electronic memory. Perhaps when things returned to anything like normal and there were jobs to be had, she could start applying for one again. In the meantime there was nothing to be done but rent her house out when she could, and sleep in Mimi's garage.

She closed her eyes and enjoyed the warmth of sunlight on her face. Spring was coming. Life would be easier. She was amazed that she'd survived the brutal winter. Truly amazed. Even proud of herself. Just as she was drifting off to something near contentment, a wind whistled down from the canyon and onto Pearl like a slap on her face. That'll teach her to relax her guard. When she raised her hands to pull up her hood her eyes fell onto a familiar face standing a few feet away, staring right at her. Wayne, her old boyfriend. She could tell right away, even with a mask, it was Wayne.

"Shelley?" he said.

Her thoughts turned to what she was wearing. It was a long time since she checked in with her looks. She felt somber and haggard, and not for the first time, glad to be wearing a mask. Her cheerless black coat was dingy from sleeping in the car, and her boots were scuffed and salt-stained. She almost turned away, but it was too late. She adjusted her mask as he stepped towards her.

"Hi, Wayne, how are you? Alice, good to see you."

Alice, his wife, nodded at her with no recognition. Why would she remember a husband's old girlfriend she'd met once at her wedding years before? "I'll go pick up our order," Alice said, and she walked over to get in the line for the West End Tavern. Shelley remembered their glazed meatloaf and her mouth watered.

"See you in a minute honey," Wayne said to Alice who gave them both a little wave goodbye. "Shelley, I'm so sorry about the house. Shit. Damn lucky you weren't in it. Poor Mimi."

"I'm lucky alright."

"Where're you working now?"

"I'm not," Shelley said, having no energy to lie. And why? It seemed that all but medical workers and grocery baggers were out of a job these days.

At that moment Les sidled up to Shelley, beaming. "Look, someone just handed me this five dollar bill." He brought with him a fog of alcohol and tobacco with a touch of grapes past their prime. She'd gotten used to him over the past few months, but she saw him now through Wayne's eyes. A weathered man with a yellowish cast to his skin and tremors to his hands, wearing an old dog's bed of a coat that clinked and sloshed from the bottles within. He wore a dirty bandana over his mouth like a bank robber.

A muscle twitched at Wayne's temple. "Are you okay?" he asked Shelley in a lowered voice. He reached his hand into his pocket. "Do you need money?"

She took a step back, almost tripping on herself. "Oh no. No no. I'm good, really." She looked at Les, who was busy going through his coat pockets. She considered how she might explain him to Wayne, but nothing came to her. There was no explanation for why Les was by her side, except to say he's the one who showed up. Lack of money had eventually created a gulf between her and her friends, even Betty-Ann, who'd been so supportive for the weeks after the fire. But as soon as Shelley started to rent out her house and needed to crash at Betty-Ann's once in a while, her old pal receded farther and farther into her own life until, with the lockdown, she disappeared altogether. "It's been good to see you, Wayne. But I've got to run."

"I'll keep an ear out if anything comes up," said Wayne. "You know how I get around." She made a wry smile under her mask and they said goodbye.

Shelley turned abruptly to head down the western end of the street, with Les at her heels. Her back throbbed and she began to limp, but she could not slow down. She could sense Wayne still standing there looking at her, wondering. She wondered herself. What was it about her that she had dumped such a nice man, one ready to settle down? Was she okay, as he so sweetly asked? She certainly didn't look it. She was as disheveled as a mop and was hanging out with a street person. She was—depending on how you defined one—a street person herself. Yet it wasn't so long ago she rejected Wayne because she didn't want to be with someone who snaked toilets. For real? It was like she'd been looking for ways to sabotage her love life. Her mother once mused out loud whether she chose men with a little glitch on purpose, so that if a relationship failed, she wouldn't have herself to blame.

"Old boyfriend?" Les asked.

"How'd you guess?"

"I thought I remembered seeing him around a while ago."

She stopped and looked at him. "That was years ago. You were living down in the creek even then?"

He nodded. "Sure. It's been a long time since I took a smoke break at the lab and never returned."

She started walking again, slowly this time. "Were you using the path behind my house?"

"I was."

"You'd think I'd notice some man walking through my yard."

"You'd think." He took a Tito's out of his pocket and drank it from under his bandana.

Had she been so wrapped up in Mimi's life she couldn't see her

own? They walked the rest of the way in silence. She was silent anyway. Les was using his empty sip as a whistle.

"Where did you live before the creek?" she asked.

"A house. Up in the canyon."

"Really? What happened to it?"

"Don't know. Maybe my wife sold it. Maybe she's still there with
the kid."

"Wife? Kid?"

"It was pretty crowded."

"You just left them?"

"As Frank Zappa said, without deviation from the norm, progress is not possible."

"Which means . . . ?"

"I met her at NOAA. She's a dust scientist. The boy with his
head in the clouds and the girl with her nose in the dirt found one
another. Somehow we even managed to have a kid, but the sound
of the baby crying tore out my heart. I heard myself cry. I saw
myself in the crib. When the baby became a toddler we horrified
one another. It was time to go."

"You left them?"

Les nodded without looking at her. "It was the safest thing to
do."

"What does that mean?" She couldn't imagine abandoning
a child. And then with a flush of sorrow, she realized she could
imagine it all too well. She had been that child.

Les opened a fresh Tito's. "It means that emotions like love
evolved so animals would fight for the survival of their family.
Fight or flight."

"Les, try to make sense. Have you seen him since?"

"Not in the traditional sense, no."

"I'll bet he wants to see you."

"Nah. But it's okay. I left an empty space for him to fill with the
compassionate acceptance of life's karma."

"Acceptance is not forgiveness," said Shelley. "My father left when I was young and I still don't forgive him. I don't even accept it." She had long ago trained herself not to think about that pain. After he left she had to make believe it didn't happen, that it was all okay, for her sake and her mother's. But it wasn't okay. It was just this big, ugly loss that followed her everywhere. It had even followed her to Boulder.

Les shrugged. "It's all part of the soup. Too late to take the onions out now."

"It's just sad," said Shelley, and she felt for the whole lot of them, herself included. "Maybe someday you'll find one another."

Les finished his sip and put the empty bottle in a pocket. It was his second, maybe even third, since they met at the bronze buffalo. Who knew how many before that?

"But it's no excuse for drinking so much," she said. "I worry sometimes."

He laughed. "I have to drink a lot. I'm an alcoholic."

Shelley hardly knew what to say to that, but they were at the end of Pearl anyway. They stood in front of the Purple Grille and looked into the restaurant through the glass door. Exposed beams, macrame, painted birds on the wall, brick floor. Booths made from reclaimed wood. Bushel basket lights.

"Still game?" Les asked.

"Game and hungry. Bring on the cult lectures."

"Purple Grille's not as bad as some cults, like the one in the White House right now. They both know that the human response to threats is predictable enough to be exploited."

Shelley had often listened to Les rant about how personal problems like childcare and homelessness were political problems, and yet as far as she knew, he wasn't even registered to vote. So, so much for that. They sat at a folding table farthest from any foot traffic, and Shelley wrapped her coat around her. The sun had moved behind the building, putting them into cold shade. A

Naropa monk passed by in his orange robes and matching orange mask.

"Why can't monks vacuum in corners?" asked Shelley.

"Because they have no attachments," said Les.

"Damn. You've heard that one."

"I told it to you."

"It's official then. I'm finally losing my mind."

"Minds are no great loss," said Les. "I should know."

An older woman in a loving-hands-at-home raw wool sweater came out to wait on them. She had a long gray braid down her back just like Les's, but neater, looking like it was spun from the same animal her sweater came from. Shelley had read that the cult members worked at the restaurant and lived on a farm at the edge of town, and this woman looked like she'd just come in from the fields. "Glad to see you hardy folks today," she said, and handed Shelley a menu. "You're new here."

"Hanna, this is Shelley."

"Les and I are old friends," said Hanna, with a wink to Les. They might have failed to convert him so far, but he brought in fresh meat, like Shelley. The menu was illustrated with lots of whimsy and a 60s vibe. "We serve the fruit of the Spirit," it read. "Why not ask?"

"A Reuben, please," said Shelley, deciding to pass on the fruit of the spirit.

"Broccoli soup for you Les?" Hanna asked. She obviously knew him well enough to know his preferences, and that soup was something he couldn't carry around in a pocket.

"Indeed."

"I'm guessing that you'd like a couple of our brochures while you wait," Hanna said, placing the material directly in front of Shelley.

"Thank you," said Shelley, who picked them up with exaggerated interest, to make sure the woman knew she intended to eat free.

Hanna smiled at her. "If Jesus were here today, you just know he'd be out on the street with you," she said, before disappearing inside.

"They use the old 'Jesus as a counterculture hero' ruse," said Les. "Then again, they also believe in a Lake of Fire for the wicked."

"Nice." Shelley paged through the brochure. It was the usual cult promises of a new life, a new you. The past erased with a prayer. Same old, same old. She looked up at Les. "She wasn't wearing a mask."

"Nah. They don't believe in protecting themselves. Hanna says if you get sick it's because God is punishing you for being evil."

"What about protecting us? Shouldn't we be worried?" She burrowed through her bag for hand sanitizer.

"The members say suffering is like sunshine to a plant," he said.

"Too much sunshine can kill a plant." Her bag, in which she carried most of her life while on the street, was stuffed with an extra pair of underpants, a spare glove, pens, a notebook filled with lists, two pairs of 2X reader glasses, one missing an arm, a half-filled plastic water bottle, a nylon bag that folded up into the size of her fist, a nearly empty wallet, her precious phone, used tissues, sugar packets, sticky pennies, and finally, a Ziploc baggie of wipes. She used to carry her old box cutter around in her bag, the one that Mimi gave her, but one day she took it out and slipped it in her jeans pocket, just in case.

She fidgeted in her seat. She had to pee, but like hot meals, bathrooms had become impossible to find during the pandemic. The public toilets on Pearl were closed. She had a five-gallon bucket up at the garage which she emptied into the sewer grate every morning, but once she was in town, there were only a couple of overflowing porta-potties set up outside of the food pantry, at the other, distant, end of the mall.

"You can use the bathroom here," said Les. "They don't mind."

"I don't have to go," she said, crossing her legs and looking at the restaurant where inside lay a real flushing toilet and sink. She imagined the sweetness of warm, soapy water flowing over her hands and between her fingers, a quick touch-up under the arms and crotch. She wondered how long the virus could live in the air. What were the chances that anyone in the cult was already carrying it? They were pretty isolated. If anything, she was more of a danger to them than the other way around.

"Go empty your bladder," said Les. "Eat in peace. I'm going to use the facilities myself before we go."

She tightened her mask and braved the inside of the restaurant, walking past a bunch of unmasked workers standing around and smiling at her. But when Shelley entered the bathroom and locked the door behind her, arranging herself on the sparkling clean toilet like a queen, she flushed her worries away. Her visit was as magnificent as she'd imagined. At the sink she washed and washed with that warm running water until her skin wrinkled. Was it safe? Safer than the porta-potties, with their open craters of crap. She turned off the taps when she smelled food from the kitchen, and hunger drove her back outside. Again, she had to pass through a gauntlet of smiling, unmasked workers, stacking dishes, and when she returned to the table she was totally refreshed but somewhat worried. What if the virus could live on a plate?

Just as she was reconsidering whether the Covid risk was worth a free meal, the free meal arrived. A woman with a galaxy of freckles across her unmasked nose came out of the restaurant with a plate in each hand. Shelley recognized her. The Wanderer. She and Les gave each other a look. She wondered if she lived with the others at the farm, or if she just showed up here to work in exchange for food, or what? She sure didn't look saved. Her face was blank, as if she'd left her soul in some dirty puddle on the street. Shelley tried to make eye contact with her but the woman kept her eyes down. Poor thing. Shelley saw that blue rag of hers in her cardigan pocket as she leaned over and put a steaming bowl in front of Les and a loaded plate in front of her.

"Oh," Shelley gasped at the sight of the Reuben with orange cheese and creamy dressing oozing from the grilled slices of rye. And fries! Dear god, real French fries. She lowered her mask and picked up a fry still hot to the touch, and when she bit into it, exposing the soft steaming potato inside of the best salty crust ever, she thought she might just be in heaven.

Chapter Twenty-One

"Sudden Infant Death Syndrome," the coroner said when Officer Iris Sokos called him early on Monday. She would have liked to be in the office with him, but everything had to be done by phone or Zoom these days. It took him a minute to pull up the autopsy report. "No substances in the system," he said. "No heart valve problems or lung defects. Just one of those things. Babies die, even the ones that seem healthy. Nature's cruel that way. The county had eight infant deaths last year."

"What about heat? Did the EMTs get the baby's temperature reading?"

There was a pause. "If they did, they didn't write it down."

"How long would a baby that size last in a hot car?" She could not bring herself to say the words "hot trunk."

"Hyperthermia? Do you think the mother left the baby in the car while shopping?"

"No. It was just so hot that day. Lots of smoke in the air too. A bad combo for little lungs."

"If it was that hot, if the AC didn't work, for instance, and all the windows were closed, the mother would have passed out too. Not to say that hyperthermia isn't tough to determine after the fact."

"What about lack of oxygen?"

"That's what SIDS is. The baby stops breathing. Researchers think they get suffocated with baby blankets but I doubt there were any on him that day. There's a follow-up report attached here from the Public Health nurse. Says she visited the child's home. Clean, functioning, no indication of neglect. The parents distraught, of course. No findings. What are you thinking?"

"Distraught isn't the word for the mother. She's out on the street all day, and I'm trying to convince her to stay home. Just looking for more information."

"The loss of a child is a huge shock," he said. "Good luck."

Iris hung up and felt the weight of an infant in her arms. Then she pulled herself together and drove to King Soopers to find the manager. She wished she'd never gone to Amanda's Facebook page. It made her feel like she knew her. There were years of posts, starting with Amanda's college days at the University, her graduation, followed by her marriage to Devin. Posts of her honeymoon in Hawaii, their first apartment. The day she got her Realtor's license. Her first sale. Their new house. Her pregnancy. Freddie's joyous arrival, followed by weeks of Freddie pictures, adorable, loving baby pictures—naked, clothed, sleeping, crying, smiling. Then, just like that, maternity leave was over, and she had to get back to work. Iris remembered that pain, like a punch in the gut, of having to return to duty and leave her baby at daycare. Amanda's last hurried post was excruciating. She was showing her first house since Freddie was born, and she was both nervous and excited, and didn't know how she'd do it, but she would! She had to run out for some groceries first, find time to take a shower, maybe even dry her hair. Bonus points for putting on makeup! She'd leave Freddie with Devin when he came home from work early, and off she'd go. Wish her luck!

Iris could feel the underlying panic. She was one of the few women on the force, and after maternity leave was over, she struggled not to show the strain of motherhood. Even now, she could feel the sheer exhaustion of those days in her bones, with the brain fog of relentless worry. She remembered more than once looking for an alley to park so she could grab a catnap at the cruiser wheel. Every shift, she'd pull herself together after being up all night with a baby, then two years later up all night with a baby and a toddler. She'd report for duty half a wreck, but she'd report if it killed her. She did not want the men to make excuses for her.

"I'd like to have a look at some surveillance tape," she said to the manager, Dave, when she found his office. "The day Shelley Price backed her car into the carts and knocked your employee to the ground. Last summer. August 8th."

"Has Trudy decided to press charges against her after all?" he asked, ushering her into his empty office.

"Actually, it's in case Shelley decides to press charges against us," Iris said, and forced a laugh, like the possibility was so absurd. "I want evidence to show how easy it was for anyone to mistake a yellow tub of kitty litter for a baby carrier."

"It must have been scary for her," said Dave, not laughing. "Stopped for nothing. Surrounded by cops with guns. Good thing she's white and a woman. If it had been me, I would have been shot dead."

"That's not true," said Iris, and he gave her a look above his mask that stopped her cold. It was true. If a black man had been in that driver's seat and not Shelley Price, that stop could have gone wrong in so many different ways. Dave had gone back to scrolling, and she was relieved he had no interest in pressing his point.

"Okay, here we are," he said. "The system doesn't usually save footage past ninety days, but I archived that day in case Trudy needed it for court. But it's a little hazy. There was a lot of ash in the air what with the fires. Let's see if it'll go back to where I left it." He clicked a few keys on the computer. "Yep. Here it is."

Iris looked over his shoulder and saw Shelley Price on the

screen, lifting the kitty litter from the cart's child's seat and lowering it in the trunk.

"The child's seat," said Iris, not really meaning to say it out loud.

"Yeah," Dave said, "It's clearly kitty litter when I look at it now, but when someone puts the idea of a baby carrier in your head, and someone's moving a yellow container with a handle from the child's seat, that's what you see. But, better to be safe than sorry, huh? A baby wouldn't have lasted a hot minute in a trunk that day."

"You did everything right," said Iris. "I'd just like to see if there's some way we can prevent this confusion in the future. Mind if I sit with this for a while? You go back to what you were doing."

"Thanks," he said. "I've got to go help with the lines outside, and we're running out of everything. I never thought I'd see the day when the store looked like a battlefield. Damaged groceries and broken glass on the floors. Empty shelves. Staff all quitting or sick. Frightened, angry customers."

"I'll come help make some order on that line as soon as I'm done with this."

She sat down at Dave's computer and rewound the video, going back to when Price pulled her red Accord into an empty spot, then went into the supermarket. In and out with a cartful in under twenty minutes. An efficient little shopper. Iris watched again as Price unloaded the kitty litter into the trunk from the child's seat. From the camera's angle, it would easily be confused with a baby carrier. Then Price squeezed in a few other groceries before pushing the cart away. Her license plate became visible. This must be the point Dave stopped watching and called the police with the plate number. Iris continued watching as the cart missed the corral. When Price went to get it, she almost walked right into a cart being pushed by a woman hurrying by. She wore ear buds, and seemed to be distracted with a phone call. Amanda Newell. A baby carrier was nestled sideways in the child's seat. A yellow carrier.

Iris took a breath and watched Amanda push the cart right to the car next to Price's Accord. Another red car. Amanda opened the back door and grabbed the baby carrier from her cart as if she was going to put it in, then paused. Probably blasted by the heat. Holding the carrier by the handle she walked around the car and popped open the trunk, then opened all the doors, one by one, airing the car out while still talking on the phone. Amanda looked like she was taking care to shield her baby from the sun as she tried to load the groceries into the trunk with one hand, but the first bag ripped. As she was doing this, Shelley Price returned to her car, backed slowly out of her space, then drove away. Amanda put the carrier on the ground, then picked it up again. It must have felt unsafe. Instead, she gently lowered the carrier in the open trunk, where the sleeping baby was shaded by the hood. Then she packed a few grocery bags next to the carrier, still talking on the phone as she worked. She walked away to load more groceries in the back seat, then the front. At some point she stopped talking.

Iris controlled her breathing to slow down her heart. Amanda look so frazzled and overwhelmed. The early years of motherhood were hard, and poor decisions were part of the territory. She once left Tatiana sleeping in a stroller outside a convenience store to grab some formula for Sharee strapped to her front. More than once she drove with the baby carrier not snapped to its base, just sitting on the car floor, because she had no time to move the base from Carol's car to her own. She was always in a hurry. There was so much to do.

As Amanda was getting the last bag out of the cart, it looked like she took another call. She was talking in an agitated manner as she circled the car and slammed all the doors shut. "Don't do it, Amanda," Iris said. "Don't."

But she did. Without looking, Amanda slammed the trunk closed with one hand and got in the driver's seat and drove off. With the baby in the trunk.

Iris saw it. There it was. And there she was, chasing kitty litter on the other side of town when a real baby was in mortal danger. In her years on the force, Iris knew about many instances where parents forgot their child. Babies left in grocery carts in super-market parking lots, sleeping toddlers left on the bus, school-age children forgotten in dressing rooms at the mall. Most often, by the time an officer arrived, so did the parent, crazed with panic. After some finger-wagging and follow-up with child services, these episodes faded from memory until the next one.

Her mind staggered down a path filled with useless "what ifs." The biggest "what if" was Amanda herself. If she hadn't been so distracted by a call to begin with, a call that was probably just some stupid bother, she wouldn't have forgotten she'd put the baby down for a minute in the open trunk. And if Shelley Price hadn't been there in her red car, shopping for a tub of kitty lit-ter for her hoarder up in the hills, she wouldn't have thrown the police off of Amanda's trail. Maybe if it hadn't been such a crazy day with wildfires breathing down on the town, with one emer-gency call after another, the dispatchers might have noticed the coincidence of two infant calls in the same half hour and put two and two together. She wondered who made the original call to 911. If someone saw a baby being put in a trunk why didn't they inter-vene? Why didn't they chase Amanda's car to the ends of the earth? Did they think it was really none of their business? It was all their business. It was certainly hers. Iris flushed to think that when she called the station to tell them there was no baby carrier, just kitty litter, they all had a good laugh. It never occurred to anyone, least of all her, that the report was real but the identification was wrong.

Although, in truth, it might not have mattered. There was so little time to save that baby. It never ceased to amaze Iris—with all the deaths and mishaps she'd seen in her career—how life, pre-cious life, was balanced on such a thin thread of chance.

She looked around the windowless office. It was a small, utili-tarian room, with metal shelves surrounding the desk, and every surface crowded with folders and clipboards. The sheetrock walls had never been painted. The only bright spot was a framed photo next to the computer, showing a slightly younger Dave with what must be his wife, both of them entwined around a smiling toddler in blue. We love them so much, thought Iris. How can such a loss ever be survived?

Iris opened the top drawer and riffled through it until she found a new thumb drive. With a bit of fiddling, she copied the video segment onto it, then, holding her finger over the key for a few moments, deleted it from the store's computer. She looked up at the ceiling, unable to move. It wasn't until Dave opened the door and said, "Oh, you're still here," that she made herself get up.

After restoring some sort of order to the crowd outside of King Soopers, she drove to Amanda Newell's house and parked across the street. Iris knew she had to do something, she just wasn't sure what. She had everything needed to go to the chief or district attorney to file charges of reckless endangerment and maybe second-degree murder or manslaughter. But why? Hadn't the woman suffered enough? Should she also be demonized and go to prison?

She thought about when JonBenét died. The police hadn't asked the parents the necessary questions because they'd just lost their child in such a horrific manner. There was pressure from prominent community leaders to back off while the family mourned. That sensitivity resulted in no justice for that child, as valuable information disappeared into time and the mother's delusion and death. Iris was barely a teen when it happened, but the ghost of JonBenét still hung over the city. Perhaps if the police had collected the evidence and testimony correctly they would have known for sure, and the family and community could have had some closure. It's what got her interested in law enforcement in the first place, thinking she could do better than that.

But no. Here she was, doing the exact same thing.

No, not exactly the same. Unlike the case of JonBenét, she, a member of the police force, knew how the baby died. And if the public knew what happened, maybe that information could prevent other deaths. Distracted parenting could have deadly consequences. You had to pay attention. You had to take care of something so precious. Iris didn't want to confront Amanda, but it had to be done.

A white car was in the driveway. The red car was gone, sold weeks after the baby's death according to the registration she'd looked up earlier. The curtains were closed. If Iris wanted to find out if she was inside, all she had to do was walk to the door and ring the bell. She would say, "Ms. Newell, I understand the terrible loss you've been going through." She would wait for some reply, imagining a pained variation on, "You have no idea." Iris practiced her compassionate nod. Then she would say, "Ms. Newell, I hate to intrude, but I need to ask you a few questions about the day in question. May I come in?"

Questions about the day in question. Not only was it some weird Escher-like phrase, but the day a mother had inadvertently killed her own child was hardly a "day in question." It was a day of unspeakable horror. Besides, Iris had no questions. She knew everything there was to know. Now all she had to do was act on it.

Iris saw a woman walking down the street, taking each step like it was her last. It was her. Amanda Newell. Agony in motion. Her freckled face was parched and drawn in on itself, and she still wore that blue swaddling cloth like a mask. For a minute Iris thought she was going to walk right past her own house. But she stopped, looked at her feet, then turned to walk to her door. Devin met her there, panic on his face, and threw his arms around her. She pushed him off and continued inside. Iris wondered what he knew. She bet nothing.

Devin glanced at Iris and gave a curious wave of his fingers, and then he closed the door.

Iris couldn't do it. None of them were ready for what she had to do. It was too hard. It was impossible. She started up the cruiser and drove off.

Chapter Twenty-Two

On Monday, after a weekend dodging showers during the day and sleeping in the garage at night, Shelley was back in her house for a few days. Dry, warm, and safe. What a luxury. The cherry on top was the leftover takeout in the fridge and a half bottle of decent white wine. She knew she should just toss it all, what with the risks, but alcohol was a disinfectant after all, and she could nuke the pad Thai until anything living in it was dead and gone. She opened a few windows and let the cold, clean mountain air swirl through the rooms. Then she went around the house spraying and wiping with Lysol, of which she had two blessed cases hidden in the basement, courtesy of Mimi, a woman before her time. Mimi would have been the unchallenged queen of the lockdown. The pandemic made Shelley see hoarding in a new light. It wasn't greed, or it wasn't just greed. It was a hard-wired survival response gone awry, a glitch in the instinct to stash away food and essentials when they were available to be ready for the day when they were not. Who knew that the day would actually come in America? What a shame Mimi was not here to enjoy her victory over the non-hoarders, but Shelley was enjoying it for her. It was a lucky thing she had not sold the Lysol back in the fall when she was doing tag sales. The two cases had been so deeply buried in the garage she didn't even find them until after Christmas. Now, she would not sell the cleansers for any price, since it was what made her rentals safe, and renter reviews these days all mentioned the sanitized smell.

As she wiped down the bathroom sink, she remembered the sweet feeling of washing her hands at the Purple Grille. The food, too, was incredible, but she had no plans to go back. Les said it was accumulative. Every time you showed up for a free meal the harder they leaned on your everlasting soul. "They'll never crack me," he'd said. "But you, you'll snap with the next French fry." She ran a cloth across the windowsill and saw him walking through her yard to his path. She opened the back door and offered, not for the first time, for Les to sleep in the basement. "You can lay down on the cold floor," she said. "I won't even give you a pillow."

"Nah. I want to be sandwiched between the earth and the sky when I sleep," he said, flipping her a peace sign goodbye.

She watched him walk to the edge of the gully then disappear down his path. It was hard to tell with his leathery face, but she was pretty sure he was older than she was. How many winters did he have left in him? She could hear him stumble and curse as he descended to his ledge. Over the sound of his complaints, she heard the sound of running water. Snow melt. Must really be spring.

When she finished cleaning every corner of her house, she stripped the sheets and put in a load of laundry. Before she turned it on though, she took a long shower. She didn't want the sheets to get more hot water than she did. It would be a long time until she was back again. Then she sat at her computer to pay some of the more dire bills, just about depleting the money she'd made renting it out that week. Nevermind Les, she wondered how much longer she could go on with this financial fast. Something had to change. This next rental was for over two weeks which would bring some real relief, and she hoped for more longer-term rentals in the summer. Maybe she could save up some cash so she wouldn't have to do another winter. She knew for a fact she did not have another snowy season left in her, living on and off the street, scrounging for food and toilets. And who knew what would happen with this pandemic? It could outlast them all.

She clicked off the computer, fed Spree, and heated the pad Thai in the microwave. A hot dinner. She hadn't had any hot food since the Grille, days ago. Then she laid down on her sofa, with her plate on her stomach, a glass of wine on the floor, and searched for something entertaining and stupid on TV. She remembered Mimi laughing it up while watching squirrel maze videos on YouTube. Shelley used to tease Mimi about it, but now she got it. Mindless. A safe place to escape her thoughts and the pandemic. She put on a cooking channel. She loved looking at food being prepared while she was eating food. Unfortunately, the pad Thai had not held up well. The noodles were tasteless glue. She spent the rest of the day in front of the TV, sipping her wine, dozing on and off. She woke up once without opening her eyes, and heard a male voice on a show say, "It's getting firm."

"Nice," said a female.

"I think we need a little more cream."

"Wow. You're good. Thank you."

"You're welcome. Anytime."

Shelley opened her eyes, thinking the TV had somehow switched to a porn channel, but it was only an old *Simply Ming* show, and he was making ice cream. The bowl of cherry vanilla did nothing for her, so she switched to a squirrel maze station on YouTube, then went back to sleep.

The next morning she knew something was wrong when she was making coffee and couldn't smell it. Didn't some people lose their sense of smell and taste when they got the virus? "Fucking cult," she said out loud. She opened all the windows, then spent the day dragging her aching body from room to room, putting clean sheets on the bed, taking care of the garbage, and cleaning the refrigerator, just in case she wasn't well enough to do it in the morning. Renters were coming the next day, and she could not afford to cancel the booking. She'd take an Uber to Mimi's garage and sweat it out there. She'd heard that many people never even got symptoms. Maybe hers would stay mild. Maybe she would be just fine.

But by the end of the day she was hot. She had no thermometer to tell how hot, but she was burning. Then shivering. She took some ancient cold medicine she found in the bathroom, but later that night she was on her hands and knees trying to find a position where she could breathe. Eventually she crawled on the floor looking for her phone on the coffee table and called 911. As the EMTs carried her out of the house, she had them toss Spree out the back door, and put the house key in the lockbox. Then she gave them a thumbtack and a note to put on the garden shed for Les to feed Spree and get tested for Covid.

Chapter Twenty-Three

Sharp rays of sunrise pushed through the low-lying cumulus, brightening what was left of the snow and poking Les awake. He tried to close his eyes against the light and slip back to sleep, but dawn won. The sun blazed like the atomic bomb it was, shaking him lucid. He sat up on his flattened refrigerator box and wrapped his sleeping sack around his shoulders. Yet another day. A single beam of light shot through the branches and illuminated something farther up the creek. It was the size of a dog house, but sparkling clear and silver like it was made of crystal. It radiated.

"What the hell are you?" he asked. "A goddamn fairy castle?"

He supposed he'd better have a look. Even if it was a fairy castle, it couldn't stay where it was. With some effort, he got up and let the sack fall from him as he walked towards this glittering vision. Staying on the creek's frozen edge, he crunched through old snow and stumbled a bit on river rocks, but on he went, drawn as if he was returning from where he'd begun. The rays shifted as the sun and clouds jockeyed for position, then suddenly the clouds made a power grab and snuffed out the rays entirely, revealing the old, sad truth of reality.

"A shopping cart." Without the other-worldly magic of the starburst sun, the cart no longer suggested the majesty of a realm outside ourselves. Yet another design flaw in human perception.

Les tread carefully to the middle of the shallow stream, balancing on exposed ledge as he reached for the cart. It had to go. The spring melt was coming and the cart would dam up the works. Besides, a shopping cart in the creek gave them all a bad rap. They were better than that. He grabbed hold of the handle with both hands and gave a yank, then another. The wheels were wedged between fallen brush and boulders. Using the good heel of one boot to break the jam, he yanked again. He freed it without getting too wet, but his hands and feet were froze cold by the time he wrangled the cart up to his tree. He planned to fill the cart with accumulated plastic crap before rolling it back to the supermarket. But not now. No, not now.

Tired and shaking with chills, he fell down to his nest on his knees, letting his forehead touch the cardboard for a minute, catching a breath. Then he wrapped his sleep sack around him and leaned against the cottonwood, feeling a surge of vernal energy radiate along his spine. No wonder when the Buddha became enlightened he was sitting at the base of a tree. Trees reach up to the life-giving sun for light, down to the earth for sustenance, their arms open to the world. He and the tree even shared a common mind. Not a human mind—what a curse that would be—but a grand arboreal intelligence. In his next life, when his atoms reorganized, he'd lobby to return as a tree, in honor of his old friend the cottonwood, or maybe an elm, to help regenerate that species. It was far too late to help his own.

He reached down into his jacket, found a breakfast Tito's and did it in. Felt some heat in his throat but no taste on the tongue. Even his senses were beat. He patted his jacket until he found the lunch from the church kitchen he'd gotten the night before, and rummaged through the paper bag. Tuna on tan bread. Easy to dissolve in his mouth. Took a bite, but no. Smelled it. Not sure they even used tuna. Damp mattress stuffing? Time to let the animals have at it, and he threw it down near the water. He considered the apple. No, not enough dentition for that. He leaned forward and tossed the forbidden fruit back into the wild. Down it bounced, landing in a hard pillow of icy-snow along the creek's edge. Some critter will find it and thank him. Any chocolate in the bag? No chocolate. Instead, a brown cookie with raisins. Not feeling like he could manage a dry cookie. Out to join the rest and await its fate. He folded up the empty bag and patted his pockets. There they were, grapes from King Soopers' dumpster, as past their prime as he was. With everyone scrambling for food these days, it'd been slim dumpster pickings. He thought of his robust *Vitis riparia*, but they wouldn't appear again until late summer, when violet berries would erupt on his ledge and halfway up the furrowed cottonwood. Each cloud-coated grape a sacred vessel for four seeds, each seed holding enough genetic material to save the world. The *riparia* tart-sweet on the tongue, but these soft King Soopers jobbies tasted like nothing. Again, out into the cosmos they flew.

He leaned back against the tree and felt himself dissolving into a warm subsystem of the landscape, his ears tuned to the trickling water of the creek, slithering down from the mountains. Such a cold snowy April, now a summery May. The world was melting. He felt the vibration of leaves unfurling. Spring, a gift from the gods. They deserve to have a Tito's sacrificed in their honor, and he found another one on his person. We have to celebrate the change of seasons before the planet becomes a flat, uniform climate of hot misery. He downed the sip. Maybe it would help ease the ache in his muscles. He looked over to where he'd thrown the food, and was surprised that the tuna and apple were already gone. What cunning critter snuck them away without him seeing? Maybe he'd dozed off. A crow poked at the grapes, tilted its head back, and swallowed one whole. Les chose only seeded grapes just for this, the miracle of gene distribution. The indigestible seeds will travel through the crow's digestive system, then get deposited wherever the crow flies, falling to the ground in a pre-fertilized package. If it landed in a spot receptive to life, the seeds would grow, providing food for wildlife and protecting the land from erosion. Even now, sprouts pushed through the soil around him. His vines. He gave them life, and they guarded his precious smattering of land, not letting it get whipped into the air by the sculpting wind, or washed into Kansas by the erosive force of water. Other crows landed, bouncing about as they maneuvered for a place at the table. Grapes long gone, now they're bickering over the cookie. As bad as humans.

Time to nap. He laid flat on his back, his head resting on his trash bag pillow, the passing clouds a blanket of love. He read the sky like a picture book, looking not for faces or elephants in the clouds, but gods. A long history of them up there. Zeus, the sky god, creator of wind and weather. Then came Baal, the Rider on the Clouds, and Hadad, with his three-pronged lightning rod, both later upended by the storm god, Yahweh, who appeared to Moses in thunder and fury. Who next? What vengeful divine will come raging and cursing from the skies to teach us our next lesson?

The crows finished their scavenged lunch and he heard them laugh. Something in their snickering tone made him think he was the butt of their joke. Then they all took off as one and soared across his line of vision, leaving white jet streams behind them, looping in the blue sky like handwriting. They were trying to tell him something. They were trying to spell out c-l-o-u-d. Wait. No. They were spelling out C-o-v-i-d.

He sat straight up. "F-u-c-k." He remembered the Purple Grille. He thought of Shelley.

It from bit.

It does not exist until It's asked a binary question: "Do I have Covid? Yes or no?"

Oh, yes. Yes indeed. And he heard the crows somersault in laughter as they disappeared into the clouds.

The world is the suffering, as Buddha liked to say.

Shelley. Her suffering would be his own. He attempted a deep breath but it went no farther than his Adam's apple. Considering the earth's mix of incompatible and unstable gases, it's a wonder breathing was possible even on a good day. He looked up the embankment and pondered. Too weak now to warn her. Would a warning matter? There's nothing to be done, and nowhere to hide. The people are to be pitied. He coughed, but his lung tissue refused to flex. Six or seven million breaths in a life span. Wished he'd kept count so he'd know how many he had left.

There's no longer such a thing as a purely natural catastrophe. Our doing is our undoing. At this late date in our species history, we're living in a viral incubator and technology will not save us. The lesson will keep repeating itself and then the lesson will keep repeating itself and then the lesson will . . .

He felt an odd pain in his stomach. One hundred million neurons control the activities in his gut, and he had no control over a single one. Our minds depend on the integrity of neurons, but the neurons are not themselves thinking. Which means, no one is watching the shop, and never has been. There is nothing in current science that rules out the brain as a radio. So what toxic station have they all been tuned in to lately?

It was getting cooler as the day wound down. Or he was the one winding down. At any rate, his thermostat switched on and he started to burn from the inside out. He looked around. The recent warm days were no match for snow patches in the shadows, and he crawled to a bit of hard-pack and rested his cheek on it, feeling relief, then the other cheek, back and forth until the pack dissolved. Today's descent into hell is brought to you by a clever coronavirus, latching onto every one of his cells with its evil little hooks. Nature is brilliant, what it comes up with to clean out the system.

So it's come to this. He closed his eyes. Time to go. We're all going, all the time. Humanity's quavering mass of cosmic gases were already halfway out the door. We're too fragile for what is coming. For what was already here. He'll be more useful not taking up any more square footage on the planet. He had tried to be symbiotic, but the default setting for humans was extractive. His family was certainly better off once he was gone from the house. His own son, as frightened of him as Les had been of his own parents. What goes around comes around. He knew from his work at NOAA how bad it was going to get, but there was nothing he could do but watch his warnings get sucked up into the great bureaucratic void. No one was equipped for the consequences of human existence, and no one was allowed to sound the bell. Scientists ignoring science. Humans diverged from great apes seven million years ago, but these days you'd never know it. He left, and once he was living in the creek, he began to love the world again. But, of course, right away the foul angels began pestering him to get back to work and do the hard job of making humans fear themselves and confront their own rapaciousness.

Just thinking about the angels made him tired and he put his brain on pause. Blessed emptiness. At some point, he opened his crusted eyes and watched the sun float down behind the mountains, turning the clouds noctilucent in yellow and gold from the glow below. Such a beautiful world. He'll miss it. He crawled his body back to his cardboard. He'd rather his sad sack of chemicals expire there, under his tree. And yet, how lovely to still have senses to enjoy it all, even now. The touch, the sights, the sounds. The smells.

No. Not smell. He had no sense of smell. What does that say

about the viral brain? Nothing good. "I'm going out on a limb here," he said to no one. "We're in some deep shit." Then again, even on a good day humans were virtually anosmic, unable to smell the olfactory symbols used by most other species to understand their world. Sapiens invested too much on intelligence, not enough on instinct.

There is a later. Much later. The world was dark and thick, and he felt a warm nose nudge his back. Was he dead? His eyelids were malfunctioning so he couldn't open them to check. Maybe it was a critter come to thank him for the tuna. Or else he was the tuna. Before he could rally a response, whatever it was decided against him and he heard the heavy steps of a four-footed animal meander away. He must still smell of life. Or he just smells. Such thin air. So little oxygen. Wonders if he could breathe easier if he could escape Boulder's altitude. Imagines sea level, but has never seen the sea. He will never see the sea.

He is alone. He is going to die alone. He thinks fondly of Mithra the cow who died in his arms and calls upon her spirit for company. *Vacca.* Latin for cow, hence the word vaccine. Cowpox cured smallpox. Could it cure Covid? He assumed scientists were working feverishly on that one, but it was too late for him. All he could do was pray to Shitala, the anti-inflammatory goddess. The crows cawed above the trees along the creek. Bad news for the planet when carrion birds are the dominant species. Bad news for him as they watch his every breath, waiting for the last. Waiting for the feast to begin.

A day. Another night? He cannot tell for the shaking. Fever or the DTs of withdrawal? A two for one clearance sale. Everything must go. Feels his body recede and his consciousness reduced to subatomic particles. He expects that when he is dust, he will be re-inhaled by the atmosphere and expelled into the infinite universe, which has no beginning and no end. What's that song? Something something, like a million suns and calls me on and on.

If consciousness is the thing that feels like something, it's lost its loving feeling. It was only along for the ride anyway, bearing the illusion of being rational, controlling nothing, hijacked by the wetware of the reptilian brain.

Wait. No. The damn angels are here. What he needed was a neon arrow pointing the way out, and he gets angels instead, and not the better ones. They glow in the bright frames of their nimbus, looking supernatural. Makes him feel subnatural. They draw straws to see who goes first, then take turns stomping their dusty feet on his chest. Won't leave him be. Wings flapping, sucking up the air. They start emptying bottles of Tito's on him, and he opens his mouth hoping to catch some on his tongue. One angel snaps his fingers and a flame appears in his hand. He tosses it on Les and he explodes in a searing burst of ignited gas. He waits to be consumed. Seventeen hundred degrees returns a human body to the elements forged inside the furnaces of long-dead stars. Wishes he had a thermometer. Wishes he had the strength to find his shepherd's crook. As he burns, the angels laugh, and images of broken light start frenetically dancing and falling apart. In a damaged habitat, all problems merge. His body a runaway greenhouse from the heat, the temperature heats up the surfaces, and the heated surfaces release more heat. His insides feel like steaming meat, his skin a burst sausage casing. Who does he have to know to buy a papal indulgence to offset his carbon emissions? What's the story? What's the scam?

Then, blessed relief from his buddies, the nocturnal clouds. Temperature falling, stars falling, snow falling, covering him with healing manna. The cooling snow, the saving snow, the fever-breaking snow. He melts and suddenly the angels depart, rising like rockets from his ledge, their exhaust cool and white. The intense flapping of their wings extinguish the rest of his flames. Nothing stirred. He was exhausted. It was daylight, but he had no idea what day.

A hawk swooped over the creek, with wings and tail fanned, pausing, then screeched on its rapid descent through the air. The crows dispersed. Les coughed. "What took you so long?" he whispered, as it was in the beginning, and for everlasting. Amen.

Chapter Twenty-Four

Shelley woke to a high-pitched sound and braced herself for a nurse to come swooping in to see if she was dead. She wondered if that's how she was going to know it was over, with one long shrill beep. But the door did not open in a flurry of protective polyester, and at any rate, the sound had stopped. The machines that monitored her bodily functions seemed to be blinking and blurting with no special urgency. With great effort, and not a little pain, she turned her head to the window, smushing her oxygen mask against her temple. "Oh! Hello."

A red-tailed hawk was sitting on an iron rod that extended out from Boulder Community Hospital, right outside Shelley's room on the fourth floor. She'd noticed the rod when she first arrived, when she still had enough breath to stand up to look out the window and get her bearings in the world. A day ago? A week? A lifetime? A narrow side window was cracked open and it had felt good to feel honest-to-god air on her skin. But those few steps nearly did her in and the day nurse, Jeanette, looking like an astronaut in her baby-blue gear, had to help her back to bed. "Nice try, Shelley," she'd said, a distant muffled voice beneath the mask and face shield. "But next time, you ring for me."

"I thought you'd say no," said Shelley.

"I will say no. That's why I say, ring for me. The last thing we need right now is a fall."

It was a moot point. After that, she never had the strength again. It took everything she had to breathe, but she was glad she got that one peek. If she hadn't, she might not know about the rod and then would have to wonder what the hawk was sitting on, and it hurt her head to think. The rod was probably leftover from some sloppy repair, but this big raptor seemed to think it was custom built for his own private perch. It was a good looking bird with its brown plumage and red tail, without which she'd be hard-pressed to say what kind of hawk it was. As it was, she didn't know her male from her female. The bird's intense, furrowed stare was aimed not at her—really, who would want to look at her now?—but at the utility courtyard below where sat a Trash Daddy dumpster, and a dumpster meant rats. Probably plenty of them. An active vermin battleground, as Les would say. The hospital's trash was a good bet for untouched meals. The medical staff didn't seem to have time to eat, and Covid patients couldn't ingest anything other than fluids by way of a vein. Garbage pickings were slim at restaurants these days, what with the lockdown, so rats across the city were starving, ravaging homes in search of food. Before she got sick she'd seen them out on the streets in broad daylight, taking risks, exposing themselves to danger in hopes of finding food. Taking risks, just like her. She'd gone to the Purple Grille in search of food, walking right inside, and fell right into the virus's trap. What an idiot. What a frigging idiot.

Rats weren't the only ones interested in the Trash Daddy. She'd seen crows, those vacuum cleaners with wings, slashing beak and claw through plastic bags of cafeteria garbage, chattering away like bargain shoppers. "Did you see this? Is there any more of that?" They soared past her view with the foul scrapings of hospital trays trailing from their beaks—a baked potato shell, some strands of fettuccini, a gray strip of chicken skin. It was a wonder they got airborne with all those groceries. With a sharp pain in her heart she thought of flightless Mimi, falling to the ground, weighted down by a lifetime of shopping.

It was a bird-eat-bird world. The crows certainly didn't want the red-tail staring down at them while they scavenged. It might get tired of waiting for a rat to dart out from the Trash Daddy and choose one of them for lunch instead. As she gazed at the hawk, a crow suddenly photobombed her view, trolling its nemesis with a swoop. But the hawk was unperturbed, and gave the crow a look that could have plucked him bald. "Stay strong," she muttered from under her oxygen mask. Just as her eyes began to flutter closed, the hawk pushed itself off the rod and shot down into the courtyard. She stretched her neck but she couldn't see if it scored a rat, and she never saw it rise.

Over the next few days the red-tail and the crows became her entertainment as she struggled to breathe, giving her something to think about other than cement-filled lungs. The hawk showed up on the rod at least once a day, but she never knew when to expect it. She had no concept of time. For all she knew, it showed up like clockwork at the same time every day. The crows were a constant, noisy presence, and the sparrows, thugs in their own right, often flew by in intimidating masses. Sometimes she felt the place was a little over-birded, but they were visitors after all, something not allowed otherwise. Who was there in her world to visit her anyway? Les? She hoped he saw the note she left him about feeding the cat. She hoped he was not holed up under his tree, sick himself, although he seemed plenty immune to anything the world could throw at him.

One afternoon, when she was feeling restless, Shelley asked Jeannette if she could sit in the recliner by the window for a bit. "Sitting up will help me breathe," she said.

"It won't," said Jeanette, "but I'll let you anyway as long as you don't dare try to get back to this bed on your own."

"Deal," said Shelley. Once Jeanette got her settled in the chair with all the tubes arranged just so, Shelley put her feet up and looked out. There was a tall man down in the otherwise empty courtyard, his head tilted up, searching. No one she knew. Visitors weren't allowed inside the hospital, so this was it, family members searching for loved ones behind glass. She was tempted to wave just to be friendly but then she decided no, he might think he'd found who he was looking for. At this distance she could be anyone. He stood between the Trash Daddy and a white refrigerated trailer, his hand shielding his eyes while the crows looked down on him from the cottonwood trees, the leaves just beginning to unfurl. The birds bobbed their heads and flew from limb to limb, making the branches bounce as if the weight of elephants had been lifted. She looked past the crows and beyond the hospital wing to the foothills and the snow-capped Rockies in the distance. When was the last time she even noticed the mountains?

When she looked back down at the man, he didn't seem so tall anymore. He looked like what he was, a small, vulnerable mammal. Sometimes she wondered if humans had any purpose at all. Keith had said we were here to protect the earth, but that made no sense. From what she could tell, the earth needed to be protected from us. In fact, she didn't see where humans fit anywhere in what he called "the great web of life". We devoured everything but seemed to be no one's primary food source anymore, unless you counted the virus. In which case, we were toast.

Jeanette came up behind her. "Shelley, we've got to get you back in bed." Shelley raised an arm tethered by a blood pressure cuff and let herself be helped up. As Jeanette baby-walked her back to bed, she could tell the moment the man walked away because she heard the crows descend upon the Trash Daddy in a noisy reunion. They were a rowdy bunch. No matter how loud it got inside, what with all the electronic squawks and hallway commotion, she could always tell when a custodian went outside with garbage because the crows made such a ruckus. Where did they find such energy? She could even tell when the hawk was coming because a military detail of crows loudly mobbed him, trying to keep him away from his perch. Every once in a while they won, and she'd see them escort the hawk off the hospital campus. Crows were persistent little buggers. But so was the hawk. She once woke to the sight of it rising up from the courtyard with a mighty flapping of wings, a limp rat dangling from its claws. As much as she'd been rooting for the hawk against the crows, she felt for the rat. She hoped the end was quick. Suffering was a terrible thing.

She remembered a long time ago, when she was down with the flu, Keith was trying to get her to sit outside in bone-chilling February weather to boost her immune system, insisting that natural settings were healing and would create a path to her soul if only she were open to the experience. It was such a Boulder thing to say. Not only that, it wasn't true. She'd been totally over-exposed to the elements this winter and it had not protected her from shit. Keith had been as annoying as a crow sometimes, constantly soul-questing, always trying to improve himself, pressuring her to come along. Funny she should think of him now. The years of her youth began spooling out in front of her like colorful ribbons, the scenes magical like a movie, and she tried to grasp her younger, hopeful self to keep her from disappearing again. Somehow in the process, she pulled a tube from her arm, and Jeanette came in and loosely tied her hands to the bed with soft bandages, and that was surely for the best.

Later, she opened her eyes and there was a crow on the rod, looking in at her, first with one eye, then turning its beak to look at her with the other. Or was it a gargoyle? The creature was all beak and wing, hunched over and ugly, spouting words instead of rainwater. "Life is a near-death experience," it cackled before flying away.

Oh no. She was hallucinating. That couldn't be good. What was that nursery rhyme her mother used to read to her about count-ing crows? One is for sorrow? She hadn't thought of her for a long time. As if when she died, Shelley's memory of her went with her. It was too painful otherwise. She missed her. It seemed she never mourned her properly, what with her rushed marriage on the heels of death. She had chosen to distract herself instead of grieve. She had filled her life with distractions instead of feeling her loss.

Suddenly her mother was in the room with her, holding her hand. "There, there," she said. "It's okay, darling."

"Mom. Shouldn't you be lying down somewhere?"

Shelley felt she had another chance to save her mother, if only she could save herself.

There was some sort of commotion going on in the hallway. She side-eyed the hall window and there were gurneys everywhere, a traffic jam of the sick and dying. She was grateful to have a bed. She heard a man call out that he was a lawyer. "This situation is actionable," he croaked. "When this is over, there'll be hell to pay."

If only she had the oxygen to laugh. When she turned back to her mother she was gone. She must have left through the window. Odd.

Someone came in to remove the bandages from her wrists so maybe the worst was over. No. Maybe just beginning. They had to untie her to flip her over onto her stomach "to take the pressure off these lungs," Jeanette said. "Keep you off the ventilator." Shelley knew the ventilator was the treatment not everyone returned from.

Being on her stomach seemed to help, but the oxygen mask dug into her cheeks. She asked an aide to turn her head to face the window, and she stared off in the distance at the famil-iar peaks and sloughs of the mountains. Spring was here. She remembered another spring, going up a trail with Keith and coming across a fresh kill. The bloody contents of a deer had been hollowed out and devoured, the insides ribbed like a cathedral ceiling. Eviscerated was the word. She was uneasy knowing there was some animal, drooling red, waiting for them to leave so it could finish the job. Keith hardly gave the deer a glance, except to remark on the different types of flies on the carcass, and kept on his steady pace to the top of the ridge, but she stopped to gape. The blood was wet. The flies pulsed with vitality, making it seem as if life was just moving from one form to another. When she met back up with Keith she begged him to take a different path back down. They divorced soon after and she never went up the mountain again.

She should have kept on hiking, even after he left her. She should have kept it up for her mother, who loved a good walk. She'd do anything to hit that trail again, to be in the mountains where life in all its pumping glory could be reconsidered. To review the options once more. She'd read the menu more carefully this time. She'd order more side dishes, and try unfamiliar entrees.

At some point a physical therapist came in to, as he called it, "help her visualize her breathing."

"Think of your shoulder blades as your wings," he'd said, putting his gloved hand on her bare back. "Now, pull your breath into your wings and feel them open. Expand your angel wings, Shelley. Good. Now let the breath go. Fold your wings and relax. Expand, and fold. Again. Good. Open your wings wide, Shelley. Excellent. You'll be flying in no time."

Just like Keith, with his Boulder platitudes. He used to always say, you want to fly, you've got to give up what weighs you down. Apparently, she was what was weighing him down. She wondered where he was and what he was doing. She wondered if he was still with Alan in Crested Butte. Or was even alive, what with his reckless embrace of the great outdoors, always climbing some steep cliff or madly paddling wild water. Then again, she, who was so careful, was the one in the hospital. Just thinking about the haphazard ways of the world exhausted her, and she felt herself falling into a deep sleep. A buzzer went off and suddenly, like a SWAT team, the entire hospital staff seemed to be in her room.

"Leave me alone," she said, her words echoing about in her oxygen mask, pushing hands away. "I'm not that interesting."

Chapter Twenty-Five

Officer Iris Sokos stood at the kitchen door of the Purple Grille, facing down Hanna in her handmade sweater, who stood just inside, one hand leaning against the door jamb, the other on her hip. Iris handed her a slip of paper. "This is a citation for not wearing masks."

The cult already walked a tight line in the city. Whenever there was a report of a missing person, especially a missing college student, the cult's restaurant and farm were the first places the police looked. The pandemic might trip the cult up altogether if it was determined to flout the safety protocols for restaurants. This was not a freedom of religion issue. It was life or death.

Iris handed Hanna a box. "Here are masks. You wear these or the Department of Health closes your operation down, period. And get rid of those folding tables outside. We don't want people hanging around and congregating."

"Where are they supposed to eat?" Hanna asked. "The people who use these tables have nowhere to go. You want them to eat from bowls on the ground like dogs?"

"Put a mask on, Ma'am. Your staff must wear them at all times and you are required to have your customers wear them for curbside pickup."

Hanna ever so slowly slipped the baby blue mask over her ears. "We need to keep one table for pick-up."

"One table, with hand sanitizer." Iris glanced behind Hanna into the kitchen to see if the staff was social distancing. There was just one person. Amanda Newell.

"What's that woman doing here?"

"Mandy is staff," said Hanna. "She's part of our community, and she's doing dishes. Hard work is good for the soul."

Amanda did not look up, and seemed not even aware they were talking about her. She had the same glazed look on her freckled face that she'd had all these winter months roaming Boulder's streets, the same vacant stare that protected her from a world in which her baby was gone, and that she was the one responsible.

Iris watched as Amanda methodically picked up a pan and sponged it clean, first the back, then the front, rinsing it under running water as if she were mesmerized by the sight. Steam billowed around her. She didn't even wear rubber gloves with such hot water. The sleeves of her sweater were pushed up to her elbows, exposing a length of badly bruised arm.

Fucking hell.

The cult had a reputation for corporal punishment, especially with children, but adults were not exempt. New members were often beaten into obedience and submission. Like most cults, they solicited compromising personal information from damaged, vulnerable people, then controlled them with manipulative doses of shame and guilt. And pain. Maybe Amanda had been looking for someone to punish her.

"If I have to come back again we're shutting you down," said Iris. "Keep customers outside, masked and moving. And keep your staff six feet from one another." Hanna did not respond, and as the door closed on her, Iris could tell that she was already taking off her mask.

Iris went back to her cruiser and sat. This was all her fault. By her inaction, she'd let Amanda wander right into the arms of predators. By not confronting her with what she'd done, she'd blocked the path to justice and her way back to the community. And it was up to Iris to clear that path. It was her job. Amanda needed to go through the legal process and come out the other side to get the help she desperately needed to reconcile herself to the death of her child. Iris had been protecting her because she'd also once felt so overwhelmed with new motherhood, juggling the balls of family, the academy, work, and the world, faster and faster, higher and higher. Breakage was inevitable, but a death couldn't be ignored. Iris had been at a loss to know what to do all these weeks, but she knew now.

Acknowledgement was the first step. She was going to have to come clean herself, tell the chief what happened, and try to explain why she'd withheld evidence. She would have to explain her actions. She would definitely get a formal reprimand, possibly a suspension, or worse. The new chief was a woman. That was something different. On her first day of duty, she spoke to the assembled department about the importance of transparency and public trust. Letting your vulnerable side show can be a good thing, Iris had heard her say. Well, she was about to be tested on that. We're all human, in the worst possible way, causing damage without intention wherever we go.

Iris returned to the station, found her reporting officer and told him everything. Then they went to the chief, who questioned why Iris had not spoken up the day she saw the damning video. Iris mumbled something about needing to do "more investigation."

"First let's get this family some help," the chief had said, "and then we'll figure out what to do with you later."

They all talked to the D.A. over Zoom, and made a plan. Before going to a judge for a warrant, the chief told her to bring

Devin Newell in for some questions, to see what he knew about that day in King Soopers' parking lot and confirm that Amanda had joined the cult. Iris called him at the tech repair store.

"Where is she now?" he asked, before she said a word.

"I need you to come by the station, Mr. Newell. Can you get away from work in an hour?"

"Has something happened to Mandy?"

"She's alive. But I'd like to talk to you in private."

When he arrived, his eyes showed alarm above his mask. He had no lawyer, which told Iris he hadn't a clue. Because of Covid, they could not use one of the small, unventilated rooms usually used for questioning, so they met him outside in an enclosed courtyard, which had barbed wire running along the top. They arranged themselves on folding chairs around a card table, and Iris sat next to him, and on his other side was the social worker who would be walking Amanda through the justice and mental health systems. The detective assigned to her criminal case sat across from them with an iPad, although he and Iris had agreed she would start the questioning.

"Mr. Newell," said Iris. "First, I am so sorry about the loss of your child last summer. I hadn't known until recently."

He nodded. "I didn't have the words to talk about it back then. It's still awful, every minute. My wife . . ." He stopped and looked away.

"Yes. I know. We need to talk about Amanda. I just saw her in the kitchen of the Purple Grille. Are you aware of that?"

"Mandy started hanging out at the cult's farm a while back, and then joined them for good a few days ago. They're taking advantage of her in her weakened state." He put his face in his hands. "The grief's driven her mad."

"I know. The baby."

"The baby. She blames herself."

"Tell me about that."

He shrugged and looked over her head, at the barbed wire. "I wish I could. She won't talk about Freddie's death. Not to me, not to her sister. No one. The few times she's actually acknowledged that he's dead she blames herself because she was with him, and she thinks she could have done something to save him. I told her, no. It was out of her hands. These things happen. Don't they?" He looked at Iris, who gave an imperceptible nod. When it was clear she wasn't going to say anything, he continued. "She won't get grief counseling. Most of the time she doesn't even think she has anything to grieve. She says she wants to live at the farm because they have communal childcare." His voice cracked. "A few months ago, she dumped Freddie's ashes into the trash claiming it was dirt and would get him sick if he got into it. *The trash.* I saved what I could. You know how her sister and I are always driving around looking for her? Sometimes we find her miles away from home in the middle of nowhere." He paused. "I think the cult beats her. Before she moved to the farm, I saw marks on her back one night."

"We're going to get her out of there," said Iris.

"I've tried. They say she's there of her own free will. But her mind's not free. It's like she's in prison. On top of that, they make them give up their worldly possessions. Their lawyer contacted me about giving Mandy's half of our assets to them. Half of our home. I'd have to sell it. It's insane. I don't know what I'm going to do."

"I'm getting her out because I'm going to arrest her."

"Arrest her? For what? Vagrancy?"

"I have something to show you, Mr. Newell." Iris saw the social worker inch her chair closer to Devin. As if this poor man wasn't in enough agony, Iris was about to open up a whole new world of horror he didn't even know existed. But there was no other way. She pulled out her cell phone and felt her stomach start climbing up into her throat. Her body was trying to reject what she was about to do. She took a breath, and she could feel the soft weight of a baby rest against her chest.

"This is going to be difficult for you to see, Mr. Newell. But remember, we are right here with you. This surveillance video was taken shortly before Freddie's death."

"What?"

She pressed the little arrow, then watched him as he watched the video, and saw the moment when he understood what was happening. His hands crept to his face. "That's not possible. Mandy would never do that." He stood up and looked around the courtyard in a panic, as if he was going to run somewhere. But there was nowhere to run, as his wife knew all too well.

"I'm so sorry, Mr. Newell. His death might be accidental, but it was Amanda's accident. She was distracted and she was careless. She didn't realize what she'd done until she was a mile away. By then it was too late."

She gave him time as he looked around at his dark, new world. The cottonwood trees around the station were beginning their annual shedding of seedheads, and white puffs floated through the courtyard like a dusting of snow. A fluff landed in Devin's hair, and he sat back down as if pressed by the weight of it.

"Show it again," he said, wiping his face with both hands.

"Are you sure?" Iris glanced at the social worker who was looking away. They were all so unprepared. She wasn't sure she could stomach it again herself, but Devin nodded yes, so she rewound it back to when Amanda started loading groceries. They watched as she put the car seat in the open trunk to protect Freddie from the sun and she could feel Devin being pulled into the past with a visible shudder. His wife and child were rushing towards him to this horrific present, where nothing could be undone, where there was no rewinding of life.

"There," Devin said, his voice clogged with tears as he pointed at the phone. "That's when I told Mandy I couldn't get home in time to watch Freddie." His hand shook as they watched Amanda hang up on Devin and make another call. "She's calling her sister to see if she can take him." His breath became so rapid, Iris was afraid he might hyperventilate under his mask. The social worker put her hand on his shoulder and his breath slowed a bit, although his whole body shook. Iris remembered her training about professional distance, how if she got sucked into someone's pain she wouldn't be in the best position to help. But it was too late to help anyone now, least of all that baby. There was only comfort. They watched Amanda end the call with her sister, and then . . . and then, they watched her shut the trunk on her child and drive away into the sweltering heat of a smoked-out day.

The screen went blank. The wind whistled through the barbed wire and they continued to stare at nothing, forced to relive the moment where it all went wrong, again and again, into eternity.

"I killed him," said Devin, and Sokos took his trembling hand and held it in her own.

Chapter Twenty-Six

Living on food and drink left near him by one of the families who lived along the creek, Les spent a week or more recuperating from the body bomb of fever shakes and DTs. He might have stayed supine longer except Spree showed up to glare at him, opening and closing his yellow eyes. "Sekhet, the lion-headed goddess," Les said. "Have you come to heal me?" He gave the matted animal an old piece of jerky he found in his pocket, and slept. Next day, Spree came and glared with greater intent, so, shaky on his legs but standing, Les followed him back to the upper world. Found renters in the house, but no Shelley. Went to look in on the cat bowl behind the garden shed. A note! To him. From Shelley. Ink runny, but legible.

"Going to hospital. Have yourself tested for Covid. Can you feed Spree?"

The bag of kibble in the garden shed was empty, drained by some critter. Not like Shelley to leave anything unprotected. Many things that gal, but she knew how to check all the boxes. She must've been burning with fever. Spree rubbed against his legs. "Can't go into the house looking for more kibble, can I, Sekhet? Can't scare the renters with Shelley so concerned about reviews."

There was only one thing left to do. He'd have to work Pearl. He was weak, but it had to be done.

The walk was difficult even with the Hop, but he got to his spot. Using a crayon he kept in an inner pocket for the purpose, and the clean side of a pizza box from the trash, he made a new sign. "Need $ for cat food." Small sympathy in this world for humans, but a cat, no, a cat can't go hungry. The sign was a real money-maker, an hour raising funds enough for him and Spree. He braved the line outside of 7-Eleven for a new bag of kibble. He coughed behind his mask and everyone gave him space. They usually did that anyway.

With bag in hand, he contemplated walking to Hazels, but no energy for that. No yen for sips either. Not sure what was going on with that, but suspected it had to do with the damn angels. Every time he thought of a Tito's, he remembered them dousing him with vodka and setting him on fire, and somewhere in that infernal blaze, consumed alive by what he once consumed, he'd sworn no more. And here he was still oddly sober. Now what? He went back to Shelley's and fed the cat. Made the top tight on the can this time, protecting precious kibble. All well again in feline world. Unlike Schrödinger's quantum cat, who can be both alive and dead, and in two places at once, Spree was very much alive and in one place. Home.

Les rested, ate some chicken noodle soup from 7-Eleven cold from the can, and the next morning grabbed the Hop to the hospital to see Shelley. But no. Talked to a guard, who put him on the phone to her nurse. No visitors. No way. But not on a ventilator yet. Asked nurse if that's because she doesn't need one or because the hospital didn't have enough to go around. She laughed, and told him where to stand outside to see her room when she was well enough to come to the window, but not today. Try another time. He checked out the courtyard. A dumpster. A refrigerated trailer. The day's quiet broken by the relentless hum of its motor. Oh, man. He pressed both palms against the white metal and bowed his head in respect to those who now understood that the laws that bound everything in the universe applied to them as well. "One lives, one dies, and the sweet elements of life are passed on and on in endless chains. Amen."

He tapped the trailer with his knuckles, then looked up at what he figured was Shelley's room. Near the window, saw a red-tail on a rod. "Okay, then," he shouted. "You're in charge, hawk."

When he returned to town, he got off the bus on Pearl and went back to work. Sitting cross-legged, eyes closed, Starbucks grande paper cup on ground before him like a temple flame. Used to be all he could find was Styrofoam cups, the hyperobject that never dies. Like plutonium, the poisoned light, from the defunct nuclear weapons facility outside of town. Now called the Rocky Flats National Wildlife Refuge. The government had some wicked sense of humor. Warehousing wildlife on toxic superfund sites. He closed his eyes and felt the sun on his face, beaming down on its helpless worshippers. He heard his lungs expand and contract with effort, but at least he was breathing. Was Shelley? Considered walking to the liquor store to quell his fears, but still seemed to have no taste for his sips. Fucking angels.

He opened his eyes and pondered the pandemic Pearl. The gods were not looking favorably upon commerce right now. Stores closed. Bars closed. Yoga joints closed. He was the liveliest business on the block. Restaurant biz takeout only but hard to do curbside pickup on a pedestrian mall. No curb. Folks left their cars on Walnut, walked by him and deposited coins in his Starbucks cup, buying Covid karma. An essential service. His cup runneth over, over and over, spilling across Pearl and flooding the great plains.

His peace was disturbed when he saw a half-dozen police cars drive up onto the west end. They only drove on the mall when something big was going down, so he got up to find out how big. Cruisers all flashing red and blue lights, glimmering like Christmas in front of the Purple Grille, police exploding from the cars like bullets. Just like when they were gunning for Shelley and her kitty litter.

"It's Sokos," he said to Hattie, who materialized next to him like a wraith.

"Sokos loves a big scene," said Hattie. "Where's your friend?"

"Hospital," said Les. "Covid."

She laughed and then they watched as Officer Sokos produced what looked like a warrant, if memory served, and then the dark blues swarmed into the restaurant. In the time it took to read someone their rights, they were back out again with their prey. The Wanderer. Her face a blank. Sokos slipped a mask on her, and she didn't react to that, or to the handcuffs being snapped on her wrists.

"Wonder what she did," said Les.

Hattie began to walk away, pulling her cart. "What have any of us done?"

Officer Sokos took the Wanderer by the arm, and talked almost kindly to her. "Mrs. Newell, you have to come with me to the station."

A man in tears pushed through the swarm and came right up to the Wanderer. "Mandy, it's okay. It's going to be okay. This was all my fault. I've got a lawyer and we'll meet you at the station."

The Wanderer did not respond. She did not even look at him. She was somewhere else, very far away.

Les wondered if that was her husband. Must be someone who loves her if he got her a lawyer. Then again, Mimi got Shelley a lawyer and he was still sending her invoices. Les always took them out of the mailbox before Shelley saw them.

Sokos bent the Wanderer's head down to get her into the back of one of the patrol cars, and she went without any fuss. As Sokos was shutting the door, out of nowhere a woman came running over, her mask wet with tears. "Mandy!" she called, pressing herself against the back window. Sokos and the man who promised a lawyer pulled the woman away from the cruiser and Sokos waved it away. The woman turned to Sokos.

"Please, she's my sister. She was a good mother. Have mercy."

The man hugged her and whispered something and they left together, everyone heading towards the police station down the block. Sokos got in her own cruiser, closed the door, and the excitement was over. Les stayed to watch as the last police car drove off of Pearl.

He put his hands in his pockets and stood watching nothing for a bit. Some basic fact about life was out of his grasp. He looked up at the mountains. A sacred land, scorched. He saw blackened trees. He looked deeper. The only living part of a tree trunk is a cell layer just beneath the bark, and he felt its pulsing energy, unfurling leaves and needles in a riot of life. The trees were so alive they seemed to move across the foothills in a slow, solemn dance. Pinyon jays flew out from branches by the thousands, trailing gusts of petals, calling with their nasal laugh. *Coming for you.* He let his gaze soften and saw two suns floating over the ridge. Twin suns, glorying in their power. He blinked and focused and the twins became a single star again. One of hundreds of billions. The trees stood still and the pinyons disappeared, but he felt the earth tremble with laughter through the soles of his boots.

Chapter Twenty-Seven

"It's so stuffy in here," said Amanda. She sat on an unmade cot, absently patting the scrap of fabric in her lap. She looked around the empty room for a thermostat, but all she saw was a vent on the ceiling, next to the cheap lighting fixture, both set behind metal grilles. What a dump. Devin had said she was here for an appraisal, but it was definitely not a property she'd be interested in listing. She'd be embarrassed to show it to anyone, no matter how modest the budget. The walls were made of cinder block and painted gray. There were no windows and the door was stuck shut. There was a cute speakeasy slider on the door but it didn't seem to work. No commission was worth having her name attached to this place. No one had even bothered to stage it. Maybe they expected her to do it.

"Just for a few hours," Devin had said. "Then I can bring you home."

Home. What was that? Hadn't he realized she didn't live at that house anymore? That they'd outgrown it? Hanna had given her a place to live at the farm. She'd been so helpful. She really seemed to get to the bottom of Amanda's problem, and offered to watch Freddie for her while she worked. What a relief. She said they'd even take care of him when she went to the supermarket so she wouldn't feel so overwhelmed all the time. She could finally catch her breath.

She stood up with the swaddle draped over her shoulder and began to walk around the stuffy room. There was no point knocking on the door again to be let out. The grounds keeper, or whatever she was, always said the same thing, that she had to stay until she talked to a doctor. A doctor would never buy a dump like this, but maybe she could ask him or her to have a look at Freddie. He seemed a little hot to her. She rubbed the swaddle against her face. Definitely warm. Then again, the room was small and poorly ventilated. A few steps this way, a few that way, back and over. A loop. Around again, and again. If only it weren't so hot. It was tiring, but movement was such a comfort to babies. It made them feel like they were still in the womb, safe and protected, lulled by a gentle heartbeat. It's why they loved a car ride. You could always count on them sleeping in a moving car.

On the third or fourth loop she had to slow down. She was having a little trouble breathing. But she had to keep walking to calm him down. He never seemed to stop crying these days. Up, over, around, and back. Up, over, around, and back. She felt a little unsteady on her feet and put her hand out to lean on a wall. Each breath was such a struggle. She had to go sit back down for a minute. Just a minute. But as soon as she sat, she continued sinking until she was stretched out flat. That was better, but she didn't want to roll on Freddie in her sleep, so she put him on the pillow next to her head.

"Hi baby," she said, and loosened the swaddle. Hanna had said he seemed small for his age. She'd have to ask the doctor about that. She couldn't remember the last time she weighed him. She couldn't even remember where she put the scale. That was something she'd left at the old house, for sure. He was definitely warm. She put her hand on her own head. They were both pretty warm.

She should take their temps, just in case. She'd gotten a fancy digital thermometer at her baby shower but forgot where she put it. It was probably with the scale, wherever that was. When had she gotten so forgetful?

She wished there was a window to crack open a bit, to let some cool air in. She should try the door again but she wasn't ready to get up. She was just so damn tired. Even her back ached. It was so exhausting taking care of a baby on top of everything else. She didn't know how she got through the day.

"Poor baby," she said, and patted the swaddle as she closed her eyes.

Chapter Twenty-Eight

In between people coming and going to mess with her, Shelley tried to sleep, but the noise seemed to ramp up every time she closed her eyes. The beeps, the alarms, the announcements. Code this, code that. The crying out. The oxygen machine was so loud. Both she and the machine were working too hard. She'd felt like she'd been circling the drain for days and she was getting tired. The machine was getting tired. She heard people out in the hall say Covid this, Covid that. Wait. Or were they saying corvid? Corvid? She pressed her mind into action until it came up with the answer. A crow was a corvid! Counting corvids. Counting crows. Counting Covids. If a group of crows was called a murder, what was a group of Covids called? A slaughter. She laughed, but it used too much precious oxygen and she started gagging under her mask and Jeanette ran in with a syringe.

> One is for sorrow,
> Two is for mirth,
> Three for a wedding,
> And four for a death.

Later, after a team came to flip her right side up, Jeanette brought her an iPad. "Someone wants to say hello."

"Les?" she mumbled from under her mask.

"Your brother Henry. But there was a scruffy character outside the hospital a few days ago. He asked if you could come to the window, but I had to say no. Maybe that was Less?"

"Les," whispered Shelley. "One 's' please."

Jeanette laughed. "I'm putting this right here," she said, tucking the plastic-covered iPad by Shelley's pillow. "Talk as long as you want. Or can."

"Here's your sister," Jeanette said to the iPad. "I'm putting you on speaker."

"Shelley?" Henry said.

"Hey," she croaked. She must've written his name down on some form or another when she was admitted. Shit. They'd contacted her next of kin.

"Shelley, it's me, Claudia. I'm here too. We're rooting for you honey."

"I love you," said Henry.

He'd never said that before. That can't be good. She didn't have enough breath to respond, but gave what she hoped sounded like an appreciative grunt. They hardly knew one another, but he was the only family she had. He and his wife Claudia, who she'd met maybe five times in her life, were falsely cheerful so she was falsely fine, then she drifted off to sleep in the middle of a sentence. Wild visions, the sound of crows infiltrating everything. Humans in her dreams began to speak in caws and clacks. Telling corvid jokes. A corvid and a rabbi walk into a bar. Then Covid followed and they never walked out. No one laughed. This place has no fucking sense of humor.

Another one: Before the crowbar was invented, the crows simply drank at home.

Silence. She looked up at the flickering TV. Maybe she could find some laughs there. Maybe there was a squirrel maze channel. It was always set on a news station, of all things. She already knew the news. It sucked. But every time an aide came in for house cleaning, they switched it on, as if she had no opinion, like she wasn't even there. She patted the rail for the control, turned on the audio, and raised it to change the channel. Then she paused. A familiar face was on the news. She held the control to her ear and watched a clip of the Wanderer being escorted into the police station by Officer Sokos. A newscaster was standing in front of the scene. ". . . the arrest of Amanda Newell today, on charges of involuntary manslaughter. The Boulder police report that she allegedly put her three-month-old baby in the open trunk of her car while loading groceries at a local supermarket, and mistakenly drove off, resulting in the death of the infant. This tragic incident occurred on August 8th of last year, but video evidence of the event has only just surfaced."

"August 8th?" Shelley struggled to sit up, pulling on whatever wires and tubes she could grab. Alarms went off and Jeanette came running in.

"What in God's name," she said. "Lie back down before I call security."

"Not a baby," whispered Shelley, pointing at the TV. "Please, not a real baby."

Shelley collapsed back on her pillow, while Jeanette did something with a syringe and the IV line.

"We're turning this thing off." Jeanette picked up the control. "The last thing you need is the news of the day. It's the last thing any of us need. Can you hold a book? We got those here. Or did."

Shelley thought of a book she'd read in high school. *Jane Eyre*? A man had run into a burning house to save his wife, a mad woman in the attic. Just like Jeremy. But in the book Rochester was smart enough to turn back from the flames. Later he married the servant girl, Jane. They could not have their own lives until that house burned to the ground, taking the madwoman with it.

She opened her eyes at some timeless point in the stuck loop in her head. What horrible thing had she been thinking about before? There had been something disturbing on TV. Then again, it was all disturbing. The TV was off. She turned her head to look for the control and saw the hawk was back on the rod. "Hello," she muttered.

"Nature is not indifferent to us, but incapable." The hawk spoke to her in Les's voice. "Life spans are too short to grasp long-term changes in the environment, and there is no time to evolve."

"Les, how do I get out of this place?"

"No one gets out alive," he said and flew off shouting "Embrace the unraveling!"

If her life span got extended, she'd see what she could do about that unraveling thing. She used to be handy with a needle and thread. She remembered her mom threading a needle for her and showing her a running stitch. Up, down, up, down.

Jeanette came in to check on her, and adjusted the oxygen. "You're a real Florence Henderson," Shelley said, and Jeanette gave such a laugh all her protective gear shook.

"I'm not the mom on *The Brady Bunch*," said Jeanette. "You mean Florence Nightingale."

"Oh no, don't let the nightingales in," Shelley said. "No more birds," and she flew off to a quiet perch in her head. Wasn't it Les who said that the network of neuronal cells in the human brain were similar to the cosmic network of galaxies? Wasn't it? Who could keep any of it straight?

At sunset, the crows were going wild and she opened her eyes. Something was up. She pressed the button to raise the bed upright. The nurse's aide had left the sides down after her sponge bath that afternoon, so she dragged one leg over the side, then the other. She sat on the edge to let the dizziness subside, then carefully plotted her path so she wouldn't yank out any wires or tubing, not wanting to set off any alarms. Jeanette would not be happy. She took her mask off and tested the air. There was no air and she put it back on. The clear tube was long enough to get to the chair by the window. Grabbing the metal tree that held her bags of precious fluids, she painfully, excruciatingly, shuffled the three feet to the chair and flopped down on it, gasping. The crows were gathered in the cottonwoods, their attention on the double utility doors of the hospital. Rats were leaping out of the Trash Daddy. Garbage must be coming. Dinner. A masked man in a black bomber jacket came out and set all the crows to cawing at once, but he wasn't carrying a bag. He didn't even go to the dumpster, but walked over to the white refrigerated trailer instead and unlocked it. When he turned to open the door she could read the back of his jacket. Boulder Coroner. He waved to someone inside the hospital, and two masked women wheeled a gurney out. They wore the same bomber jacket, like a sports team. The Boulder Coroners. Their slogan, "Nature always bats last." On the gurney was a human-sized white plastic bag, and the crows went silent. The three coroners quickly maneuvered the body into the trailer, and when they stepped out, one of the women looked up at the hospital and seemed to sigh.

What had Shelley thought was in there? Had she never wondered? The women wheeled the empty gurney back into the hospital while the man stood guard at the trailer and they rolled out another body bag, and then another. The crows muttered. Finally the man closed the trailer door and locked it, and the team went back into the hospital and the double doors closed behind them. One by one the birds raised their wings and floated down to the Trash Daddy.

Alpenglow radiated pink behind the mountains and she yearned to be walking the foothills to be awash in that healing light, to be so high up she could turn around and view her life from a distance. She wondered if she could locate that trail again after all this time. She wanted to find the spot where the deer had been and collect the weathered bones in a pile, then top it with the skull. She wanted to sit and wait for the mountain lion who'd killed it, who surely watched her every move. There was a lightness in her chest and she felt herself glowing with a yearning for them both, the killer and the prey. They were all related, even the flies in the flesh. It was a circle. She wanted to hug them to her body and let them know how much she loved them. Time was not on their side, but she was here to help. She might have been too late to save Mimi, and she couldn't save the baby, but she would save them.

Mimi suddenly appeared in front of her, looking down into the courtyard with her binoculars. "It's all over but the crying," she said, shaking her head. "Poor baby."

Shelley reached out to touch her and missed. She did not know how she ended up on the floor. She did not remember falling. Jeanette ran in and said "What the hell," and called for help on the intercom. Shelley's mask must have slipped off because she couldn't seem to breathe. She felt like she didn't need to breathe either, like it was all being taken care of by someone else now. She felt so free. More nurses in protective gear arrived and surrounded her. One nurse pushed the chair out of the way and glanced out the window. "I hear they have to bring in another trailer."

"Don't be looking out there," said Jeanette. "Get me the paddles."

Shelley didn't know what the rush was all about. She felt so happy exactly where she was, feeling the soft caress of the world as she floated around her body. Poor body. She wasn't in any pain, although she sensed her limbs weren't arranged quite right. Maybe her wings were in the way. She heard a long shrilling sound.

"Oh, the hawk," she said. "The hawk is here."

Chapter Twenty-Nine

Les was on Pearl, curled on his side with his cup sitting by his face. Officer Sokos, masked like the Lone Ranger, stood over him. "You okay?"

"Yeah, yeah, yeah." Les sat up and rubbed his face, wondering how long she'd been watching him.

Sokos pointed at his cup. "Don't you worry about the virus on that money?" she asked him. "How do you sanitize it?"

"I'm immune," he said.

"What do you mean you're immune?"

"Had myself a good case of Covid."

"What? You were in the hospital?"

"Didn't need it. Biology rarely rests on a single solution. Stayed down at the creek and filled my lungs with the stars and they crowded out the virus. I should patent it."

"Why didn't you go to the clinic? Or try to find some shelter?"

"Not for nothing, I could've dragged my ass to an overpass, but they're full of kids. And that guy in the wheelchair. Didn't want to be a contaminator."

"Do you know where you got it? Have you done your two-week quarantine?"

"Time is a mental construct, officer, not a measurement. If you want to know the current human time, go down the street to the National Institute of Standards and Technology, with their cesium atomic clocks. Amazing machines."

"The city has some hotel rooms for unhoused persons to quarantine in. Wouldn't you like that? They deliver meals to you."

"I'm safer here, outside."

"Did you get the virus from the Purple Grille? We closed them down. They were a hot bed."

"Saw you there yesterday, arresting the Wanderer. What'd she do?"

Sokos paused. "It'll be in the paper later today." She looked away and adjusted her glasses. "She put her baby in the open trunk of her car and then forgot he was there. Shut the trunk, drove off. The baby died."

Les stared at her until she looked back at him. "Let's take a wild, wild guess. Last August? The day you accused Shelley of putting a baby in the trunk of her car?"

Sokos nodded. "The day the city was full of wildfire smoke. When air quality is poor, everyone makes mistakes. Even crime goes up. It was an accident all around."

"Life is an accident all around," said Les.

"We were holding her for a psych evaluation before bail was set, and then she got Covid. Not doing great."

"She wants to be with her baby." Les pulled a cigarette stub from a pocket and lit up. He coughed, but with effort he was able to get some smoke into his tired lungs. "If only someone had reported seeing her put the baby in the trunk, maybe you could have done something about it."

"Don't get smart with me."

"Shelley's sick too. The Wanderer served us outside at the Grille, and we both used the facilities indoors. Probably not one of my smartest decisions, but wouldn't have happened if the city hadn't shut down the public johns. Shelley's at the hospital. She's had a few rough spots, but with any luck just needs a little oxygen and care." He shook his cup. "We all need a little care."

"I'd like to stay and chat with you all day about toilets, but I have an appointment to get tested for Covid. I've been in contact with Amanda Newell too. The Wanderer, as you call her. She has a name."

"So did that baby."

"Freddie," she said his name so quietly it might have been lost in a breeze. Then she reached into a pocket and put a dollar in Les's cup, like a prayer box.

"Freddie," said Les.

Sokos turned to leave. "If you decide you want that hotel room, come down to the station and we'll set you up. I'm not going to force you to go, since you'll walk right out. I don't think I have to worry about anyone getting too close to you. Just stay outside, and keep that mask on."

She walked away, and Les was glad. Not just because she was a jerk but because her presence kept his donors away from him. As soon as she left a woman inched over and put a five dollar bill in his cup.

"Stay safe," she said.

"Will do, darlin'," he said. That fiver would guarantee him a pint. He imagined the heft of the bottle in his hand, the magic sparkle of the liquid on a sunny day like this, the first drops on his tongue, the numbing heat in his throat. The release of the tight grip of consciousness on his brain. He used to love that, used to live for it. Vodka had the constancy and comfort of a best friend, and the all-encompassing surrender of a great love. Now his body grew hot in revolt at the thought of booze, like he'd become allergic. Fucking angels. What was he supposed to do with his time now? His life?

He closed his eyes. He was still pretty knocked out by the virus, and as he felt himself drift back to sleep, the image of the Wanderer wandered into his mind. Oh yes, she was one sick puppy. She was barely on the earth before in her wide-awake coma, now she was hanging on by a silver strand, ready to return her borrowed atoms to the universe. What to do? Should she even be saved? Or was this the merciful end of her suffering? He hovered. Viruses mutate more often than any other organism. In evolutionary terms, they will always adapt faster than we can, so in the long run they'll always come out the winner. Still. He decided that any healing that takes place can contribute to a larger healing.

So. His eyes fluttered open and he looked up at the sky. No life. Not even a moth. He closed his eyes again. He worried that with no alcohol to lubricate his system, his delicate algorithms no longer functioned. When the equation changes, everything changes. He sensed the Wanderer inching farther and farther out on her thread. He stepped into her soul for a moment but it was a ferocious place to be and he was thrown back out on his ass.

He opened his eyes and searched the sky again. A big old redtail up there, been around for a long time, enjoying the miracle of flight, awake to the wonder of aliveness. The birds, they have it all over us. They soar and do not give a thought to the nature of gravity or the origin of a curved universe, do not struggle with the unrest of a human mind. He laid back on the pavement and stared up at the hawk wheeling in the sky above him, forming a hypnotizing circle, around and around, making tighter loops with every swing. He asked for a ride, and it is allowed. He steps into the hawk's head. He soars with the raptor and they break out of their cyclic pattern and rise on the wind. "Road trip," Les says, and the hawk dips and banks, dips and banks, racing to the north edge of town, feeling the magnetic pull of rats and dumpsters. Better hunting. The hospital. Through the walls, they see not the Wanderer, but Shelley, and suddenly they are aware of a scarlet fist faltering, blood pooling in the chambers. With a stomach-lifting drop they enter predation speed and head for a window, the talons go out and the wings arch back, the avenging angel, and for a brief second they think they will crash through the glass. They screech, they screech again, as they grasp the rod with a strength Les has never known. A pulse begins and a pulse stops. Life and death, side by side. Then a rat appears below and they were off again, diving in a free fall to the asphalt. The hawk snatches it with his feathered claws and rises up, weighted down with a squirming dinner, weighted down with survival.

Les jolts upright on the mall flailing about like a snared animal. Someone has not survived.

Chapter Thirty

Shelley sat on a bench outside Boulder Community Hospital waiting for her ride. The hospital had a specially-fitted van to bring Covid patients home so they wouldn't infect friends and family in a car, or infect what was left of the Lyft and Uber fleet. The weather was warm. Pigeons strutted with purpose near her feet, combing for food, sneaking glances at her bag. It had rained in sheets the last couple of days, clearing the air. She'd be feeling pretty good except for the Wanderer. After she recovered from her fall the other day, which seemed to slam the virus right out of her, she'd been obsessively following the Wanderer's story. It was like reading her own. Baby in trunk, life falling apart afterwards, Covid. The only difference was that the Wanderer did not survive Covid. And the baby did not survive the car.

His name was Freddie. He died of heat and asphyxiation in the trunk of his mother's car. How much did he suffer and for how long? Shelley kept putting herself back in time to the parking lot that day, trying to change the end of that story. But the story only got worse with repetition, because at every turn, his death could have been prevented. Most of all, she could have prevented it. She remembered seeing a woman with a baby in a carrier, loading groceries in the car next to her. A red car. The Wanderer. Why hadn't Shelley offered to watch the baby in the shade somewhere while she took care of her groceries?

But even as that thought went through her head, she knew she wasn't the sort of person who helped complete strangers. Her mother was. Shelley always found it annoying every time her mom would stop to help people with crying toddlers or tumbling packages. She once made Shelley late for school when she stopped to help some old guy find his keys on the sidewalk. Shelley was pissy about it and her mom laughed. "It's the human community, honey. We have to help one another carry out the plan."

"What plan?" Shelley asked, and her mom scooted her through the door and into school.

What had been obvious to her mother was lost on Shelley, but maybe she could change. Maybe she could become that person who helped others she saw struggling. Heaven knows there were enough of them. She had struggled herself, and had been helped. She thought of Les, who she ignored for years until she needed him. She'd spent so much energy helping Mimi get what she wanted, it seemed there was no room for others. If she hadn't been at the supermarket that awful day, doing Mimi's relentless shopping, the manager would have kept looking through the surveillance tape to see who actually *did* put a baby carrier in a car trunk. The police would have surrounded the Wanderer with a SWAT team instead of her and saved the baby. Maybe. In truth, considering how hot the day was, she doubted Freddie could have survived the time it took to review the tape. And yet. She could not shake the feeling that her decisions had cost him his life.

Life. She'd taken it for granted before. She wouldn't do that again.

"You must have some angel watching over you," Jeanette had said when Shelley was coming to after her fall. "The woman in the next room wasn't so lucky. Passed away just as we were bringing you around. We need a million arms these days."

Shelley looked out the hall window to see a sheeted gurney go by, and it was like watching her own body being wheeled away. Now she realized it was probably the Wanderer. If so, her deranged decision to get out of bed might have kept the staff from helping her instead.

But maybe it was just as well.

She stood when she saw a hospital van turn in, causing the pigeons to rise up. There was a hand-lettered sign in the windshield that said "Special Carrier." Who knew what all this cost? Thank the sweet gods for Obamacare. Health First Colorado was paying for her hospitalization, and while there were co-pays, the discharge nurse told her to ignore any bills, that the Feds were going to pick up the whole tab during the emergency. As she walked gingerly to the van, the shadow of a large bird flew over, but when she looked behind her, all she saw was a few pigeon feathers suspended in the air. She nodded to the fully masked and gowned driver who slid open the door until she got herself in and buckled. Before the driver closed the door on her, she gave him the address on a piece of paper. Talking was too difficult through the double mask Jeanette attached to her face on her way out of the hospital. The driver glanced at the address and nodded as he got into the driver's seat, which was separated from her with a wall of plastic sheeting. They were going to Mimi's garage, since Shelley couldn't go to her own home quite yet, because the renters wouldn't be out until tomorrow. She had tried to appear sicker at the hospital so they'd keep her for one more day, but she could breathe on her own now, and they needed that bed.

The discharge nurse had asked if she had a safe place to go. "I have a house," Shelley said, not going into too much detail. She knew the city had some rooms at the empty hotels for the homeless, but then she'd have to admit that's what she was, and she knew they'd keep her there for the quarantine period. She'd survived Covid, she could survive a night in the car up at Mimi's. The good news was that she wouldn't have to rent her house out for a while, because while she was sick, stimulus money arrived in her bank account. Just like that. Magic money. It would give her the luxury of recuperating in her own home, once she got there. She hoped she'd find Les at the creek. He'd been well enough to try to visit her, so that was a good sign.

As they drove through town she gazed at the mountains. She'd moved to Boulder for the beauty when she was young, and then had promptly taken it for granted. No more of that. She'd been so careless with it. Careless with the stacked boxes, careless about her part in the hoarding. Careless with the world. The little recycling she did to save the planet at Mimi's had burned the house down. She had to get off her butt and do more. Not only was time not on her side, she knew now it never was. She'd gone into the hospital in winter and come out in spring, as if she'd been away for months rather than weeks. Boulder looked like she felt. With the snow gone, it was all dark and damaged around the edges. Winter had come early that year and covered the scarred and burnt land beneath, making it easy to forget the devastation of the wildfires. Mimi's death seemed like another lifetime in another world.

The van stopped. A demonstration? She hadn't seen that many people in the street since the lockdown began. Young folks, but not all. A few gray heads, some middle-aged folks like her, some children. They were all masked, distanced, and angry. Many were holding "Black Lives Matter" signs, but some had handmade ones. "That's not a chip on my shoulder. That's your foot on my neck." "The law was built on white supremacy." "George Floyd: I Can't Breathe."

Floyd? Must be that man she heard about on TV while waiting to be discharged, crushed to death by a cop a couple of days ago, a knee on Floyd's throat as he called out for his mother. She knew the fear of not being able to breathe. She thought about her own inter-action with the police. What if she weren't a white woman? What if she were a black man, stopped by the police, them thinking she'd kidnapped a baby? She'd be dead. Killed over a tub of kitty litter. Being targeted had been scary enough, but it was just her pride, not her life. She really hadn't felt the same about law enforcement since. Then again, she hadn't really felt the same about anything since that day, what with death, poverty, and pandemic entering her life.

When they started moving again, she did a double-take. The Wanderer, holding a baby, walked through the crowd and disap-peared. Either she was feverish, or she was doomed to be haunted by them forever. As the van inched forward, she recognized a masked face that wasn't some apparition. Trudy, the cart girl, still staring hard at the world through her round glasses. She held a sign. "Enough."

Shelley tapped on the window and gave Trudy a thumbs up, but Shelley couldn't tell if she saw her. Poor Trudy, out under the sun in roasting heat pushing carts around at a supermarket, just doing her job, and Shelley had come gunning for her in a stupid rage. Had Shelley apologized when she saw Trudy on the bus a few weeks ago? She'd said it was an accident, but it wasn't the same as an apology. Trudy looked at her and squinted. Shelley pulled her mask down. "I'm sorry," she mouthed as the van broke free of the crowd. "I'm really sorry."

As they pulled away, she saw Trudy wave and she waved back. She adjusted her mask, closed her eyes in exhaustion, and the next thing she knew she was at Mimi's.

The driver slid open the door, and helped her down the best he could without actually touching her. He looked around at the bull-dozed rubble of what had been Mimi's house. "Are you sure this is the place?" he asked from under his mask.

"Don't worry about me," Shelley said. "You go." She shooed him away, then headed to the garage. She hoped the neighbors didn't see her get out of a medical van. That would raise some questions, and not the sort she'd want to answer. But that worry didn't last long because it was replaced with another, bigger worry. The garage was padlocked, posted, and camera'd. Friggin' lawyers. Probate must've reached a state where someone was given power to do something, and this is what they did. Well, she used to work here, so it was natural for her car to be stored there. Wasn't it? She'd contact Mimi's shark Frank and see what he knew and who she could talk to about getting her car out. It wasn't registered anymore so she'd have to get it towed. And she'd have to leave it at her house which wouldn't make renters happy. Welcome back to life, Shelley, and here's your shitty basket of worries that comes with it.

In the meantime she was weak and tired and had no place to sleep. She could throw in the towel and call the hospital about getting a hotel quarantine bed, but she didn't want to be under house arrest. She sat on the curb and did her pondering away from the cameras. Being in the hospital had done a number on her back, and she wanted to lie down flat somewhere for the night. Her garden shed? Was there room? She could scrounge a blanket or old sleeping bag to bring with her. The food pantry, even now, kept a random pile of donations by their back door.

The bigger problem was that the renters might see her, but if she was quiet and arrived after dark that shouldn't happen. A whole afternoon stretched ahead of her until then. She had no strength or lung capacity to walk anywhere, so she'd have to take an Uber to town. She'd hold her breath to protect the driver for the short drive to Pearl, where she hoped to find Les. She hoped there was a Les to find, and that he wasn't in the hospital by now too. Or worse. She thought about the white trailer in the hospital's courtyard. Anyone could be in there. She knew now, it was all just a matter of time.

Chapter Thirty-One

Shelley found Les on Pearl by the bronze buffalo and she was greatly relieved. Alive. He was alive. He'd gotten the virus too, but he just pushed through it alone in the creek and survived. Considering the smoking, drinking, and a diet of old grapes, it was a miracle. Just goes to show the randomness of life. And death.

"Spree missed you," he said. "But he got by. Came to tell me food was gone. A real survivor, that one, and healer too. I was better after his visit. Sekhet, lion-headed boy goddess, the powerful one."

"His cat food was all gone?" said Shelley.

"You didn't close the canister all the way when you left."

"I guess I was in a rush to die."

"Critters ate it, but I got more."

"Expensive stuff. What do I owe you?"

"Nada," Les said, pulling a bag of grapes from his pocket. "I raked in the cash with a kibble sign. Everyone asks about him. I might have to take him down here sometime for a victory lap." He tossed a grape in his mouth. "Did you hear about the Wanderer?"

"Yes, arrested. And now she's dead."

"Dead? Fuck all."

"I feel awful," said Shelley with a cough. "I was next to her in the parking lot when she was struggling with groceries and a baby and didn't do anything about it. For all I know I was next to her in the hospital."

"We are an endangered species."

"I'd fallen on the floor, and the first thing I saw when I came to was a body being wheeled down the hall. That could have been her."

"I knew it. I sensed death all around you."

"Les, it's a hospital during a plague. It doesn't take any special talent to sense death there."

They were silent for a while, except for coughing. Shelley watched people amble down Pearl, occasionally dropping some coin or bills into Les's cup. They all seemed to be a bit out of it. Their minds elsewhere. Distracted. She wanted to tell them about the white trailer, how it stood there waiting. She wanted everyone to start paying more attention.

"My nurse said you called and tried to visit," she said. "Thanks. Sorry I was too busy hallucinating to come to the window."

"See anything interesting?" asked Les.

"Mostly talking birds. And Mimi. I think she tried to kill me."

"Birds," Les said, and smiled. "Nice."

"Not particularly. Most of them were downright scary. It was not what I would call a good trip."

"They have to be scary sometimes. Like angels. It's their job."

As if on cue, a hawk screeched overhead in a heated interaction with a jay, then the birds went their separate ways in a huff. The sky was so beautiful that Shelley wondered if she had ever really seen it before.

"Why is the sky blue?" she asked.

Les cleared his throat and coughed. "Blue is the light that stays behind, hanging out in the atmosphere. It doesn't quite touch Earth in its journey from the sun."

"That's sad."

"No. It's glorious." As they stared, a blue jay feather drifted down towards them, like a piece of sky gently falling. Les stood and snatched it out of the air, and they laughed, which set them both coughing.

"A keeper," he said, and he tucked it into one of his many pockets.

"I'm going to lie down," said Shelley. "Too much excitement."

She'd swung by the food pantry and picked up a half-decent sleeping bag out back. Her sense of smell was still off, so she examined it for vomit or worse as she spread it out on the bench. And then she stretched her tired body out. There were so few people on Pearl and she was so heavily masked, she felt she could do what she wanted, and did. She closed her eyes against the bright sun and let it warm her all over. It was a gorgeous spring, and here she was to enjoy it. Achy, but here. She spent an uneventful afternoon drifting in and out of sleep as Les tended to his cup.

At some point, she woke up with a start and thought she saw the Wanderer out of the corner of her eye, walking down Pearl, but there was no one, just a few pigeons fluttering in place. When it started to get dark, she rolled up her bag and Les counted his money. "Let's get some takeout to bring with us," he said. "My treat."

"I'm not going to argue with that," said Shelley. "Surprise me. Maybe I'll even be able to taste it." She waited on the bench while he went to the outdoor table at the West End Tavern. She'd never known him to buy takeout before. All his money was invested in those little glass bottles of Tito's, and he scavenged for eats. Maybe the government found him and sent him stimulus money too.

He returned carrying a bag, and they took the Hop back to her house. They usually walked it, but they just couldn't muster the strength. There was no one else but the driver on the bus, separated by a plastic wall. She felt guilty about getting on public transportation while possibly being contagious, in fact, probably still contagious and coughing to boot, but what could she do? Even the short walk back from the bus stop was hard going. They tried to stay quiet as they walked in the purpling light, not wanting to bring attention to themselves, but they had to keep muffling their coughs and clearing throats. With everyone at home now, people had nothing better to do than stare out the window, and she and Les sounded like a walking TB ward. They held their breaths as they tiptoed around to the back of her house, hiding from her renters, until they got to the garden shed.

"Night then," she whispered, and patted her sleeping bag.

"Come on," whispered Les. "I'll give you the good spot on my ledge. You can lay down straight. You'll wake up a pretzel in there. And not for nothing, but we already know there's critters in there."

Spree sidled up to her and rubbed himself against her legs.

"You made it, Spree," she croaked. "I was so worried. Thank Uncle Les for taking care of you. He was pretty sick himself."

She opened the shed door a crack and the three of them looked in. Les was right. There was rustling in the corner under the plastic pots. She put Spree down to see if he would go after whatever it was, but no. Spree sat and looked at the open door, making no motions to enter, which made Shelley think it was something more than a mouse. The weather was warm enough, it could even be a snake. Or snakes. She envisioned herself sitting up all night in fear.

"Besides," he said. "I got your favorite. Meatloaf. You don't want to eat it in there, do you?"

"You're not going to be up all night dancing and shouting are you?"

"There's no telling. Maybe if you start listening carefully enough you'll hear the music too."

She coughed into her sleeping bag and saw the shadow of her renter pass by the kitchen window. If they called the police, dear god, it would be the end of her business. She could not keep from coughing all night, she knew that much, and she could make as much noise as she wanted down by the creek. The weather was warm and dry. "Alright," she said, lowering her voice. "Let's give it a try." By noon the next day she would have her house back. Just hold on for a few more hours. It couldn't be worse than what she'd just been through in the hospital.

"Follow me," whispered Les.

Shelley turned to Spree. "Let's go," she said, and they headed down the path. It was steep, uneven, and slick with snowmelt but exposed roots acted as footholds. The brush had fully leafed out making it hard to see, but she stayed near Les. She heard the creek before she saw it, and soon they came to an old cottonwood tree, high enough above the water to have survived this long. Holding its ground. She knew this tree, or at least she knew the top of it, since it was one of the few along the creek tall enough to peek above the edge of the ravine. There was a bit of dry, flat ledge around it. Les's home, for lack of a better word, was smaller than she'd thought. Funny, here she lived right on the edge of the creek and had never followed his path all the way down. She was always afraid of falling, and more. It was spooky, a human wilderness, with no homes and no rules and a whiff of urine. She had qualms about sleeping so close to Les, but knew that the chances of sleep were almost nil. He'd never tried anything with her, but he was a man after all, and they would both be horizontal. She weighed her options yet again, considered the meatloaf, and all in all this was still the best bet. Besides, she was too tired to climb back up the embankment anyway. And she would hardly be alone with Les. She could see small fires up and down the creek. But would they come if she screamed? She'd never come when they screamed.

"Nice," Shelley said.

"We mill trees and cut stone to create something we call home," said Les, spreading out his arms. "But it is already here, ready-made. The original ones say that just sitting under a cottonwood can cure what ails you." He took off his mask and pointed to a five gallon bucket in the bushes. "For when nature calls," he said. "Don't squat bare-bottom around here or you'll get your ass bit by a rattler. I know."

"Where do you empty that?" Shelley looked at the creek.

"The sewer grate in front of your house." He unfolded a big piece of cardboard and spread it out for her.

"My house?"

"Don't worry. I move it at night, just like the nocturnal dung beetle."

She sat. There was so much right in front of her eyes she never saw. Her sleeping bag had no zipper, so she arranged it under and over herself like a taco. Then, from a black plastic bag that had seen better days, Les pulled out some sort of covering for himself, almost like a black cape.

"Pillow?" he asked.

"Please," she said, and he handed her a wadded up t-shirt he pulled up from the dregs of the bag. She knew she was getting better because its scent was something powerful. She waved it away. "Know what? I think I'll just use my bag."

"Best thing for your back is no pillow. Go to ground, feel the earth." He leaned up against his tree, using his black bag as a cushion, then pulled the cape over his knees. He reached into the take-out bag and handed her a cardboard container and bamboo utensils. Spree sat in between them, waiting.

"Yum!" she said. The meatloaf was still warm, with mashed potatoes and green beans, all covered in a dark gravy. Les got the same except with peas, which she supposed were easier to chew with so few teeth. She heard rustling in the bushes. Spree turned to look but did not investigate.

"What's that?" she asked.

"Critter," said Les. "Wildlife knows us by our garbage, and they're waiting for it."

When they finished eating, Shelley gave Spree a chunk of

meatloaf, and Les took her empty from her. He pocketed the cutlery, then walked to the brush where they'd heard the rustling and tossed their trash into it. "Someone will even eat the cardboard containers. Perfect recycling."

He sat back down and took a bottle of water out of his bag and drank. She'd never seen him drink a liquid that was not alcohol. Maybe it was lucky water, as they called it on the street, a bottle filled with vodka.

"What's that?" she asked.

"Aqua," he said. "Haven't felt like my Tito's lately. Had a vision while I was sick. I think it was a vision. Wasn't pretty."

"Good on you," she said, amazed. A sober Les. She wondered what that would look like and how long it would last. She drank just a sip of her own water. She didn't want to have to get up in the middle of the night and find that bucket, and meet whatever was between her and it.

"I'm going to sit up," said Les. "You sleep." He searched through his pockets and brought out a few half-smoked butts and lit one with a match. The glow reflected on his face, then disappeared.

"I'm not sure I'll sleep," Shelley said, "but I'll rest."

She adjusted her body on the ground, feeling some sort of vegetation cushioning her aching back beneath the thin bag. It felt cozy and welcoming, and she kept very still to take it all in. After clawing the sleeping bag, Spree curled up against her side, unconcerned about the night noises around them. Shelley was watchful, waiting for something to happen, and soon enough she no longer expected anything to happen and relaxed. As the night sky got darker, the fish, swans, and archers of the sky got brighter. She'd spent so many nights on the street the last few months that the stars had become as familiar as her hands and she did not need or want anything more. Not a bed, not a roof, not a house. She was entirely happy. She had felt this briefly in the hospital after she fell and before she came to, when she felt alive and part of something bigger, more whole. There had been a flood of emotion filling her heart. She wondered if she had died. She wondered if that was heaven.

"I feel like I could touch the Moon," she said. She raised her hands up and framed the Moon in her palms. "It's like holding a ball."

"Hold on tight," said Les. "The Moon's moving away from Earth about as fast as your fingernails grow."

"I think I can keep up. Look at all the stars. I've never seen so many."

"You'd see more if it weren't for the light pollution. And satellites. Many stars are too far away to be seen directly, but you can see them out of the corner of your eye." He paused. "That's true about many things."

She thought of the Wanderer, how she thought she'd seen her and her baby on Pearl that day. "There's some things I don't want to see, straight on or not."

"Everyone should be made to lie for an hour under the stars every night," said Les. "Breaks up the old pattern, thinking humans are the center of the universe."

She turned on her side. Yes, the universe. What about it? Why was there something and not nothing, as she'd heard Les ask more than once. There was no answer, he'd say, answering himself, but the something was definitely all around us. Like now. The snow had disappeared while she was gone, and in its place the green things were saying hello. There was a tangle of leaves in front of her face. "What are these plants?" she asked, trying to remember if she knew what poison ivy looked like.

"Grape vines." He patted the leaves.

"Your grape vines?" She propped herself up on her elbows and looked around.

"Mine," he said.

The moon provided enough silver light to see how much earth

Les had covered with his crazy project. The vine, with its new leaves and tendrils, crept far from the tree along the embankment and climbed halfway up the tree as well. She thought of all the months she'd been hanging out with him, and everywhere they went he was always pushing grape seeds into the ground. Now look. That was some real faith in nature, for you.

"Tell me a story," she said. "Tell me the story of Les."

Les coughed, and then she sat up to cough too. He rummaged around his jacket and took out two cookies. He offered her one, and she accepted. If she couldn't sleep she might as well eat. In the dark his hands looked like roots, the swollen knuckles as knobbed as tubers. He poked around in his pockets again and found a few half-smoked butts. He laid them neatly on the ground. Then he pulled out an old bread bag full of mangled greens and emptied them out on the ground. He took off his boots and the blood-stained cloth wrappings that served as socks. Even in the darkness she could see that his toes were overlapped and deformed. The nail beds were gone. A pinky toe was missing. Two pinky toes.

"That's some frostbite," she said.

"No, it was some childhood," he said. "Pain was encouraged in the hope that ordeal would lead to illumination. That's the story of Les in a nutshell." He then went about rubbing his feet with the crumbled leaves. "First mint of the season."

She might have guessed his story would be more like a dark fairy tale, with tortured yellow-eyed creatures lurking in the woods. "Why mint?" she asked.

"Healing." He held the crushed leaves in both hands and brought them to his face, then offered them to her. "Breathe in. Even if you can't smell yet, it'll help the lungs."

She inhaled. She could smell. Or was it just a memory of a smell? A memory of scabbed knees cushioned by mint along a culvert, catching tadpoles with her brother. Behind the old house, before the move. Before her father left. Those were sweet days, weren't they? It had taken her a long time to get back to them. "How did the boy Les survive this illumination?"

Les put his wrappings and boots back on. "The boy wandered the hills looking at plants and bugs. He studied the clouds. The violence at home eventually became just a painful annoyance. He knew it was not the real world. The real world was the sky, and the running water, and the beetles living their best lives under leaf litter." Les paused to light a cigarette stub.

"What happened to the parents?" Shelley asked.

"Don't know. Bones got broken and the boy got taken away to a Home. He wrote them a letter to free the turtle he kept under the bed. They never wrote back. He still wonders if the turtle made it out alive."

"The boy did," said Shelley. "The boy made it out alive."

"I suppose. Science released him from the pain of living in an inexplicable world. The day he was taught that humans were made of eighty-four minerals, twenty-three elements, and eight gallons of water spread across thirty-eight trillion cells was the day he finally made sense of life."

Les coughed and put out his cigarette butt. "How did that boy become this man?" she asked, and gestured at him with her cookie.

"The creation of a coherent environment out of chaotic stimuli is one of the brain's primary activities, so I studied the clouds for what they had to tell me."

"Which was?"

"The clouds aligned themselves and told me that I was a creature of organic matter and electrical energy that will be absorbed and spit back into the arms of the cosmos, the sooner the better. I took that to mean I should come here, to this ledge of repose."

"Here? I'd have gone back to the clouds and asked for a roof with that repose."

"Shelter is an animal need, but home is a state of mind. I could reconcile with the Earth here and make myself at home."

There was some trembling noise in the thickets. A critter? "I prefer a place with a few walls."

"When walls fall the mind opens to the brilliance of totality."

"Totality," Shelley said, coughing on the word. "I don't like the sound of that."

Les coughed out a laugh. Shelley finished her cookie, then leaned back to watch the sky. The moon was so bright it lit up the passing clouds. "What do the clouds say about the future for Les?"

"They tell me I'm just like them. Just passing through. A brief visitor on Earth."

She wrapped her sack tighter around her body. "When I thought I was dying, I sort of thought I should be doing more for the Earth."

"First thing, you're going to have to learn to fly."

Shelley thought of the planes dumping red liquid on the wildfires. "I'm a little long in the tooth to be getting my pilot's license, Les."

"If you need a plane to fly, you're not doing it right."

She laughed, then coughed. A low animal noise came from the underbrush, and she held her breath. "What's that?" she whispered.

Les shrugged. "An animal. Enjoy the sounds of whatever it is. The day is coming when there will be no wild creatures without our intervention." A man started screaming farther up the creek, then silence. "Now, those human sounds, worry about them. After you master flying, the next thing to do is learn to fight with knives."

She smiled, reached into her pocket and pulled out her trusty knife and clicked it open, brandishing it in the air. Moonlight caught the metal blade and made it sparkle. "I'm pretty handy with this baby."

"Good," he said. "You'll need it."

She put her knife away. "The story of Les was sad."

"Don't go to sleep with thoughts like that. It doesn't help. Here, I'll tell you a joke."

"Okay," she said, pulling up her sleeping bag. "Go ahead."

"Why can't you trust atoms?" he asked.

"Why can't you trust atoms?" she asked.

"They make up everything."

She groaned, then coughed a little, and closed her eyes.

Les sat for some time, finishing the last of his butts, watching the smoke rise like an offering. His connection to the astral plane. There was no sound or breeze other than that stirred up by the wings of nocturnal insects. Shelley's breath got slow and steady, then she was asleep and it was not so quiet. A snorer. He could have guessed that. As if orchestrated by her snorts, spring peepers began their nightly chorus, followed by the wingbeat of a large nightbird overhead, a big fan of bite-sized frogs. He reached into a pocket and pulled out the jay feather he'd snatched from the sky that afternoon, that expansive blue veil of the goddess. He dragged a finger along the feather's edge, letting the stiff barbs spring back to perfect order. Soft but with a spine. Had we the wings, many would fly, as old Emily once wrote. He leaned over and carefully, carefully tucked it in Shelley's hair, then smiled. Oh yes, he thought, you'll survive.

Chapter Thirty-Two

It was a day that began with an owl. Shelley had never been woken up by an owl before, but one was sure enough hooting in a tree not far away. *You-uu, You-uu, You-uu*. Not enough light to see it. The moon had run off behind the mountains.

"Flammulated owl," Les muttered, stirring in his nest of blankets.

She nodded, but realized he couldn't see a nod so she added a grunt. She watched where she thought the hoot had come from, and when the first glimpse of daylight broke, she saw it, the feathers blending with the filtered light. It was far closer than she had imagined, practically right over her. How many times in her life had she been near some wondrous creature and not known?

"Hello there," she said. She felt that ever since her experience with birds at the hospital she was now on a first-name basis with the species. At the sound of her voice the small owl's eyes opened wide, like dark pools of water, but did not look at her. It was thinking of down-lined grass and speckled eggs. Moss, peeling bark, beetles, leaf litter. It thinks patience, it thinks hunger, it thinks survival. It senses a small vole scurrying in and out of the brush, then dives with silent wings. She hears only the humming buzz of spring insects.

"That was odd," she said. She touched her forehead to make sure the fever wasn't back.

"It is odd," said Les. "That owl shouldn't be down here. He lives in the mountains. Wonder what he knows that we don't."

"Everything," said Shelley. "With those big eyes, he can see everything."

"If our eyes were in that proportion to our heads they'd be the size of oranges."

Shelley sat up and saw her sleeping bag was covered in white. "Snow!"

Les rolled over and opened his eyes. "Not snow. The cottonwoods are releasing their fuzz. It's May. It's what they do. Distributing their DNA."

Shelley brushed the fuzz out of her hair, and examined one of the seedheads up close. Did she know that? Had she really lived in Colorado most of her life without realizing that cottonwoods snowed in May?

Les got up with a great deal of moaning, pulled his bandana up over the lower half of his face, and wandered up the creek, presumably to pee. She wasn't ready to get up. It was chilly but not cold. The morning air was so clear it felt like a soothing solid against her skin. She'd slept in all her clothes, and with the sack she'd been warm, even toasty. She buttoned her coat and raised her arms to stretch, bracing herself for a sharp pain in her back, but nothing. A miracle. Not only that, but she'd slept through the night. Outside, under the sky. She didn't just sleep, she slept like some sprite had fluttered by and sprinkled fairy dust on her. Her dreams were settled and comforting. Her mom had showed up in one, and just sat there, smiling at her. She had a baby in her lap, rocking it back and forth, back and forth. There was no sorrow. No loss. Just love. She gathered her sleeping bag around her and sat up and coughed. Even her cough felt better.

Les returned with two banged up tin cups of steaming coffee.

"Where'd you get those?" she asked.

"The families under the bridge. I bring them stuff, they give me stuff. They said welcome."

"It's barely even dawn," she said. Les handed her a mug. The sleeves of his jacket were pushed up and there was a scarred print of a perfect set of teeth marks on his lower arm.

Shelley thought about his mangled feet inside those boots. People walk around with such pain, hidden away where no one could see.

He returned to his tree, stretched his legs out in front of him, and coughed. "It's civil dawn," said Les. "The sun is six degrees below the horizon, enough light for outdoor activities to commence. They're getting their kids off to places where there's Wi-Fi for remote school. No working or learning from home if you don't have one."

"Work?"

"Service jobs. Construction. A lot of people here work, but their wages don't cover housing."

Shelley sipped her coffee, which was amazingly good. It didn't seem right that you could work and still not afford a place to live. Then again, if Keith hadn't paid up her house as the divorce settlement, what sort of place could she have ever rented on Mimi's salary around here, nevermind bought? She couldn't have. She couldn't even maintain her house without renting it out half the time and putting herself on the street. Maybe she should rent out her basement to one of the families here, just accept what they could afford and hope it would cover expenses. Work out something to keep each other safe, what with the pandemic. There was a toilet down there, and they could use a hot plate or toaster oven to cook. Maybe there was one kicking around Mimi's garage, if she ever got access to it again. She thought of the dozens of expensive countertop appliances she'd helped Mimi buy and then pack into storage, unopened. What was that all about? Had she never thought to ask Mimi why? Maybe if they'd ever talked about the why sometimes and not always the what, she could have been some help and not an accomplice.

Having renters under the same roof would be a big change in her life, but she was ready for it. She'd been through so much, she could do this. She would make herself ready. As her mother used to say, if change were easy, it wouldn't always be depicted in the Bible as a miracle.

"I'd like to meet the folks who made this coffee," she said.

Les looked at the sun. "They're gone now. They have to drop the baby at daycare first."

"Baby?" It was frightening to think one lived here, along the creek. She looked around her. Now that the snow was gone, the winter's trash was exposed. Up and down the creek, a tumble of broken lawn furniture, plastic bottles, shreds of clothes, and pieces of bikes. "We need to clean all this up."

"After the spring melt, volunteers come with a couple of dumpsters and we all work to clear it out," Les said.

"They do?"

"They do," said Les, lighting up his first butt of the day, and they both coughed.

In the growing light, she watched small children trudging out of the creek and up to the street, weighted down with backpacks. Off to school. She looked at her watch.

"Just a few more hours and I can get my house back." She finished her coffee and reached for her boots. "I'm going to go whizz. I'll be back."

Les watched Shelley walk away. The sun was finally up enough that he could see it reflected in the newborn leaves overhead, glistening. The wind picked up, sending a warm gust down the creek. The owl commented. *You-uu, You-uu, You-uu.* Les closed his eyes and smiled at the sound of the gentle hoot, then sat upright in a panic. He sniffed the air then stood up, studying the clouds.

"Altostratus," he said out loud.

It was coming. *Coming for you.*

"What's wrong?" asked Shelley, making her way back through the brush. "Who were you talking to?"

"The sferics were talking to me," he said. "Electromagnetic waves of atmospheric origin. Usually associated with thunderstorms. Or the first sign of the foehn."

Shelley sat back down and wrapped the sleeping bag around her shoulders. "Les, it's too early for a complicated weather report. Just tell me if it's going to rain or not."

"The foehn is here. That's the report."

"The what?"

"The Chinook. It's not the fresh wind that blows against the empire, it's the ill wind that blows hot and dry down a mountain, driving everything mad before it. Plays hell with serotonin levels."

"The Chinook comes every year," she said, going through her bag for some food. "I haven't snapped yet."

"The temps could rise forty degrees in minutes, then the adiabatic compression accelerates the melt. The fires destroyed the undergrowth that might have soaked up water and slowed it down. And we're all downstream. So the answer to your question is no, it's not going to rain. It's going to flood."

"Want a granola bar? Peanut butter crackers?"

"I'm going to wander up the ridge a bit, try to get a bead on the clouds. Come along?"

"You go. I'm going to have a snack and rest a bit. I don't want a relapse."

He looked up the creek towards the canyon, then bent his head back and studied the sky. "The trouble is, as the Buddha said, you only think you have time."

"Oh, I know I have time," Shelley said, opening up some crackers. "The renters don't leave til noon."

Chapter Thirty-Three

When her renters vacated, Shelley returned to her house, tired as an old turtle. She hadn't rested at the creek as planned. Mid-morning, she heard the horns and shouts of the Black Lives Matter protest in town, so she put on her mask and wandered over. She found a secluded place to sit and took it all in, inhaling the energy. She was surprised how many people she knew, store owners in town, workers from the University. Street people. High school kids. The crowd was some angry, but full of life, and by the time she got home, she felt strong enough to strip her bed and put fresh sheets on. That didn't last. By late afternoon she curled up on the sofa with Spree. She was better, but far from her old self. She'd felt so good when she woke up that morning she was tempted to sleep outside again. The ground had been healing, and she needed healing in all sorts of ways.

Spree rubbed his face against hers, and purred heavily under her touch. There was so much pleasure to be had in the world. He would have enjoyed watching the birds with her in the hospital. "How'd you heal yourself, Spree? Last fall you're burnt and bald, and now look at you. All big and furry."

He stopped purring and stretched his neck, listening to

something outside. "It's a car, silly," Shelley said. "Just a car turning around in the circle."

But in a few short moments there was a knock on the door. Spree jumped off the sofa and Shelley peeked out the window. Officer Sokos.

"Now what?" she said. She put on her mask and opened the door, but the wind practically blew it out of her hand. What had Les said about the wind today?

"Here to have a look in the trunk of my car again?" Shelley asked.

Sokos stepped back, away from the door, adjusting her sunglasses over her mask and looked around. They both stared at the curb, where it all started last August, as if reliving it. The guns, the helicopter, the fear. "I'm sorry that happened," said Sokos. "I should have said that back then."

An apology. Shelley never thought she'd hear that from her. The pandemic was creating all sorts of changes. "I'm sorry that happened too," said Shelley, not feeling like she had to be all that gracious about it.

"I wasn't sure you were home," said Sokos. "I didn't see your car."

Shelley looked at the empty driveway. "My car," she said. She almost forgot she had to deal with getting her car out of Mimi's garage. Maybe she could use a little of the stimulus money in her account to have it towed back home where it belonged. One day she might even be able to afford to put it back on the road. Who knew what amazing things might happen in her life? "My car is elsewhere. I heard you finally arrested the right person for the kitty litter. Oh, wait, it wasn't kitty litter after all, was it? It was a baby."

Sokos touched her sunglasses, and then adjusted her black mask. "It was a mistake all around."

"Now they're both dead."

"I keep going over what happened that day and wishing it had gone differently."

"Wishes can't change the past. How'd you finally figure out there was a real baby in a trunk somewhere?"

"Chance," said Sokos. "More crimes are solved by luck than we'd care to admit."

"Did you have to arrest her? Hadn't she suffered enough?"

"I didn't arrest her soon enough. I let her fall into the hands of that cult. I increased her suffering when she might have gotten some help."

Shelley was surprised that Sokos was taking so much responsibility for what happened, but then again, there was a lot of it to go around. After all, Shelley could have kept that baby out of the trunk in the first place if she'd only offered to help. In spite of herself, she softened a bit.

"What did the Wanderer say happened? With the baby?"

"Freddie. She didn't say. Every question was met with a vague look. We told her we knew it was an accident, why hadn't she said so? She said, 'No one asked.' It was her only lucid moment. The officer who arrived at the scene that day had told me she was in no state for questions. It was not great policing."

Shelley was quiet. They both looked up the street, as if waiting to see the Wanderer plodding her way down the sidewalk. Shelley hoped that wherever she was, she could finally sit down and get some rest.

"Now the husband is in jail on assault charges and a suicide watch." Sokos cradled her arms. "He blames himself for making Amanda rush that day in the parking lot, scrambling for child care when he bailed. He attacked his boss this morning, the one who had kept him from going home on time that day. Tried to run him over with his car." She looked at her hands and let them drop. They listened to the wind. "But that's not why I'm here." She reached into her jacket and pulled out a piece of paper, then stepped forward and handed it to Shelley. Then she stepped back. "There's a flash flood warning for the next twenty-four hours and the city wants you to evacuate. That sheet will tell you everything you need to know."

Spree came to the door and sat, staring down the street. Shelley looked behind Sokos. Police were going door to door. Sweet mother of the mewling baby Jesus. Can't there be just one disaster at a time anymore?

"I can't," Shelley said. "I'm supposed to quarantine. Besides, spring flooding tends to veer up on the other side of the creek."

"This will be an exceptional event," said Sokos. "There are road closures all along the creek, from Nederland to Gunbarrel. Call the number at the bottom of that sheet to find out where to go if you're under quarantine. There's a hotel or two set up for that sort of thing."

Shelley leaned against the doorframe for support. She was so tired. She'd gone through so much to get back in her house, she wasn't going to leave it. She could weather a flood. She'd been through worse.

"No. I won't go. They might not let me back out, and they probably won't let me take the cat. Don't worry about me. Have you gotten everyone out of the creek? You know there are children down there? Les told me there's even a baby. A guy in a wheelchair too."

"I am well aware of who lives there. They are not invisible to us. Les has been helping the Homeless Outreach Team, convincing the squatters we aren't here to deport or institutionalize anyone." Sokos took off her sunglasses. It was the first time Shelley had seen her without them. She looked tired, and vulnerable. Almost human. The wind blew her clay-colored hair out from under her cap. "The problem is, he won't go. Maybe you can talk to him."

"I'll do that," Shelley said. "But you and I both know he usually only follows the voices in his head."

There was a moment when they almost smiled at one another. Sokos nodded, then tucked her hair under her cap and put her glasses back on. The light caught on them funny, so they weren't that reflective blue anymore, but bands of colors.

"Get to safety and take Les with you. And one more thing," Sokos said, pointing at Shelley. "There's cottonwood fluff in your hair. And a feather."

Shelley ran her fingers through her matted mess as she watched Sokos walk back to the cruiser. The wind caught her cap and blew it across the lawn. Sokos had to get on her knees to retrieve it.

Shelley scooted Spree into the house and shut the door. She looked in the hall mirror and brushed the fluff away, then plucked a blue jay feather from her head. She twirled the feather between her fingers, amazed that such a color could be on a bird. That it even existed. She tucked in her jeans pocket and went to talk to Les.

Chapter Thirty-Four

Shelley made her way gingerly down to Les's spot under the tree, grabbing onto a low branch here and there to steady herself. Not only did the wind throw her off balance, the steep banks were still slick from the recent rain, and if she fell in the creek, she'd have no strength to fight the rising water. It was alarming how much higher the creek was now than just a few hours ago, and she knew how much higher and ferocious it could get. A few years ago a flash flood took a bite from her backyard. Maybe she should evacuate after all. Then again, she'd just come so close to death from Covid, what were the chances of death by drowning now? The world wouldn't pull something like that again on her in the same breath, would it? She calculated how much backyard stood between her house and destruction. Enough, she hoped. Enough. The garden shed could be a floater if the worst happened. Maybe she should move the mower to the front lawn for the duration.

"I know, I know," Les said as she approached, before she even had a chance to open her mouth. "You want me to leave."

"Sokos asked me to talk some sense into you. You can't stay where you are."

"None of us can stay where we are," he said, with a cough. "Thermodynamics 101. All living organisms must constantly exchange a flow of matter and energy with their environment, or die."

"Good to know," said Shelley. "Sokos wants me to leave too, but I'm thinking I'll hold down the fort. They give us these warnings all the time and it's usually nothing."

Les sniffed the wind. "This is not nothing. Don't mess with nature."

"I don't want to go to a quarantine hotel. The nurse at the hospital told me that once I'm in I can't just check out."

"So?" asked Les. "Rent your house out while the city puts you up for a couple of weeks. Assuming the house is still standing."

"I've waited a long time to sleep at home. Come stay. You put me up last night. I can put you up tonight."

"Do you have an attic? With a window where you can pull yourself up on the roof if need be?"

"A crawl space. Maybe there's a vent. But it doesn't matter, I'm not climbing up on any roof."

"Climb high or die as they say in the business. I'm waiting on a family that went off this morning and hasn't been seen since. The people who gave us coffee this morning. They might be afraid that if they go to a shelter they'll be deported."

"Bring them. I'll leave the back door open for you." She stopped. "Promise to get out in time, even if they don't show up?"

"I do. And you? Will you get to safety in time?"

"I'll try," she said, and started her climb back up the embankment. The ground was as slick as snot, and she nearly fell right on her face.

Les licked the air, then stood up to assess the situation. The breath upon the water was becoming a violent exhalation. He knew it was going to be bad when he saw the National Guard swarming around that afternoon, accountants and bank tellers in soldier garb unloading sandbags, trying to save downtown at the cost of intensifying the blast here in the creek. They knew. Oh, they knew. They had come to move everyone out, shouting orders from beneath their black masks. He could feel their fear. Could feel his own fear now. Water was already grinding away at the earth beneath his ledge. Wished he had some sips.

No. No he didn't. What was needed was a clear brain to wait on that last family. Quick decisions might have to be made. Life or death. Or life and death.

He leaned against the tree and closed his eyes, saw the silver dragon charging down the canyon on the hot wind of the foehn. The red dragon had burned all the trees and shrubs in the mountains last summer, allowing snow melt to rush down the sides of the canyon with nothing holding it back. Then there's the secret ingredient to any disaster. Dust. Ashes to ashes in the worst possible way. Dust and ashes rise in the wind from exposed ground, get blown on top of the snow, accelerating the melting, which exposes more ashen ground, which blows more dust on the snow, accelerating the melting. The system will keep repeating itself, and then the system will keep repeating itself. A lethal loop. A crazed red and silver striped dragon chasing its tail, creating dust devils. *Chiindii.*

After the Hayman fire, a couple of inches of rain fell and it took under an hour for the flow of water to rise from 62 cubic feet per second to 2170 cubic feet per second. There had been a shitload of rain the other night, and now a foehn-induced melt. He sensed the transformative cycles of birth and death riding the current with a whip, slapping the water. Turbulence was the best way of moving energy across spacetime, a fundamental organizing principle of physical systems, creating unimaginable power. What was coming was explosive.

In other words, if he stayed too much longer he was fucked.

And Shelley? He considered the safety of her house. He considered the safety of anyone in the flood plain. They were now like the Pleistocene people, born during the Ice Age twelve thousand years ago, then the great melt came, an inundation so sudden and cataclysmic it decimated the human population, leaving behind widespread oral histories of a flood, and more besides. The people are to be pitied, and it's not over yet. Les used to believe that it was only the futility of the first flood that prevented the gods from sending a second, but now he was not so sure. Water carves canyons out of deserts, swallows whole cities and continents, but with any luck it will also destroy our stupidity and greed.

If that's what had to be, let it be. Two hundred thousand years of human existence and here we were, ready to dissolve like salt in water.

An angel arrived. Not one of the bullies, but a quiet one, wings slender and slate-gray, folded like a dove's. He was surprised the angels knew how to find him without following his trail of empty Tito's. They were smarter than he thought. She waited with her head down. She has all the time in the world she says. All the time. He has none, he says, and she laughs, raising her head to look him in the face. He sees eternal love in her eyes, and pity too. "Climb high or die," she says. "When the water comes down from the mountains it will be like a fist."

She turned and stepped into the roiling water, walking away on the turbulence until she disappeared in billowing clouds.

Better go. He turned to leave, but a dark, smirking angel rose up in front of him.

Coming for you.

Les found his shepherd's crook on the ground and brandished it at the angel. He had always held out hope that if he kept his demons at bay, he could buy time for someone to rescue him. He imagined he would be saved by love washing over him, but he saw now, he could only be saved by letting it flow through him. It was time to go with the flow. He put his crook down. "I'm done fighting," he said, and the angel shrugged and disappeared, sinking with a smile beneath the roiling surface of the creek.

He leaned on his crook like a cane and examined the flashing water, then looked up at the crazed birds flying up and out of the canyon. The sun was setting. He sensed brush snapping, animals running for high ground, and knew water was now rushing like a freight train through the burnt mountains. A hawk, its screech silenced by the noise, snatched a rabbit driven out into the open by fear. Les could feel the talons dig deep into the animal's flesh. And then he felt the land breaking beneath him.

It was late enough now that the family he was waiting for must have gone elsewhere. But then, as he turned to make his way to Shelley's, he finally saw what he'd been waiting for. In the dimming light, he made out a woman lugging a baby carrier coming down the main path, oblivious to the danger. As he opened his mouth to scream at her, she slipped on the wet mud and lost her grip on the carrier as she stumbled. As she bent to retrieve it, the flood waters blasted out of the canyon and lifted it away. It floated. It was floating, even as the mother disappeared. As if he had wings, he used his metal crook to pull himself up into the cottonwood tree, then leaned over the rapidly rising water, his body draped along a branch like a sandbag. He held tight as he lowered the hooked end of the crook into the water. The baby carrier was a swiftly moving thing, and he saw his life condensed to the few seconds he had to save it. In defiance of Heisenberg's uncertainty principle, it was indeed possible to calculate speed and position simultaneously. It was almost dark, but he could see well enough to align the handle with the hook, and caught the carrier, which nearly pulled him off the branch and into the water. He suctioned his armpits to the branch to free his hands, then pulled up the crook until he could grab the carrier's handle. Once he had a firm grip he released the crook so he could use both hands to yank it on the branch with him.

Saved. The baby was his. He did not want to think of what happened to the mother. He had not seen her float by, so there was a chance she got blasted out of the water. He looked into the baby's wide eyes and open mouth. Crying. It was alive. The long cone of history condensed into that single sound. "Welcome to Earth, little one," he said, and with that, another wave came out of the canyon. The tree shuddered from the force, and the water was now halfway up the trunk. He hoped the grapevine was still doing its job of holding the earth. As the water splashed his heels he thought of the dry shrubland of the front range. Red dust. A rattlesnake rubbing itself against a jagged stone, emerging into a new life. His life. He climbed higher, holding the carrier in one hand, pulling himself up with the other. But the higher he climbed, the more the tree bent closer to the water. The tree couldn't save them both.

Extinct. Latin for "wipe out."

Not on his watch. He deserved to go extinct, but not this baby.

He balanced his torso on a branch, holding onto the carrier with one hand and using the other to grab perforated grape bags out of a pocket. With his teeth and the one hand, he tied them together, end to end. Then he stood and attached the carrier to a branch above him with the chain of bags, feeling the tree wobble under the pounding pressure of water. He had to get his weight off of it. He loved this old cottonwood, but the roots were shallow and the wood brittle. They were a bonded pair, him and the tree. All these years, he breathed out toxic carbon dioxide, and the cottonwood sucked it up through its heart-shaped leaves and released oxygen, which he breathed in. Its chlorophyll shared chemical kinship with the hemoglobin in his blood. They were part of one another. They were one. He would not pull it down with him. When he finished securing the carrier, he touched the baby. It had exhausted itself with screaming and its eyes were closed. The

233

snowsuit was dry but the blanket was wet. He removed it and tied it to the branch like a flag, so someone might see. He removed his jacket with a struggle, and draped it around the carrier. The baby opened its eyes and looked right at Les. He remembered his own baby, his fearful love for him so intense he had to leave before it consumed him. He had so completely fucked up his life. Even if he had to leave, he should have stayed a father to his child. He should have stayed at NOAA and worked for the progress of humanity instead of wandering off in surrender, and into the arms of sips. All that time carelessly loitering beyond the dust and the dirt when he could have saved lives.

He still could. But for Covid he would have kissed the baby goodbye. Instead, he tested the carrier with a tug. The water was trying to grab him now, his boots pulled off by the force of it. He had to let go and give the baby a chance. It might not be a great chance, but it would be something. He checked that the baby's harness was secure so it did not get catapulted into the air when the tree sprung up, and then he got ready to leave the world. He envisioned not a point but an expansion, pulling him out into the cooling cosmos. He felt the terror of being physical, of being trapped inside something so mortal, and then thought of his afterlife body riding through the skies in the mouths of crows, and that put a smile on his face. He was ready to be reconstituted into other life, in another place, with the rapid annihilation of the self. In Buddhist terms, not such a great loss. Better than being found dead in a pool of bloody vomit. Wished he could have stayed long enough for quantum computing to reconcile Einstein's theories with particle physics, solving that space-time thing. Wonders if he will be returned to the energy of the universe as a wave or particle. Wonders where he put his lousy wax wings.

"Good luck, baby, I did what I could," he said as he opened his arms as if to fly but embraced gravity instead, then fell backwards, letting liquid chaos suck him under and pull him away. I am the water, a voice said. Wait for me, thought Les, and then there was no me. Just us. All of us, everywhere, reabsorbed into the universal flow. The toad and the prairie dog. The jackrabbit and butterfly. All the owls, the grapevine, and the primordial ooze under the flat, water-worn stones. A cottonwood. Back to nature, while it lasts.

.

Chapter Thirty-Five

Shelley heard the roar of the water as it was coming down the canyon, then felt the ground shiver as it walloped the banks of the creek. The ground shook. She could see water. She shouldn't be able to see the water, which was not brick red as in previous floods, but black like oil from the burnt canyon. It was horrifying. It was rising faster than she'd ever known and she thought it was the end. It might already be the end for Les if he hadn't hauled his ass up from his ledge. Not even his tree could survive the power of this flood, and had probably already washed away. Her house might too, but she prayed that being on the inside of a slight bend would save it, and her. She ran to find the cat carrier, and packed up her laptop, but by the time she looked out the window again it was too late. The water had torn through the neighbor's yard and was rushing across the street. She was an island now, and there was no escape.

"Let's go, Spree." The crawl space it was, and using two hands, she yanked the attic stairs down by its cord. Carrying her phone, her laptop, and a framed photo of her mother, she pushed Spree ahead of her, step by step. She pushed aside Christmas ornaments and boxes of clothes that no longer fit, then they sat on the floor and waited. The house rattled. She felt the water tear away at the creek bed as if it were her own body. It was unrelenting, it screamed outside the little slatted window vent in the crawlspace. She'd seen pictures of houses washed away in floods, torn off their foundations, and wondered how long hers would hold together. It was the sort of thing that happened all the time in the canyon. People survived. The creek bed was not wide enough for her house to float away, it would just slip in and get jammed. And then what?

Get battered to pieces by the water.

She felt dizzy. She was still not well, and decided if she was going to die, better to be lying down. She ran down to her bedroom and grabbed a comforter. There was no room to stand in the crawl space anyway. There was nothing to see, and nothing to do but wait. She worried about Les, but the man was resilient if nothing else, and he was probably holed up somewhere enjoying the show, muttering about system failures.

She kept checking her phone for news. It was chaos all over the city. She wondered if she should call for help, but she did not want emergency workers to risk their lives for hers because she'd ignored their advice. She'd wait until the water reached the house, then she'd call. Would that be too late? She looked out the slatted vent to the back yard. Clouds had covered the moon, but at least it wasn't raining and making things worse. As she knew so well, things could always get worse. She could not so much see rising water, as sense it. It would not take much more to bring it into the house. How much more to pull it off its foundation? She eyed the vent and assessed its size. Could she fit? Could she even break it open? She'd have to maneuver her body through the opening to the roof peak a foot or so above. With Spree. In the dark. She bet that if water were lapping at her butt, she'd find a way fast enough.

She heard a crashing sound nearby, like a house being eaten

alive. Spree sat up. "Don't worry, Spree. You survived the fire, you'll survive a flood."

She pulled Spree closer to her. Surviving one catastrophe didn't guarantee surviving another, but he didn't need to know that. He only needed to know she had some hope.

Chapter Thirty-Six

"Look, Mommy, you're growing a leaf!"

Iris ran her hand through her short hair and sure enough, a narrow blue-green leaf fell on her pants. Sharee picked it up then climbed onto the armchair, making room for herself on her mother's lap. Iris was still in her uniform. Why change when there was a good chance she'd be called back in later that night when the flood broke? The force was dangerously understaffed with officers sick with Covid. She'd tested negative so far, but it was probably just a matter of time.

"Can *I* grow leaves instead of hair?" Sharee asked, twirling the leaf by the stem.

"No," Iris said. "Only trees and plants grow leaves." She buried her nose in Sharee's red hair, still damp from bath time. Five years old. How did that happen? Both girls were redheads like her in spite of the convoluted way they were created, using her egg for Sharee, Carol's egg for Tatiana, and donor sperm for both. And yet the determined red genes had advanced through the ranks, producing hair the color of Colorado earth.

"What kind of leaf?" Tatiana asked. She got up off the floor where she'd been lying on her back, staring at the ceiling. When she turned seven last fall she'd announced she was too old to be read to at bedtime, she could read one herself, thank you, but now she showed up for anything. It had come to that.

"It's mine," said Sharee, clutching it to her princess pajamas.

"It's a bush leaf," said Iris.

Carol came to the living room door, wiping her hands on a towel. "A *bush* leaf? Really?" She was smiling but looked exhausted. After the kids were down she would have to get back on the computer and finish the paperwork she never got to during the day, what with having to supervise the girls. It was all hard, but the worst, she said, was having to watch Sharee attend kindergarten on a screen, sitting all by herself. "Do I want to know what you were doing in this bush of yours?"

Iris shook her head, and picked up *Charlotte's Web*, the book they'd been reading all week. "The wind blew my cap under a bush."

"Bad wind," said Sharee.

"What kind of bush?" asked Tatiana. She examined the leaf in her sister's hand, already a little worse for wear.

When Iris had helped Tatiana with her homework earlier, she couldn't identify any of the leaves on the worksheet. Maybe she'd been paying attention to the wrong things in life. "It was a medium-sized bush. It's time for bed, let's get this story going."

Tatiana walked over to the computer and came back with some loose papers. "Look! It's Rabbitbrush! Can you get more leaves? For school?"

"Rabbit! Read a story about a rabbit!" said Sharee.

"We have to finish the one about the pig first," said Iris. Why was it that every time she was in charge of bedtime, it dissolved into bedlam?

"Let's settle down," said Carol, and they did. Iris had authority at work, but at home she might as well be talking to hamsters. Sharee cuddled deeper into Iris's lap, and Tatiana sat on her heels with her chin on Iris's knee. "Call for backup if you need it," Carol said, and returned to the kitchen.

"'Chapter twenty-one,'" Iris read out loud. "'Last Day.'" She paused. They were almost at the end of the book. When she pulled it from the shelf a few days before, she'd forgotten how sad it could get. How real. Maybe it wasn't the right story to read during a pandemic. But then Tatiana looked at her like something was wrong, and she continued. It was the last day of the fair, when it was just Wilbur the pig and Charlotte the spider alone in the fairgrounds stall, reminiscing about how she'd saved his life with the words she'd woven into her web. Charlotte was wistful about the coming seasons that Wilbur would now live to see, rather than be butchered before Christmas. "'All these sights and sounds and smells will be yours to enjoy, Wilbur—this lovely world, these precious days . . .'"

Iris paused again. She felt a tight knot in her chest and had trouble breathing. She sensed Carol at the door again, staring at her, so she forced herself to go on. Wilbur and Charlotte were discussing their fondness for one another, and expressing their gratitude, but then Charlotte said, apropos of almost nothing, "'What's a life anyway? We're born, we live a little while, we die.'"

Fucking spider. Still, Iris continued to read, even as her voice shook. The room got small and hot. She wondered if it was time to take the storm windows off. What season was this? Sharee looked up at her with a concerned little face. Iris took a breath and read of Wilbur's excitement about returning home, to the barn. He asked Charlotte wasn't she excited to go home too? "'For a moment, Charlotte said nothing. Then she spoke in a voice so low Wilbur could hardly hear the words. 'I will not be going back to the barn.'"

Iris choked on the last words, and she felt Carol's hand on her shoulder. "Why?" asked Sharee. "Why isn't she going back home?"

Iris let the book close in her lap so she could pull her girls to her and hide her tears in their hair, but when Carol began to massage her shoulders with both hands, she sobbed. She convulsed with grief.

"What is it, Mom?" asked Tatiana, clutching her. "What's wrong?"

"It's my fault," Iris said, trying to control herself, and failing. "I killed her."

"Who?" said Tatiana. "What do you mean?"

From the depths of Iris's arms, Sharee began to whimper. Tatiana pushed herself away from her mother and stood. She looked in horror at her other mother. Carol came around and sat on the arm of the chair, pulling Tatiana close. She put her other arm across Iris's shoulder. Her hand rested on Sharee's head, and she muttered, "It's okay. It's going to be okay."

Chapter Thirty-Seven

When the first smudge of morning sun finally appeared, Shelley peered out of the vent at the yard. The water had receded. The air smelled of raw sewage. It was over. She'd been saved by the whim of the water, which must have decided she wasn't worth the trouble. She climbed down the attic ladder, holding Spree in her arms. Dry. The floor was dry. Spree jumped down and sniffed the air, then sauntered to the kitchen as if nothing had happened. There seemed to be no end to how many lives that cat had.

The roaring of the water had stopped in the middle of the night, so the worst must have been over by then. How could something so violent and destructive be the act of a few hours? She stepped out the back door, and saw where the torrent had taken a mouthful out of her yard and carried it out to the plains. The garden shed was gone. She hoped Les had not been in it.

She walked around the house and out into the street, where neighbors were just returning from the shelters, braving the mud and debris to see if their homes survived. One did not. The house next door, the only other one on the circle that directly abutted the creek like hers, had been knocked off its foundation and was upended in the water. Wires and pipes spilled out like intestines. The owners, an older couple, were standing very still next to their car. They had survived, but they didn't know that yet. The Red Cross was setting up a table with coffee and doughnuts out in the street, and one of the volunteers carried two cups of coffee to them.

Shelley heard the sound of ambulances and emergency vehicles. One neighbor told another that a cemetery downstream had been gutted by a spur of redirected water. Coffins had floated away, settling in yards across town.

She needed to find Les. "Let's go," she said to Spree.

Spree shook his paws crossly, but followed her anyway. Les's path was washed out, but she could see the top of his old cottonwood and headed in that direction. As she found her footing, she grabbed onto what sparse brush remained to steady herself as she slid down. They came upon a drowned bird in a cage. Spree nosed it quizzically, wondering for what strange reason the bird refused to move. She had to climb over black, burnt trees that had washed down from the canyon. There was a car on its side, and random pieces of homes, a window frame there, some porch steps there. Buildings that had survived last summer's fires only to be washed away this spring. From now on, maybe survival would only mean living long enough for something worse to come along.

And yet, when she finally got to the tree, it was amazing, a miracle really, how much of the creek bed had been saved here. Elsewhere the earth had been torn away, but wherever the grapevine had taken hold, so had the earth. It was what probably saved her house and her life. Except for his cottonwood, almost all the other trees were down or gone. But did Les still stand? Did he get to high ground in time? The ledge was full of crap, but no Les. His black bag, gone. The bucket, gone. She pried his shepherd's crook out of the mud. Where were his angels now? She looked up the length of the creek to the bridge, and became disoriented until she realized it was gone. Crumbled into the water and gone. She hoped the families who lived underneath it got out in time.

Spree meowed. "Okay, we're going soon. It doesn't look like he's here. Let's hope he's somewhere." She poked around the best she could, climbing over lawn furniture and playsets, using the crook to steady herself, checking to make sure he hadn't been trapped in the mountain of crap. His tree had acted as a catcher and it was all gathered here on the ledge. A King Soopers shopping cart was crushed against its trunk, smothered with loose rope and assorted clothes. Milk jugs and plastic bags were hanging from its branches like a Christmas tree. She looked up, and was surprised to see debris even in the very top branches. Either the violence of the water threw it all in the air and that's where it landed, or the tree itself had been bent over in the torrent and had swept up the flotsam. She heard a sharp whistle as a winged shape appeared overhead, landing on the top branch with such force the trunk swayed.

A red-tailed hawk. "Hello there," she said, and wondered if it was her buddy from the hospital. Spree rubbed up against her leg. The hawk was hunting the disturbed landscape. It raised its wings but instead of flying off, it did a controlled drop to a lower branch, which shuddered from the weight. Was he after Spree? The hawk jumped down again, landing a few feet lower, where some fabric was stuck on the branch, fluttering in the breeze.

Wait. No. It wasn't stuck. It was tied. It was a blue baby blanket, and right next to it, tightly bound on the branch, was a yellow baby carrier. A baby carrier. The arms of a blue denim coat hung over its sides. Les's jacket. She started shouting for help, but the sound of emergency vehicles up on the road drowned her out. The hawk pushed off the branch and disappeared towards the canyon.

"Please let it be empty," Shelley said, but she knew Les would not have gone to all that trouble for an empty baby carrier. Where was he? Why didn't he stay in the tree too? The carrier was too far up to grab, and it was leaning over the rushing water to boot. She looked around the creek. No one. She took her phone out of her pocket to dial 911. No battery. She'd used it all up last night. She could hear sirens up on the road. "Turn off the fucking noise for a minute and listen!" she shouted, but nothing. She dropped the crook and began to climb. The shopping cart at the base of the tree gave her a good head start, and there was so much crap caught in the tree, hanging from every branch, she could practically pull herself up with debris, and where there wasn't garbage there was grapevine creeping up the trunk, creating stirrups for a toehold here and there. God bless Les and his grapes. She wished she had more breath, more strength, but she was doing it. She pulled herself along the branch towards the carrier and felt it bend, but she was close enough to lift the jacket and see inside.

"Oh," she said. "Oh." A baby. Sleeping or dead? She didn't want to know, but her hand went to its cheek. Cool, but not cold, and she thought she saw the eyelids tremble. She was so light-headed she felt she was going to fall or throw up, but she could not do either of those things. She reached for the handle and yanked it towards her, but it was tied too firmly to the branch with a length of knotted grape bags. Where was Les? She looked down into the raging water, but there was no time to think about what might have happened to him now. She had to get the carrier down and get help. She looked up and down the creek and shouted, but still no one. She tried to untie the knot with one hand, but it was too tight. And she couldn't reach in to grab the baby with one hand either. Then she remembered. Her knife. Carefully balancing the trunk of her body on the branch, she reached into her jeans pocket and pulled out her trusty box cutter. The blue feather was stuck to it, then fell off into the water. Oh, Les. With a single swift slice the carrier was free. She grasped the handle with her left hand like she'd never grasped anything before, put her knife back in her pocket, then carefully shimmied back down the tree, changing hands on the carrier as needed, feeling for places to put her feet, slowly, steadily.

She waited for the old familiar ache in her back to stop her cold, but the pain never came, and she finally took a breath as her feet touched the shopping cart.

When she hit the ground she almost landed on Spree, who had not moved from his spot the entire time, as if he were prepared to catch her. She put the carrier on the wet ground and pulled back Les's jacket, and they both looked in. The baby must have come from the settlement up the creek where the families lived, under the bridge that was now gone. One of those families made her coffee just yesterday morning. Spree licked the baby's face and she thought she saw movement. She tried to get the baby out of the carrier but the seatbelt was jammed with mud. She slashed the restraints with her knife then pulled the baby out and shook him. She put her mouth over his mouth and nose and blew. The eyes flickered. Maybe. She made a sling from Les's jacket and tied it around her neck and waist, and rested the baby inside. But as soon as she tried to scramble up the muddy bank on all fours, the earth slipped out from under her feet. She found the crook and used it to ratchet herself up, step by step, and even then, she could only get a foothold by climbing where the grapevines grew. Spree was more sure-footed than she was, and he led the way.

"Be alive, little one," she said. "We're almost there."

Voices. She heard voices. People.

"Help," Shelley shouted. "Here!" But her voice was drowned out by a roar of noise that came from the canyon. Another flash flood? Really? "Climb high or die," Les had said, but she could not move faster than she was already going. She was trapped. She was going to die. There was no way out of it for her, but maybe the baby had a chance. She dropped the crook and untied the jacket from her body, then just as she was getting ready to throw the bundle as high up on the bank as she could and hope for the best, she saw a helicopter overhead. Not another flood, a helicopter. She heard a woman screaming and looked up to see people in the distance running along the torn banks of the creek, searching. They did not see her. She thought she felt the baby move against her chest, and then she was the woman screaming. Gathering Les's jacket in both arms she held the baby to her and tried to run, but the wet earth slipped away beneath her and she fell to her knees. With one hand, she grabbed a handful of vines to pull herself up the embankment, and with one step up was surprised to find something solid as her feet touched the exposed roots of a tree to ground her. And then she flew.

Acknowledgments

Excerpts and stories derived from *Arroyo Circle* have been published in *Novel Slices, Stonecoast Review, Terrain.org, Still Point Arts Quarterly, Short Editions*, and the anthologies *Among Animals 3* and *Awake in the World V3*, as well as the author's collection of short fiction *Highwire Act & Other Tales of Survival*.

As always, so much gratitude to Raymond Street Writers, my first and best readers. Thanks to Dede Cummings and Rose Alexandre-Leach at Green Writers Press who shared my love and vision for *Arroyo Circle*. Kisses to Catherine Parnell and Britt Lange for helping to bring the book to the light. And to Robin, hugs and apologies as needed.